SONG OF CURSES

BOOK 3 | THE SIREN'S CALL SERIES

KRIS FARYN

Copyright © 2022 by Kris Faryn

Nimbus Brands Publishing

All applicable copyrights and other rights reserved worldwide.

No part of this book may be reproduced in any form or by any electronic or mechanical means, including information storage and retrieval systems, without written permission from the author, except for the use of brief quotations in a book review. This book is a work of fiction. Names, characters, places, and incidents either are products of the author's imagination or are used fictitiously. Any resemblance to actual persons, living or dead, events, or locals is entirely coincidental.

First electronic edition: February 2022

E-Book ISBN: 978-1-7331869-7-1

Paperback ISBN: 978-1-957870-02-1

Hardback ISBN: 978-1-957870-03-8

Printed in the United States of America

Cover design by Covers by Combs

Copy editing by Julie Glover

Visit our website at KrisFaryn.com

PRAISE FOR THE SIREN'S CALL SERIES

Song of Destiny by Kris Faryn was a compelling and emotional read. It left me craving more.
Seventeen-year-old Korrina fights a constant compulsion to sing, a battle she refuses to lose because when she sings, people die. Her world shatters when she discovers she is a mythological Siren, and her destiny demands she use her song to kill. She has a decision to make. Should she walk into a future that seems preordained, or choose instead to save those she loves? Exciting and fast paced, Song of Destiny is a winner.
NINA BANGS, NEW YORK TIMES BESTSELLING AUTHOR

~

Kris Faryn's debut really sings—an exciting heroine's journey with humor and heart.
JAYE WELLS, USA TODAY BESTSELLING AUTHOR

~

Kris Faryn has cultivated a fascinating drama that readers will not want to put down until every last word is devoured. While sirens are often depicted as mermaids, she takes the classic Greek portrayal of bird women and runs with it, crafting it into a modern high school world in a very believable way. The plot is fast paced and riveting....For the reader who loves YA fantasy with a spunky heroine, Ms. Faryn is a must read.
IND'TALE MAGAZINE

FREE NOVELETTE

Want more of The Siren's Call world? Sign up for my newsletter and receive a free novelette!

Sign Up For Kris Faryn's Newsletter And Read A Free Novelette Today!

CONTENTS

Chapter 1 *Korrina*	1
Chapter 2 *Jared*	8
Chapter 3 *Korrina*	13
Chapter 4 *Korrina*	20
Chapter 5 *Jared*	26
Chapter 6 *Korrina*	32
Chapter 7 *Korrina*	39
Chapter 8 *Jared*	46
Chapter 9 *Korrina*	53
Chapter 10 *Jared*	61
Chapter 11 *Korrina*	69
Chapter 12 *Korrina*	74
Chapter 13 *Korrina*	80
Chapter 14 *Jared*	86
Chapter 15 *Korrina*	92
Chapter 16 *Korrina*	100
Chapter 17 *Korrina*	108

Chapter 18 — 113
Jared

Chapter 19 — 118
Korrina

Chapter 20 — 123
Korrina

Chapter 21 — 130
Jared

Chapter 22 — 135
Korrina

Chapter 23 — 142
Korrina

Chapter 24 — 148
Jared

Chapter 25 — 153
Korrina

Chapter 26 — 158
Korrina

Chapter 27 — 164
Jared

Chapter 28 — 166
Korrina

Chapter 29 — 171
Jared

Chapter 30 — 173
Korrina

Chapter 31 — 178
Korrina

Chapter 32 — 183
Korrina

Chapter 33 — 188
Jared

Chapter 34 — 190
Korrina

Chapter 35 — 194
Korrina

Chapter 36 — 201
Korrina

Chapter 37 — 208
Korrina

Chapter 38 — 214
Korrina

Chapter 39   220
Korrina
Chapter 40   227
Korrina
Chapter 41   233
Korrina
Chapter 42   239
Korrina
Chapter 43   245
Korrina
Chapter 44   251
Korrina
Chapter 45   257
Korrina
Chapter 46   262
Korrina
Chapter 47   266
Korrina
Chapter 48   271
Jared

A Note From Kris Faryn   275
Korrina Wants To Know - Book Discussion   277
Korrina's Mythological Cheat Sheet   279
Also by Kris Faryn   291
About the Author   293

CHAPTER 1

KORRINA

Becoming a martyr to save my turned-evil boyfriend was probably a bad idea.

I curled my toes inside my sneakers. The wind kicked up dusty sand around the high Sedona mesa and briefly obscured my view of everyone I was about to leave behind.

Crannik and the priests, huddled together in their robes like a rugby team of monks. Cloud and Danica, sorely out of place in this group of mythicals. Tanzy and Amity with their Siren auras burning brighter than the desert sun. And Dave...

I wasn't sure I'd miss Dave.

But the rest?

The rest...I'd have to store them away, lock them in a hidden spot in my heart to keep them safe, protected.

Okay, fine. Even Dave.

Tanzy froze. Her eyes went wide. Her Siren gift of seeing the future gave her a split-second head start on being really upset with me.

I shoved one of Hestia's last three dimension-crossing treats in my mouth and held tight to the thick cord that tied my heart to Jared's.

Tanzy's scream split the almost-peaceful scene before the world went silent.

Hopefully my dramatic exit wouldn't distract my friends from the very real threat of the Greek god civil war that I'd just helped start.

The spirit void whipped around my body, and the powers-that-be strengthened their efforts to rip my soul through my skin. *Yeah, yeah, I get it. Bodies. Not. Welcome.* But maybe this trip would be shorter than my last few visits.

A cold film slid over my body, slippery and soft, and my feet hit solid ground. The darkness faded, the room came into focus…and there he was, his back turned to me.

The room pulsed a hazy purple light. I straightened my legs, willed them not to tremble. Smooth stone walls, a high ceiling, worn floors, they all radiated this gently pulsing light. It was a steady and rhythmic heartbeat, but the heart it mimicked couldn't be mine. My heart sputtered erratically like a near-empty spray paint can, a clogged-up mixture of adrenaline, inter-dimensional travel, betraying my friends, seeing *him*.

Hestia's cookie rested on my tongue. I swallowed it and closed the gap separating me from Jared.

His shoulders heaved as if he was having a hard time catching his breath.

I reached for him, and the spaces between the pulses of light grew longer, as if being this close to him slowed time.

His shirt was slicked through like he'd been running, and I distantly recognized weapons on the walls, workout machines, fighting dummies, training equipment. None of that mattered. I breathed him in, pressed closer, afraid to touch, afraid to not be connected. My fingertips grazed the air between us, tracing the outline of his spine, his hard muscles.

He inhaled, his back shuddered. "Korrina," he whispered.

I leaned closer, the distance between us pushing and pulling like two magnets fighting against opposing forces. Every life-saving instinct I had shouted to run, fight, save myself. I ignored them all. In this moment, this splice of space that existed outside of time, Jared was mine.

Slowly, he turned, and slowly, I met him, each of us moving with aching caution, as if any sudden movement would break this bubble, would send reality rushing in.

He reached up, and my gaze found his blissfully brown eyes, not a trace of the poison that had turned him into a red-eyed, Siren-killing machine.

His hand cupped my cheek, his thumb grazed my skin. "Are you real?" he said, his words quiet.

I found his other hand, interlaced my fingers with his, and raised to my tiptoes. The thread of fate connecting my heart to his grew stronger, more intense, corded and braided into something unbreakable. Even if I could snap myself free, it'd leave a wound so big I'd never survive.

He leaned in, his thumb traced my lips, and still, I didn't answer him. This didn't feel real. I didn't feel real. The distance between us closed, and his breath warmed my lips, a featherlight tease. I ran my fingers up his arm, noting each hard curve, every new muscle, memorizing this body that housed the heart I loved, convincing myself I was really here, he was really here.

His lips pressed into mine, and an electric current coursed through my bones. Our feet left the floor, the gravity-defying effect of a Siren's unabashed love. He pulled back, and his eyes searched mine. "You really are here."

I smiled, and my eyes filled with tears. "I made you a promise." I pressed into him, covered his lips with mine, buried my fingers into the loose waves of his dark hair.

He deepened the kiss, and every bit of restraint he'd shown over the past year, every ounce of confusion, every trace of the new creature he'd become, it all turned to mist.

Time slipped away. The colors in the room shifted. Jared

broke away from me and looked around like he had just woken up.

I didn't want him to wake up.

"You can't be here," he said, a roughness filing the edge of his voice. He pushed me back, but held on to my shoulders, and his gaze darted around the room. "Korrina, you have to leave. Now." The roughness in his voice turned sharp, fine-tuning the rising panic in his tone.

"Where are we?" I probably should have asked when I first landed here.

"Phorkys's fortress. And if someone sees you…" His panic was addictive.

I took out Hestia's two remaining cookies and shoved one into his hand. "Come with me. Place this in your mouth and hold on to my hand, and we'll leave here. Forever."

His hand clenched around the treat. Some emotion crossed his face—one I couldn't identify, making me even more aware that he wasn't fully my Jared. "You shouldn't have come here." He let me go and stepped away.

Immediately, I felt his absence, like I was standing on the edge of a bottomless hole. "Jared, please. We'll figure the rest out once we get away from here."

He ran his hand through his hair, pulled at the ends. "I can't leave, Korrina. Don't you get it? He *owns* me. Body, mind—"

"Heart?"

He pressed his lips together. Anguish filled his eyes. Anguish, and something else.

The cookie in his hand crumbled, fell to the floor. The brown in his eyes dimmed. Reddened.

My Siren voice sensed the danger scenting the air. Honey filled my mouth, burned against the taste of his kiss. A red light began to flash inside the walls, faster and faster.

"The intrusion alarm has been triggered." Jared's fists

clenched, and he took a step toward me, but this time, intimidation filled his every movement. Power. Strength. That *otherness* he'd become. "You're leaving me without any choices."

"You are my choice, Jared. Always."

Pain etched his features as he took another step.

My Siren song coiled in my throat, but I stood my ground. I'd come here with one intent. Save Jared. That hadn't changed. That wouldn't change.

"You never did make good choices." He grabbed my hand and wrenched Hestia's final cookie—my one ticket out of here—from my grip, threw it to the floor, and stomped it to crumbs.

Shock wrapped around my throat, held on tight.

"What is *she* doing here?" A new voice entered the room. New, but not unfamiliar.

Jared went at-attention straight, tightening his hold on my hand. He spun me around, locked me between his chest and arm.

Colin stood at the entrance to the stone gym. The scars my mother had given him shortly after I'd been born pulled at his expression, giving him a permanent cockeyed sneer. Little punishment for being a terrible ex-boyfriend to my mother, and being an even worse father to me.

I didn't give Jared a chance to answer. I grabbed his arm, threw my weight against his grip, and slipped out of his embrace. My song sprang free, a dark purple beam of power that shot straight at Colin and hit him in the chest. Not as thick as it usually was, not as verdant with my newly discovered dyad power. A knot of concern curdled in my stomach.

Colin's feet left the ground, and he flew back through the doorway.

Jared growled, put his head down, and tackled me to the floor. My song wrapped around him, picked him up, and pinned him high on the wall. My power stretched between the guy I loved and the father I hated, with nowhere to go and no way out.

And I was getting weaker. I could no longer hear *Ania*, the dark counterpart to my *Elpida* power and a surprising source of unrelenting strength.

Footsteps, many footsteps, thundered closer and closer. Footsteps that could not belong to any human smaller than Shaq.

Colin got to his feet, returned my power with his own green Siren Hunter magic. My power strained against his assault, and I fought the urge to manifest the scepter of power attached to my soul. It was the one thing Phorkys craved above all else. Using it now would be as good as gift-wrapping and delivering it to him.

Though maybe, just by being here, I'd already done so.

"Give it up, Daughter," Colin snarled. "Your power here is dampened. You cannot fight all of Phorkys's children at once."

At his back appeared a multitude of misshapen, malformed monsters. Cyclops, half-crab creatures, snakes that hissed and fluttered wings on their backs.

Colin took another step forward. Jared slipped a foot or two down the wall. My power faltered. Colin noticed.

"Do you really think Phorkys would not have defenses at the ready to stop another Siren attack? Your ancestors fooled him once. It will not happen again." He gestured at the walls. "His power is infused throughout this fortress, and you, by yourself, are far too weak to resist."

My power flickered. Jared fell to the ground. Colin rushed forward, pulled out his dagger.

I pulled my song in close, coated myself with its purple energy, created a forcefield of protection.

It didn't matter. The room flooded with Phorkys's monstrous warriors. Jared tossed a rope around my middle. Colin grabbed the other end and tied my arms to my sides.

Green fire flickered at the end of Colin's blade. Green fire that had the power to curse me as it had cursed my Siren ancestors, as it had cursed my Siren cousin Amity, as it had cursed my mother.

Jared was right. I didn't make good choices.

Becoming a martyr had been a super-bad idea.

CHAPTER 2

JARED

Korrina was here.

Stunned, I tightened my grip on the end of the rope that held her captive and followed a step behind Colin. She gasped. I bit my tongue, gave her a little slack, and tried to ignore the hint of her taste—a honeyed heat that had proven impossible to forget.

Why had she come here?

I knew why. Somewhere deep down, I remembered her. Beyond all the tales Colin had spun into my head about the treachery of Sirens, I had locked her away and kept some echo of her memory safe.

A procession of Phorkys's lesser-known children—the Horde—trailed behind us as Colin led the way to Phorkys's throne room. The mood was celebratory, though the hisses, growls, and shrieks might convince Korrina otherwise. This was a huge boon to Phorkys's plans.

Capturing Korrina was the equivalent of taking possession of our enemy's strongest weapon, but my thoughts were at war. The militant part of me, my role as Colin's *strategos*, was fast at work, mapping out all possibilities of using this new weapon.

But with each new battle strategy, every new plan that formed in my mind, all circling around breaking Korrina, using her, weaponizing her, my stomach churned. Begged to reject my breakfast.

Colin pushed open the black onyx doors to Phorkys's throne room. The reflective surface caught us in a watery snapshot.

Korrina was the only creature who shone.

"Thanos." Colin gestured at one of the guards, an unbeatable poker player covered in thorned carapace with black eyes that gave away nothing. "Watch her."

Thanos stepped next to Korrina, took the ends of the rope from mine and Colin's hands, and held her tight.

She looked at him, shivered, then shifted her gaze to me and swallowed me with her help-me eyes.

"*Strategos*," Colin snapped. "With me." He spun on his heel and headed for a side exit. The door opened into a meeting room. I followed and shut the door behind us. It clicked.

Colin slammed his arm into my throat. Pinned me against the door, lifted me to my toes with a super-human strength I'd not been granted. Shock charged through my body, but lasted only a moment. I should have expected this.

"Tell me you didn't know she was coming here," he demanded, choking my air supply.

"I didn't know," I rasped. Pressure built in my head, and the room went dark at the edges.

"Then you let her in. How?" His fingers sharpened, and it felt like he held a blade to my collarbone.

I shook my head. The room swam. Consciousness held on like a fraying thread.

He let me go.

I fell to the floor, hands and knees, retched. My throat and lungs burned.

Colin paced away. "How long was she here before I arrived?"

My fists clenched. I forced in a bladed breath.

"How long?" he asked again, his tone leaving no room for mercy.

"A minute. Maybe two," I confessed. "She gave me one of two tokens. Said they would allow us to escape."

He crouched in front of me. I met his unblinking gaze, and in that moment, I had a hard time believing Colin was ever fully human.

"She has a token that allows her to go wherever she wishes?"

"Had." I forced myself to stand. Now that I could breathe again, my voice grew stronger. "I smashed them both. You can find the evidence on the training room floor."

He crossed his arms, stepped closer, and gone was the brotherly camaraderie we'd often shared. I wasn't sure what had taken its place, and I sure as hell hadn't thought it was this fragile.

"I will do that, while you stand with her in front of Phorkys and explain yourself. Korrina Lore could have destroyed us in those two minutes." Colin stalked to the other side of the room and rested his hand on a door that led out to the hallway. "Pray that Phorkys shows you mercy. The punishment for treason is worse than anything you could possibly imagine."

A scream erupted, followed by a loud boom, both from the throne room.

His eyes narrowed. "Take care of it," he snapped and whipped out of the door.

This was Colin's way—giving me a chance to prove myself after a miserable failure.

I reached deep, found the source of my Siren Hunter power, and dragged it through my veins.

Korrina always seemed to come alive when she used her power. Mine felt like death.

It slicked through my fingers, a frosty cold that burned around the edges and glowed with liquid green fire.

I pushed through the door into the throne room, green fire

blazing around my hands, looking every bit the fearsome Siren Hunter I was supposed to be.

Korrina was a ball of purple energy.

What was left of the rope lay on the floor, useless.

Thanos got to his feet, looked more dazed than when Colin had punched him out in the annual Dark Depths fight night. Other guards scattered around her. The rest of the Horde kept their distance.

Korrina crouched where I'd left her, a kitten with her claws extended in a room full of nightmares.

Impossible.

That was the position she'd put me in.

"*Elpida*, stand down," I roared and fueled the flames at my fingertips. They blazed into a bonfire.

Her eyes met mine, a vivid violet dyed by the aura of her power. My flames wavered, but no one noticed. No one ever saw anything other than the deadly flames, a gift from the goddess Demeter to our primordial god Phorkys as a thank you for intel on her daughter's whereabouts. Flames that held the dual power to avenge Demeter's loss and to curse, transform, and kill Sirens.

Flames that were at once attracted to and repulsed by a Siren's power.

Flames that had a mind of their own.

Mine stretched toward her, and a need to consume, to control, filled my lungs like water. My power licked the edges of hers, and it at once stung and made the flames crave more. They arched from my palms, encased her purple light in a seamless cage, and for a split-second, our powers combined, turned as blue as Korrina's endless eyes.

A bright flash of light burst out from her, collapsed on itself.

Everyone ducked, me included.

When the sparks disappeared, my power was banked, hers

had vanished, and she was crouched on all fours, gasping for breath.

I closed the distance between us, grabbed her arm, and hauled her to her feet, hoping she could feel the apology in my gentle grip. "Any more displays like that, and we'll find a way to silence your power," I growled, channeling my inner Colin.

"From your mouth to my ears," a voice boomed from the throne.

Slowly, my focus widened. Away from my grip on her arm. Away from her elegant profile. Away from the room full of Phorkys's children and allies who now bowed to the throne.

I looked up, dropped to my knee, and forced Korrina down with me.

"A truly inspired idea, *Strategos*." Phorkys loomed at the front of the room, seated firmly on his throne made from the bleached remnants of his defeated progeny as if he'd always been there. Gray-haired, long flowing beard, at first glance he looked like someone's grandfather. But his appearance shifted like dappled sun on water, highlighting his armored and clawed hands, the red spikes along his skin. The scars that rippled down his face, his neck, his exposed chest.

Eons of living.

Eons of surviving.

Eons of being forgotten, ignored, discounted as an old man. Dismissed as powerless, irrelevant, not-a-threat.

The god of the deep, dark, dangerous waters.

The god of monsters.

My master.

CHAPTER 3

KORRINA

Jared's hand dropped from my arm. My knee was going to sport a shiner from hitting the ground, but that was the least of my concerns.

Jared hadn't run away with me.

He had threatened me. Tied me up with a rope and brought me before his god.

I was numb.

"*Strategos*, bring her forward," Phorkys commanded.

Jared wrapped his hand around my arm again, not tight but a gentle coax. I got to my feet and let him tug me toward the Friday Crab Special sitting on the throne. I'd thought my previous visions of the ancient god would have prepared me for this moment.

Ha.

I felt like I was looking at a Magic Eye poster, and if I stared at him long enough and let my eyes cross, he'd turn into something else. Phorkys's body was mostly human, but he had crab-like features that poked out of his skin, claws that clicked instead of hands, and a serpentine tail that waved behind his back.

I held my chin high, refused to look away from his intense gaze. There was something otherworldly in his eyes, something that would have been more at home in the stars than here on earth, no matter which side of the Veil I was on. I'd been around other deities, but Phorkys was something else. Something more.

He stood, walked down the three steps that set his throne apart. Close up, I could see his skin was not soft but hardened, like a shell that had been molded to fit his exact form.

"Finally, I see you with my own eyes," he murmured and looked me over, head to toe. "For one so small, you have caused quite a bit of trouble."

I bared my teeth. "Best compliment I've had all day."

He held my gaze for a moment longer, chuckled at the back of his throat, then sat back down on his rib-boned throne. "Bring our other guest."

Other guest?

A few minutes later, one of the guards returned with a guy about my age. Hair matted with dried blood, bruises covering his cheek, one eye swollen, arm in a sling. It took me a second to realize who it was.

My stomach twisted. "Luke?" I whispered.

He'd been gone less than a day. Taken from Tanzy's home, he'd allowed himself to be caught, planning to use what he'd learned getting close to me and the other Sirens to win back Phorkys's trust. Not that we'd told anyone else. They'd have locked him down tight and thrown away the keys. Perhaps that's what I should have done, but…despite my doubts, I'd hoped he'd found a way to get back in Phorkys's good graces.

Given the bruises, things seem to have gone as well for him as they had for me.

Luke bowed deep to Phorkys, ignoring me entirely, and Jared stood at our backs. It was surreal, this moment. Surreal because a year ago, we were in high school together, having petty fights and thinking our little world was too big.

"One must wonder at your timing," Phorkys said. "Either you are very poor conspirators, or this is complete coincidence. And I do not believe in coincidences." His voice dropped an octave, and he tapped his chin with a sharpened claw. "However, I know the *Elpida* to be quite devious."

I couldn't help it. I grinned.

"So the question becomes, what are the two of you planning?" He went quiet for a moment as he studied us.

The grin fell from my lips. I did not like the cunning look on Phorkys's ugly face. Not one bit.

Jared cleared his throat. "My *dimiourgós*, if I may interject."

I startled and looked between Jared and Phorkys. Neither one acknowledged my stare. In Ancient Greek, *dimiourgós* meant creator. It was an early word for father.

That's how Jared thought of Phorkys? Not as slave to master but son to father?

My stomach sank even further.

Jared waited for Phorkys to nod. "The Betrayer has been persistent that he has important intelligence to share, upon his reinstatement to the family. Since his arrival, he has said nothing else, despite our…encouragement."

Luke's jaw clenched. This wasn't the first time he'd been tortured by Jared and Colin, but it didn't mean he'd gotten used to the abuse.

"Additionally," Jared continued, "the *Elpida* brought tokens for her escape. Hers and mine, and no one else. Surely if they had planned an attack together, she would have brought a way for the Betrayer to escape as well."

Phorkys leaned closer. "We'll discuss that matter in further detail privately, but please, my son, go on."

My son? I was going to vomit.

"Perhaps there is a way for the Betrayer to prove that he is not here on behalf of the *Elpida* and is true to his claim that he acted as a double-agent to gain the Sirens' trust and report back on their weaknesses." Jared bowed his head and stepped out of my line of sight.

Phorkys seemed to chew on Jared's suggestion. "A show of allegiance to gain back our trust. A briefing on our enemies' secrets in exchange for a renewed bond."

Luke bowed his head. "I have been lost without the family, my *dimiourgós*."

Luke too? Blurgh. Though in his case, he actually *was* related to Phorkys, albeit very distantly.

"Allow me to prove myself, so I may be accepted within the fold once again."

Phorkys chuckled. "This has been a very interesting day. I do enjoy interesting days. Tell me, what can you possibly offer to show your allegiance?"

Luke took a breath. "My power silences a Siren's song."

My breath caught, despite knowing that this was part of the plan.

Phorkys sat straighter and pointed at me. "That Siren's song?"

"Any Siren's song, but it seems most effective on the *Elpida*. As one of her guards, I can make sure her song is tethered at all times."

I mentally cheered him on. As my guard, we could plan how to take down this sadistic crab-dad without suspicion.

"Why was this not revealed before now?" Phorkys glared, looked around the room as if searching for someone to blame.

Luke shrugged his one uninjured shoulder. "By the time I discovered it, it became impossible to tell you without blowing my cover. Then I lost my position as one of your trusted, and it seemed the wisest course of action to keep my strengths hidden."

"And so, you tell us now?" Phorkys suddenly seemed larger, the room seemed darker, and my song readied at the back of my throat.

"And so, I tell you now," Luke confirmed. "I needed to come to you with more than this information to earn back your trust. I needed to come to you with real information, information you could use to act against the Sirens and the Council, as well as to wield the scepter once more."

Phorkys's head jerked up. "The Council?"

Luke's spine seemed to grow stronger. "I have met with them. I have learned who occupies which seat, which way the power leans."

A burning hole began to eat at the bottom of my stomach. The Council hadn't been part of our plan. The scepter attached to my soul had definitely not been part of our plan. Giving Phorkys real information he could actually use against my Siren family had been nowhere near the plan.

A smile stretched across Phorkys's face. "I accept your proposal, my son. Now come and extend your oath finger to me."

Something passed over Luke's face, but he steeled his expression and walked forward as best he could with the manacles around his ankles. He reached the base of the throne, carefully unwrapped his injured arm from the makeshift sling, and extended his hand.

Phorkys took his ring finger in between his massive claws and lifted Luke's arm high. "And so, the lost son returns."

Snarls and grunts met his words.

"My son, you will be the *Elpida's* constant leash. Your sacrifice will silence her song." A deep undertone entered Phorkys's voice, and with it, something inside me shivered, wanted to hide.

He lifted Luke's arm even higher and snapped his claw closed.

Luke fell to the ground. Red liquid spurted over Phorkys's chest, and from Phorkys's claw dangled Luke's finger.

There was no controlling it this time. I turned and vomited

all over someone's bared talons. I looked up into a sea harpy's evil gaze, and she gingerly stepped back, shaking off one talon, then the other.

Phorkys crushed Luke's finger between his claws, called for a bowl, and ground up bone and blood and skin into a powder. He whispered some words over the bowl, light flashed, and he poured the contents into a coiled shell. He raised the shell to his mouth and licked it. The shell sealed closed.

"Isamarine, your chain," Phorkys called out, and a small creature wearing a food-stained dress made her way through the crowd. A long braid fell to her waist, and two scraggly, bat-like wings fluttered sporadically at her slightly hunched back. She shuffled past me, and I got a whiff of onion and garlic. Her skin was tinged green, as if she were part seaweed, her eyes a sunset orange.

She met my gaze for a second, and something close to pity shone out of her copper eyes. Once close to Phorkys, she held out a chain that was wrapped around her waist like a belt. He snipped off a section, and the chain reformed and adjusted itself to her hips as she stepped back into the crowd.

Phorkys attached the shell to the chain, and Jared pushed me forward and lifted my hair. Phorkys leaned close, and fastened the chain around my neck.

"In time, *Elpida*, I hope you come to think of me as Father as well. Until then, may this charm silence treacherous thoughts and allow you to see the truth."

The chain slithered against my neck, cool and metallic, and tightened itself against my skin. Phorkys stepped back, and I fumbled for the shell at the base of my throat. I couldn't even slip a finger between the necklace and my skin.

I reached for my song, an energy force that was always coiled in my chest, ready to be sung into power, but for the first time since the last time Luke touched me, my song was gone.

No one was touching me.
And my song was gone.

CHAPTER 4

KORRINA

The crowd parted as if my real name was Moses, only instead of parted waters full of fish, this crowd was teeming with teeth and talons, night terrors and monsters scary enough to start new legends.

They hadn't seemed so scary before.

Phorkys took his seat on his throne and clicked his pinchers together to get the room's attention. "Treacherous maidens who betrayed their sacred oath gave birth to ones such as this. And now they come, in the guise of innocence, to take even more than what they have already stolen. My children"—Phorkys rose, seemed to gain ten feet in height, lifted his arms in the air—"gaze upon the *Elpida*, the living embodiment of the scepter of time and memory, a gift from the titaness Mnemosyne, mother of memory, time, and tales, a gift given in exchange for our stories of the deep and dark, stories that no light can see. This scepter is our inheritance, and this Siren is our prize. Together, may we be restored."

The room broke into loud cries, stomps, and adrenaline-fueled, testosterone-filled shouts. The floors shook with their enthusiasm, grew even louder when Phorkys rested one heavy claw on my shoulder.

"Take her to the Grotto," Phorkys said, his voice low yet somehow ringing through the crowd, and an exuberant chaos erupted. "We will not suffer a Siren in our presence." He gave me a push, and I stumbled forward, fell to my knees.

I stood, took a deep breath, and dragged in as much dignity as I could gather. Jared gripped my shoulder and strong-armed me through the crowd, out of the throne room, and into the hall. Behind us, the crowd followed, a mob intent on vigilante pursuit, held back only by the glow of Jared's Siren Hunter magic centered in his palm.

"Don't look back," he whispered. "Keep your head high. They won't come closer." He pressed his unmagicked hand against my lower back with a gentle touch, guiding me forward, down one turn, then another, and another.

Anger should have coursed through my veins. Betrayal should have burned my skin. Terror should have shaken my bones.

But all I could feel was gratitude. Gratitude that Jared had blocked everyone from seeing my face. Gratitude that even he could not see the few tears that had escaped.

Gratitude that despite all the hellacious things that had happened between our kiss and my silenced song, his words proved that somewhere down deep, he cared.

For now, that was enough.

The crowd grew quieter and quieter. Jared slowed, dropped his hand from my back, and let his green magic fade. "They're gone. We've gone too deep. Very few creatures dare venture this close to the Grotto." He let out a breath and rubbed his hand across his forehead and through his hair. "Why, Korrina? Why did you come here?"

"You have to ask?" Wonder filled my voice, but it shouldn't have. The poison that had turned him into this creature, this enemy by force, had also stolen his memories and warped his beliefs, specifically his beliefs about me.

He pressed his lips together.

"How can I be who I'm supposed to be, and do what I'm supposed to do, if half of my heart is buried here, with you?" I took a step closer.

His eyes went shiny. "But I don't have a heart to give you," he said, his voice low.

I smiled, not surprised. "Doesn't matter. You have mine, so this is where I belong. With you. And you don't belong here, Jared. You know you don't. There is something inside of you at war, and I'm here to help that part of you, the part who knows you don't belong here, win."

He shook his head, looked away. "And Luke? Why is he really here?"

As much as I loved him, I didn't trust him. I couldn't trust him until I knew he belonged to himself once again. "Luke is here because he's doing what Luke does best. Betraying everyone to keep himself safe." I made my face go angry-Korrina and looked away.

The polished walls and floors had long disappeared. The corridor he had led us to was dimly lit with smoky torches and the occasional pulse of light through the rough-hewn walls. It smelled damp, and pressure had begun to build in my ears. Ahead of us was an iron gate, all pointy-edged with an old-fashioned dungeon lock.

I gulped. "Is this the Grotto?"

Jared nodded.

"Looks homey." I straightened my spine, walked to the door, and turned the big key to unlock the gate. I wasn't about to make Jared lock me in a scary dungeon. The last thing he needed was additional guilt added to his already heavy burden. Anyone who knew him could see that the weight he carried was too much.

Jared cleared his throat and followed close behind. "It's not homey, Korrina. The Grotto is where Phorkys sends those he cannot kill but needs to forget. Prisoners down here have died from lack of food and water. Not out of cruelty, but because once here, you are forgotten."

"Anyone ever tell you that you've got a great bedside manner?" I let out a nervous breath. "Phorkys doesn't want to forget about me. He wants to use me."

Jared nodded. "Which is the only reason I have hope that you'll be okay, for the moment. There is one other prisoner here who is cared for with purpose. Colin sees to her needs. And so, I'll see to yours."

I looked at him, but he wasn't looking at me. I followed his gaze.

We'd crossed what looked like a guard room or common area to a bank of barred cells that lined yet another hallway. All empty, except one.

I couldn't feel my feet, but somehow I still moved forward.

It was her hair that I first recognized. Red, curly hair that she'd passed on to me. Mermaid waves of it spilled around the floor, curled past her pale, sun-deprived shoulders, past her white wings all the way down to her feathered knees. Her eyes were closed, the lids so translucent I could see the blue veins that ran under her skin.

My heart was going to punch out of my chest. Trembles shook through my fingers as I wrapped them around the bars of her cell.

"Mom?" I whispered, only half believing that I wasn't dreaming.

"She won't wake," Jared said. "Not until her medicine wears off. And then you'll wish for her to sleep again."

I turned in time to catch his shudder. He'd gone all watery. His words hadn't quite processed. Tears streamed down my face, but I didn't care. "Open her door. Please. Let me see her."

His long lashes shuttered his eyes. "Only Colin has her key. Colin and the guards."

I looked from him, to her, to the empty cells surrounding her. "And who holds my key?"

He didn't answer.

"Let me stay next to her. Please. I can't…knowing she's here, I can't not see her."

He looked around, but we were alone. "I'm not sure that's wise."

"If she can't wake up, then what harm is there?" A pleading tone had entered my voice, but it didn't matter. This was my mother. My mother whom I'd only recently discovered was alive.

"She's sick, Korrina. It'd be easier for you if you couldn't see her. Trust me." He began to walk away, to lead me down another hallway, *away* from my mom.

I stepped into the cell next to hers, slammed the door closed and held onto the bars. The lock engaged, the clunk-clunk echoing through the Grotto. "She's my mother." I glared at Jared, who should have understood.

But again, there I went thinking he was the old Jared I'd known since preschool.

I softened my tone. "We don't abandon those we love. Not when they're sick. Not when they've forgotten who they are."

He stepped close, wrapped his hands around mine, and leaned his forehead against the bars. I leaned into him, our heads barely able to touch through the thick, metal rods of iron.

"You need to forget me too, Korrina. If you get the chance, you have to leave this place. I cannot help you. Leave me here and forget I ever existed."

I leaned back, gazed into his eyes. "I don't abandon the people I love, Jared. Not ever."

He pressed his lips together, let me go, and turned his back to me. His shoulders lifted, and he walked away.

I sank to the floor, reached through the bars that separated my cell from Mom's, and grazed the tip of her closest feather, the only part of her I could reach.

The Grotto. Phorkys's prison. For those he didn't want to kill.

Yet.

CHAPTER 5

JARED

The gloom of the Grotto clung to my back, a slick, oily gunk I couldn't shake. Cheers echoed through the fortress—the Horde celebrating Korrina's capture. My back was clapped, my shoulders squeezed, my arm lifted in triumph.

They credited me.

I turned down an empty servant's hall in the fortress's ever-winding maze, ducked behind the corner, and doubled over. My breath wheezed and my chest tightened as if tentacles had wrapped around me to liquify my insides.

"Is the Siren secure?" Colin's voice entered my hidden space.

I straightened, coughed as if I'd swallowed something wrong, composed my expression.

If he suspected my feelings, he didn't show it.

"She is," I said, and felt for her. Somehow I could sense her, moving in her cell deep below, as if she was tied to my soul. Had something happened during that nanosecond when our powers combined? Or had this connection always existed?

"Follow me," Colin snapped. His tone said I still wasn't forgiven, and if past experiences were anything to go by, the next few hours would be painful.

We reached the training room where a fighting ring had been set up in the center and a crowd had gathered. Colin surveyed the audience, smiled, then turned to me. Not a friendly smile.

"You better be glad I found this." He sprinkled the crumbs of Korrina's token into my hand, then stalked forward and ducked under one of the fighting ring's ropes. "Today's challenge," Colin shouted, projecting his voice above the Horde, "is in celebration of our own *strategos*'s victory over our ageless enemy. The first to defeat him will feast with me tonight." Colin beat his chest, and the gathered guards and creatures roared.

Thanos picked me up by the back of my shirt and tossed me into the ring. "I will bring this boy to his knees," he growled.

I picked myself up, brushed an invisible fleck of dirt of my shoulder, and cracked my knuckles. "Got something to prove, thorn-face?"

The crowd laughed, elbowed each other. Thanos's men—other creatures made from rock, shell, and thorn like him—rumbled on the front row to show their support. This was his chance to redeem himself after Korrina had kicked his hide. It was mine to retain my status, to prove to Colin that I belonged here.

To prove it to myself.

Korrina was wrong. This was the only place I belonged.

Thanos leaped over the ring's ropes and landed in the center with a shaking stomp. He rose slowly, breathed in deep, and pushed out the spikes that were buried just under his hard skin.

I brought the fire to my hands, my own built-in defense system and weapon.

The Dark Depths fight rules were simple. Use whatever you had to win. A knock-out was encouraged. A kill was rewarded.

Thanos tucked himself into a ball and rolled forward, an unescapable death boulder. I threw out my flames, reached through the ring and grabbed a two-headed axe out of Crox's belt, and swung. Metal hit indestructible shell, and the impact shot up my arms, a muscle-punch followed by a shudder. My flames poured around Thanos, and he came out of his defensive position with a pained grunt.

The fight was on.

Aiming for his knees, I swung low. Thanos jumped out of the way, shooting spikes from his wrists mid-air. A sharp sting glanced against my shoulder as I rolled away.

Thanos landed with a ring-shaking thump and roared.

I closed my eyes, felt for Thanos's vibrations, flipped to my feet. I swung Crox's axe around my head as I moved and hit solid flesh.

Thanos cried, went down to his knees. The axe stuck out of his chest, his carapace cracked. He sucked in a breath, pulled the axe loose, and tossed it out of the ring.

With his carapace weakened, I had one shot.

I grabbed my power, yanked it through the center of my palm, and shot a beam straight for the crack.

Thanos lit up green as he flew into the air then landed on his back.

He lay there, still.

Colin leaped into the ring, checked for a pulse, counted to three.

Thanos didn't get up, but he was at least alive.

"*Strategos* wins," Colin yelled.

The crowd's roars deafened, but they would have cheered no matter how the fight went. They just liked the violence.

"Who's next?" I called, strengthening my voice, letting adrenaline fuel my blood. My hands buzzed. I couldn't keep still.

Someone pushed their way through the crowd. Smaller than the rest of the Horde, but determined.

"Let's see how you do without flames to hide behind,

Hunter." His voice preceded him by a second, and it settled like a knot in my chest.

"You sure about this, Betrayer?" I snarled and wiggled my intact oath finger.

Luke's violet gaze darkened, and he grinned. "Just like old times."

He grabbed two bostaffs from the cache, climbed in, and tossed me one. The thick wood slapped against my hand like a fastball in a catcher's mitt. The crowd grew quiet, pressed in.

Thanos had his reputation to defend. He'd shown a good fight and earned back some of his street cred.

Luke had his reputation to defend as well. Only instead of street cred, he was defending his right to be here. To be one of us.

I flipped the bostaff around in my hands a few times, making adjustments for the weight, for balance, while keeping my focus on Luke. He favored his left, uninjured hand. His right was swollen and red.

In other places, maybe they granted mercy for the weak. Here, weakness was a sin.

Without warning, I leaped into the air and slammed my bostaff on his injured hand.

He cried out and a dull slice of pity dug through my gut. Blood dripped from Luke's cauterized, now-cracked-open wound.

Something deep inside me awakened, not just determination to win, but a dark and delicious need to settle scores.

Luke was the reason I'd transformed. I brought the bostaff down on his arm.

He'd given me everything I had today. I swung it around and slammed it into his spine.

And then he'd betrayed Phorkys—bam—*Colin*—crack—*his own family*—thump.

He'd abandoned us. He'd abandoned me.

I paused my assault. Before me, Luke writhed on the ground. I stepped closer, breathing heavy, and stared down at him.

He'd betrayed Korrina.

Rage broiled my blood. Hunter power radiated out of me in crackling sparks of green lightning. The green flames were dialed in to hunt Sirens. But focusing them on Luke was an easy task.

I raised the staff high above my head, and green flames licked up my arms, curled around the worn wood without burning it. Burning was saved for the one curled at my feet.

Luke lifted his hand, as if to defend himself.

"No mercy," I whispered.

His hand shot up my pants leg, past my boot, and wrapped around the bare skin of my calf.

My shock at the move lasted only a millisecond.

The flames disappeared. The center of power that was my strength vanished.

Its absence let something else rush in. Relief, a break from the constant tension, and memories.

Flashes of Korrina growing up, us playing together, me falling in love with her the moment some bratty classmate in our kindergarten class dumped spaghetti on her head, a kiss.

The staff dropped from my hand.

Luke released me, and with a snap, my power came rushing back, pushing away emotion, refocusing my drive.

Too late.

Luke leaped up with his staff. He slammed the wood under my chin.

Starry pain buzzed around my head, and through the haze, I realized I'd hit the ground and Colin was counting me out. Disappointment filled his eyes.

The crowd shook the room with cheers, growls, screams, excitement.

"...three. Luke wins," Colin shouted. "*Strategos* has been defeated."

Numbness tamed the adrenaline pulsing through my chest. Defeated. For the first time, I'd been defeated.

And Luke had secured his place in the Horde.

CHAPTER 6

KORRINA

The Grotto had fallen dark. The walls pulsed with a faint, sunset orange light, but it was barely enough to trace the outline of my mother's sleeping shape.

It was quiet in this dungeon. I'd have anticipated the comforting screams of fellow prisoners, but not here. Here, either everyone had already been quelled into submission, or Mom and I were the only captives.

I pulled my hand back into my own cell, away from Mom's soft feather.

A feather.

Never in my endless childhood dreams where I got to meet my mother had I imagined her covered in feathers. But then, what Brooklyn-born girl suspects her mom is a Siren?

I felt my way around my new home. The floors were surprisingly soft, as if coated in moss rather than stone. In one corner, my hand sunk into the floor. I yelped then poked at it. The floor dipped where I poked then sprang back like a water mattress. A sleeping area?

Cool.

Also curious. What did Phorkys hope to accomplish by making his dungeon comfortable?

Or maybe this comfort was only granted to long-term inhabitants.

Like my mother.

Hopefully not me.

For only the billionth time since coming here, I regretted not cluing in Tanzy and Amity to my plan. If I'd had, they'd never have let me come. But also if I'd had, they could have helped me find an eventual way out.

I was wily, but even the wiliest needed help every now and then.

When I was an active member of Mischief and Mayhem, our high school's prank gang, Cloud ran us through drills based on various situations. One of those happened to be "lost and alone." I never did well in that scenario.

Nevertheless, here I was, lost and alone.

I closed my eyes and summoned images of Cloud at his bossiest.

He stood in front me, Jared, and Danica as we relaxed on the grass in the park. "This was not a drill, people."

I raised my hand. "Uh, yes, Cloud. It was."

He glared. "The exercise was to act as if it was not a drill, Korrina. And you failed. Miserably." He flicked his gaze to Danica. "Dan here is the only one who would've survived."

She wiggled her lip ring at me and batted her heavily lined eyes.

Jared shifted and his hand grazed mine, causing all sorts of imaginary, electric butterflies to tickle my skin. Had that been on purpose? Oh please, let it have been on—

"Korrina!" Cloud shouted.

I sat up straight. "I was listening."

He rubbed at his head as if he had a headache. "The next time we do this, please remember that even when you are stripped of all your weapons, your tools, your allies, and the high ground, you still have this." He tapped his brain.

"And lucky I am that we have you," I said, stroking his ego. It was like a cat and needed constant attention.

He crouched in front of me, stared into my eyes with a tangible strength. *"No, Korrina. You have yours. And your brain will always provide you the way to safety. Give your brain the puzzle, and it will piece together the way home."*

The memory dissolved, and I tapped my fingers against the bouncy floor. "Here I am, Cloud, weaponless, songless, friendless," I whispered. "And even with my brain, I'm not sure I can pass this not-a-drill."

The rustle of movement came from Mom's cell. I crawled over, reached through the bars, and felt for her. She'd shifted closer, and more of her wing was in reach. I petted the hard muscles under her feathers.

I could do this. I had to do this. For me. For Mom.

Use your brain, Korrina. I didn't have my song. I didn't have Hestia's cookies. I was pretty certain I didn't have Jared.

But there was a chance I still had Luke.

And I could still dream walk.

Dream walking was the one piece of magic that was completely mine. It didn't come from my Siren power, and it wasn't a symptom of the scepter. It was all me, and even when Luke had silenced my song before with his blood, he hadn't been able to stop me from dream walking.

I stroked Mom's wing one last time, then got comfortable in my cell. She'd had the power to see into the future. I had the power to dream walk into memories and dreams.

No one could take that away from us.

I briefly considered trying to contact Neri—my meditation game had gotten strong with her help—but the last thing I wanted was a lecture. Even if I deserved one.

I let those thoughts float on by, slowed my breathing, focused on my mother, and felt my spirit leave my body.

A velvet blackness swirled around the essence of what made me *me*. Here, I had no Siren collar. No voice box. No arms or legs. No body.

Spirits tumbled about, spilling as if caught in an invisible, intangible current.

The Void.

Why was I here and not in Mom's dreams?

I'm here, Elpida. Ania, my shadow side and the sorrow to the *Elpida's* hope, squeezed the place where my deepest emotions hid. Her face flashed in my mind. A carbon copy of my reflection but with silver eyes, dark auburn hair, and a knowing raise of her shaped eyebrows.

"Why can't I feel you with me anymore?" I asked. Not my voice—voices didn't exist here—but more of a thought sent through the strong thread between us.

I felt her shake her head. *I'm not sure. Something blocks me from you in the waking world.*

"Luke's power? They made me a collar that won't let me use my song."

Maybe. No matter. This will not last. Nothing does. And my time here has not been idle.

Her thoughts always trended dark. "I'm supposed to be in my mother's dreams."

I felt Ania nod. *She does not dream. She is here.*

Ania gripped me tight with her dark strength. Once I'd allowed her to, she had given me control and a depth of power and experience I would never have guessed possible.

Sorrow had matured my power.

And it was Sorrow that now guided me through the spirit void. I wove my essence with hers, tightening our bond, hoping that I could somehow keep her with me in Phorkys's fortress and, together, take the place down.

I'm afraid it will not be that simple.

"Nothing ever is."

A silver flame burned against the endless ebony of the Void, like the pinprick of a distant galaxy. Ania pulled me closer and closer, and instead of the flame breaking apart into countless stars, it concentrated, burned deeper.

I knew that flame.

The day Jared had turned into a Siren Hunter, I had lost myself. My broken heart had thrown my spirit from my body and I'd been set adrift here. The Void was a place for lost and restless souls, a space between dimensions. It lived inside the Veil that separated the human world from the mythical world and acted as a defense system to keep humans where humans belonged and mythicals where mythicals belonged.

But Mom's spirit had found me. She'd been this blindingly bright flame and had filled me with all her love.

I wasn't certain that I had died, but I knew without a doubt that she'd pushed me back to life.

"Mom?"

Her spirit's flame stilled.

My own flame was a bright bluish-purple. A brilliant light that attracted spirits like suicidal moths, only I couldn't hurt them.

I batted at one, and a sharp slice of pain ripped through my spirit.

"Yewouch," I thought-screamed, and the sadistic spirit fluttered away, but not before flaring the same color of my own spirit flame.

Other lost souls began to trickle closer.

Mom's flame stroked one, and she shuddered, I guessed with pain. Like the soul that had touched me, this one flared with Mom's silver light, and...

"Ania, did Mom's flame just dim a little?"

Yours did as well. Lost souls steal from the living. It gives them the sensation of living again.

Well, that was just freaking-fantastic.

"Mom, it's me. Korrina. I need you to wake up." I tried to keep the panic from my thoughts, but with no body, my entire spirit was like a giant neon-flashing sign for my emotions. Souls stealing from the living? I had so many feels about that. None of them good.

Her flame came closer, inspecting mine.

My star. Her thoughts rushed over me, a wave of longing and love. *You shine so bright.*

"That because I'm alive, Mom. Just like you. We need to go back to our bodies. We need to wake up."

Mom's silver fire twisted into a skinny flame, and she backed away. *Impossible. Must sacrifice. Too much pain.* Some emotion darkened her thoughts.

"Sacrifice? No. No, Mom. That's not an option. You don't get to choose death over waking up." I reached for her, expanded the shape of my spirit so I could envelop her like she'd once enveloped me. "We'll manage your pain, okay? Just wake up with me. I'll be right there when you open your eyes."

More souls cascaded around us, and it felt like a firefight with a stampede of baby dragons. Death by a thousand burns.

I cannot return. She twisted so fast she became a tornado of light. Souls fled from us, and before I could react, she was nothing more than a distant, fading light, growing smaller, smaller, smaller.

"But I found you." I pushed all my energy into the thought and tried to chase her. "We're finally together."

Ania gave me a push, rocketing me through the Void in the opposite direction. *You stay too long. Too many have sensed your presence.*

The darkness faded, my body swallowed my spirit, and my toes tingled. My stomach clenched, and a wave of nausea rocketed through me. I creaked open my eyes to see dark violet light pulsing through the walls, slowly uncurled my body, and tried to come to grips with a new truth.

Mom was dying.

Her breath stuttered. A red light began to pulse through the walls and threw her skeletal figure into a harsh relief. Her talons jerked, her shoulders thrashed, her breath panted in pained gasps.

Footsteps thundered down the corridor and echoed around the stone walls.

Mom's back arched up, her spine almost bent in half. Her wings brushed the floor, and a noise rumbled against her throat.

Not a Siren song, but a high-pitched keening in a minor scale. A scream that grated and screeched.

CHAPTER 7

KORRINA

Mom thrashed in her cell, and her scream grew more and more pained.

"Help!" I lunged for my door and shook the bars as if I could break the lock, my muscles trembling, the taste of stomach acid at the back of my throat.

Colin skidded into view, followed by the thorny guard I'd incapacitated in the throne room and two others just like him. Colin's sea-green eyes held no trace of red now, but the scar going from his cheek to his mouth was as gruesome as ever.

Not because of the way it looked.

Because of the way he got it.

He caught my gaze, and his expression almost held an apology—*almost*—as he unlocked Mom's caged room and scooped her into his lap. He laid her head on his thighs while two guards held down her arms and talons and forced her mouth open.

"What are you doing?" I threw my weight against the bars separating me from them, but they didn't even rattle.

A vial of some liquid was held tight in Colin's fist, and he shoved a dropper inside the glass bottle, then pulled out her cheek. Poison? Is this how they got rid of their dying prisoners?

"Don't kill her! I can help bring her back, I promise." I watched, helpless, as he dripped a few drops into her mouth then held his hand over her nose and lips so she had no choice but to swallow.

Colin spared me a glance. "It's her medicine," he grunted out.

I swallowed back the panic rising like vomit in my throat. "Medicine?" Doubt came through strong. "Why are you giving her medicine?"

"Give it a minute," he said.

I had no choice but to give him as many minutes as he wanted.

Mom fought him, never once opening her eyes. That awful screaming continued without break deep in her throat.

It was only minutes. Felt like hours.

Another scream pealed out of her lungs and whistled to a stop. Her body relaxed. She slumped against Colin. The guards let her go and walked out of the cell without a word.

My muscles went limp, exhausted from my dream walk, monkeying my cage, and tensing up my whole body while Mom's medicine worked its way through her body. But it had worked. And it appeared that Colin had been telling the truth.

Colin let out a puff of breath, then found my gaze again. "I'm sorry you have to see your mother like this."

I snorted and waited for the punch line. "Oh, you're serious? Huh. And here I thought you didn't have feelings."

He pressed his lips together, drawing the scar my mother had given him tight. "I'm disappointed you think so little of me."

"What's wrong with her?"

"I've had the best minds this side of the Veil try to help her," Colin continued, as if I hadn't spoken. "Something went wrong when she was cursed, and I can't—" He rubbed at his scar, then picked up Mom's hand and pressed his lips to it.

"I'm going to hurl." Bile rose in my throat at the sight of his lips on my unconscious mother, but he was right. Something had gone wrong. Mom was supposed to be a fully-fledged cursed Siren, thanks to an ex-lovers spat with Colin.

But instead of a bird body with a human head, she lay there, half-human, half-Siren, full prisoner. Feathers draped her like a strapless dress, feet curled into talons, wings spread underneath her back. Trapped in the spirit world's void for lost souls.

Yet her arms were still human. Her shoulders. Her pain.

"You know if she was awake, she'd kill you."

"You don't know Raelynn." He stroked her cheek. "She is… very special."

I gagged, making sure it was loud enough to echo. "Thanks to you and being a bad ex. She fell in love with my dad pretty quickly after she left you. I can't imagine that you knew her too well."

Colin jerked. His eyes flashed red. "Careful, daughter," he hissed, his Scottish accent battling the danger in his voice. "You are only safe as long as Phorkys deems you of use."

He gently placed Mom's head on the cushiony floor, folded her hands on top of her stomach, and arranged her hair so it cascaded over her shoulders once more. He got up, walked out, and locked her door behind him.

"Thanos," he called out to the guards as he disappeared around the corner. "Bring her."

"I'm not your daughter," I yelled after him and wrapped my hands around the bars, my too-late denial bouncing off the stone walls. "My dad is dead," I whispered, my heart breaking in all the familiar patterns.

Thanos and the other two guards advanced.

I backed up as far from the door as my cell would let me.

Thanos unlocked my door, and the other two guards entered my room. Their faces looked carved from stone, a total lack of expression. Each grabbed one of my arms and puppet-walked me out of the cell, down the hall, and out of the Grotto.

The walls had turned from dark violet to a pale, butter yellow.

We stopped in front of a cavernous room, where it seemed every creature who lived in this underwater hellhole had gathered. Servants brought in food on trays and set the dishes in the middle of long tables. Monsters of various shapes and sizes began to serve themselves, family-style, from the dishes.

I smelled bacon.

Bacon?

It began to hit me that this was breakfast time, that the lighted walls in this place acted as some sort of communication or time-keeping system, and that I was starving.

Were they actually going to feed me real food in this place?

I was way more excited about that than I should have been, but…

Bacon.

And dare one hope, coffee.

One of my guards stuck his thick thumb into the base of my spine and prodded me forward. I lifted my chin, kept walking, and tried not to have the first-day-of-school jitters. I'd matured past cafeteria table hierarchies, hadn't I?

Rows of monsters stopped eating as I passed, and one by one turned to give me their full attention as I was forced to the front of the room. A sinking feeling in my hunger-center began to burn.

This didn't feel like an invite to breakfast.

Someone stuck their foot out, and I stumbled. Caught myself before I fell down. I met my bully's gaze and stared deep into his violet eyes.

Luke. Enemy turned ally turned undercover agent.

I hoped.

I glared at him. He snarled, elbowed a buddy, his damaged

hand now sporting a clean bandage, and a cruel laugh escaped his lips.

"Laugh it up, Chuckles," I sneered and channeled Danica—toughest chick I'd ever met. "Let's see who's laughing once I rip off this collar." I yanked at my new accessory, my skin already raw underneath from futile attempts to free myself.

My guard and I approached the raised platform at the front of the room. It was a simple stone structure, polished smooth from centuries of footsteps. Phorkys wasn't there, but Colin was.

And Jared.

Don't look at him.

If I did, my tough girl act would melt faster than licked cotton candy.

Colin shifted on his feet, his hands behind his back in an at-attention military pose, and the room went silent. All attention focused toward the front of the room. Toward me. Toward Colin.

"*Elpida*, daughter of mortal and monster, we have brought you before us today to offer you a choice."

Choice? I almost choked.

The room rumbled with tension, and the sharpened stare of a hundred fangs on my spine sobered my mood.

"Join our family or return to the darkness of the Grotto."

"I'm not giving you my finger," I snapped. "And I'm not joining your cult."

Colin's eyes darkened. "You would be wise to reconsider your options. An immortal life is a long life, even when it is not imprisoned in darkness."

"Well, good thing I'm not immortal then." I was half-human. Not a demigoddess like my Siren ancestors, not a direct descendant of a Muse, and not godlike in the slightest.

Colin's face tightened, and something glinted in the depths

of his irises. "Are you so certain?" His voice was soft, but it carried a dissonant note and a hint of threat.

I blinked. No, I was not certain. But given that there were few other Sirens walking about, our lifespan couldn't be long. Especially with the Hunters killing off most of us. Immortals didn't die. Sirens living in the human world had been dying for centuries.

But if he was right…could I spend eternity locked in a cell?

Was that what I'd committed myself to? Not saving Jared, not saving my friends, but wasting away in a dungeon next to my slightly insane, comatose mother?

I lifted my chin. No. That scenario was not an option.

"Our master is giving you one week to decide. Join our family, gift us with the blessing of the scepter eternal, or be forgotten in our dark depths."

One week?

My stomach slid out of place and landed somewhere near my toes. A lot could happen in one week. For better or for worse.

Colin stepped down one step from the top of the dais, bringing him within arm's length. "Perhaps you will be lucky and discover you are not, in fact, immortal." The room chuckled. Colin stepped closer, leaned his head close to my ear, and dropped his voice. "But I do not think that will be the case."

My legs trembled, a low vibration that shook my marrow. Colin's head shot up, and the voices in the room grew louder. It took me all of one second to realize it wasn't me shaking, but the room.

And my guards were distracted.

I narrowed my eyes, tightened my muscles. Colin might be my birth father, might be Phorkys's top Siren Hunter, might be lethal to his bones…

But he was still human.

I lunged for his throat.

A staff slammed into my stomach. My feet flew eye-level, my breath erupted from my lungs, and I landed on my spine at the bottom of the steps. I gasped for air as Colin's face came into view, as Jared stepped back to the background, his staff resting at his side, as what little fight I had left started to shrivel.

The fortress shook as if it was being bombed, each quake shaking rocks loose from the high ceiling, shoving cracks into the tiled mosaics on the walls.

Colin began shouting commands, ordered my guards to take me back to the Grotto, and Phorkys's collection of monsters and adopted children fanned out with military precision, grabbing weapons, forming ranks, and filing out of the banquet hall.

I really hoped I was mistaken, but I had a sinking feeling we were under attack.

CHAPTER 8

JARED

Ordered chaos.
It was what I loved most about battles. There was structure, but also unknowns. We had a strategy, but accepted risk. We'd trained, but didn't know how much pain was at stake. And pain was a soldier's drug. Pain made us feel alive.

Pain could almost make me forget the look on Korrina's face when she realized it was me who had hit her with my staff.

I tightened my grip around the leather hilt of my sword, shoved thoughts of Korrina to the side, and led my company up the sloping sides of the fortress. Protected inside a forcefield, so far down in the ocean that undersea mountains surrounded us, no light reached us, and without Phorkys's protection, we'd all be crushed thinner than pancakes by the dense water pressure.

Sparks of light from deep-sea fish lit the dark ocean around us. A flare here, a flash there. Sometimes I caught the gleam of deadly fangs. Sometimes one of Phorkys's many children. Sea serpents with human heads, poisonous fish with knife-like fins, and on rare occasion, the skolopendra would do a swim-by. Larger than a small cruise liner, its rows of webbed feet were enough to make me train harder during the day, pull the covers up tighter at night.

Phorkys's forcefield kept the water out and the oxygen in. It did not, however, keep out weapons. Not that many weapons—or attacks, for that matter—could survive the trip here.

We stormed onto the parapet, shields up, crossbows ready. Those with supernatural powers balled them in their fists.

The ocean was empty.

"Form up," I shouted, and my company drew into position. I walked to the edge, scouting for our enemy. Outside the forcefield, Phorkys's deep-sea children snaked around the fortress, providing our first line of defense.

Not a single one was engaged.

I peeked over the edge of the stone wall into the courtyard below.

A giant boulder had crushed the center fountain. Around the yard, smaller boulders had cracked statuary, punched holes into walls.

"Look out!" one soldier cried, and adrenaline spiked my veins.

I looked around.

Nothing.

I looked up.

The bioluminescent lights spotlighted another stone falling from above, plummeting directly for my creatures.

"Fall back," I screamed.

We could fight anything but the ocean crushing in on us. The ocean and whatever was happening above.

I dove after the last of my company, my feet sliding into the protected part of the fortress just as the stone pierced the forcefield and left a bloody gash in the left wing.

A boulder, smooth and polished, and littered with spikes.

This wasn't an earthquake.

This was an attack from the surface.

The war between the gods had begun.

THWACK.

I lunged again at the training room dummy, harder, faster, relentless. Sweat poured into my eyes, but I let it burn.

Thwack.

My staff jerked in my hands, resonated in my bones.

Thwack.

The sound almost drowned out the noise of crushing rock that had been pulverizing our home for hours. The left and right wings had been evacuated, along with the upper levels. And we were stuck down here like rotting corpses, helpless.

Thwack.

The dummy bounced back, and Korrina's fragile body flew through my mind. The painful sound of her breathless gasp. The dimming of fire in her blue eyes.

I had done that to her.

My gut curdled. My hands tightened around my staff. I couldn't protect my home. My body no longer obeyed me. I no longer belonged to me.

All I had left were my thoughts, and even those I couldn't force my mouth to speak.

Thwack. Thwack. Thwack.

I hit the dummy until the room went fuzzy, until black roared at the edges of my vision, until my arms shook, my legs trembled, until I had only moments before I collapsed. I sank to the floor, rested my arms on my knees, and let my head fall forward.

"No woman is worth this amount of punishment," Colin's low voice rumbled somewhere close.

I reached out for the hand I knew was there. "Even your daughter?" I retorted. He gripped my wrist and pulled me to my feet.

"Especially my daughter." Colin clapped his hand on my shoulder. All, it seemed, had finally been forgiven.

If Phorkys heard us, he'd have my head. But my dark transgressions were safe with Colin. He was the only one who could possibly understand.

"He wants to see you," Colin said, the tightly stretched words tense.

The breath in my lungs solidified. "Just me?"

Colin jerked his head, then half-pushed, half-guided me out of the training room. "I've been ordered to take my contingent to the surface to stop this attack."

I nodded. Of course he had.

Deep in the bowels of Phorkys's stronghold, among the weapons, torture devices, and machines that turned our muscles to iron, that's where Colin and I had found our comfort zone. My room was steps from the training room and below the banquet hall—not the best location but I didn't complain.

I had no idea where Colin slept.

Maybe outside Raelynn's cell, watching her sleep.

We turned down a hallway that would lead us past the barracks and gradually slope upwards to the next level of the fortress. Soldiers had been stationed in this area, prepared for an attack. Colin and I stepped past a group of human-like men sharpening axes. They saluted us as we passed.

I glanced at Colin without turning my head. His profile was jagged and sharp, like a pro-wrestler's face that had been strategically rearranged. By the time I had his experience, my face would be no less ragged. No less wrong.

He'd had a life before all this. I didn't know much about it, other than what Korrina had told me before, but even that was like an echo. A life I could barely remember, the only bright spots being her. I had faint memories of Mother and other people my age, but they were steadily becoming less real.

I didn't recognize the boy that used to live above the surface. I only knew the creature that lived here, deep in the dark.

Too soon, we arrived at Phorkys's war room. Colin and I had been here frequently over the past year to discuss strategy.

But never had I been in this room with the primordial sea god himself.

Colin stopped at the entrance, gestured for me to go in, then left me alone, waiting for Phorkys.

The room was a testament to Phorkys's eons of deeds. Battles his children had won were depicted in murals, his monsters portrayed as heroes. The heads of ancient beasts poked out of the walls, preserved by some magic that stopped them from decaying. The busts of his official children—those he'd legitimately had with his sister-wife Keto—were set into stone alcoves around the room. The Graiai triplets, Skylla, Thoosa, and finally the three Gorgons with their famous little sister, Medusa.

Phorkys was a family man.

Everything he did, he did for his children. Legitimate, bastards, and adopted alike.

He treated us well. We never wanted for anything. We were happy to serve him.

And yet...

My palms sweated. I felt sick.

I wouldn't have worked myself to this point had I known I'd alone been summoned by Phorkys. It might be cowardly, but I'd feel stronger with Colin by my side.

The door connected to the throne room opened. Next to the door was a tapestry of Phorkys with his scepter and his torch, full of power and might, long before the Sirens stole the source of his strength and fastened it to Korrina's soul—so it could never be separated from her.

She was now his weapon, his strength, his mission to break. In spite of Colin's threat, I could not imagine Phorkys allowing her power to be forgotten in the Grotto.

Phorkys appeared in the dark outline of the open door. I dropped to one knee and bowed my head. His presence filled the room, wrapped me in his power, strengthened my trembling muscles, my fragile bones. I breathed deep, found my center.

"Stand, my son," he commanded, and I had no choice but to rise. "Are you ready to take your place as my champion?"

"Champion? But Colin—" I protested, despite the stupidity of doing so.

"Colin has my love and my loyalty. But he cannot do what you can do."

My chest squeezed tight. "I am your servant," I replied, accepting without knowing.

Phorkys nodded. "Bring me the *Elpida's* heart."

I froze. "Her heart?" My eyes darted toward the exit, as if I could run. "But if she dies, doesn't the scepter cease to be?"

"You hold her heart." He dipped his chin, his beard brushing against the waving tentacles at his waist. "She came here with the valiant but naive intention to rescue you. Only you can bring me her loyalty, her desire to serve, her willingness to use the scepter under my command."

My shoulders relaxed. He wasn't asking me to kill her.

"I demand her love," Phorkys continued. "And you will deliver it to me, or she will pay the price."

"What price?"

Phorkys's dark eyes sharpened. "The scepter is most powerful when it is willingly used. But it does not have to be willing. It just has to obey."

My body tensed.

Korrina didn't have a week until she was forgotten in the

Grotto. She had a week until she was made prisoner and mindless slave.

I bowed my head, accepted my mission.

Phorkys wasn't asking me to kill her.

But it might have been better if he had.

CHAPTER 9

KORRINA

The floor rumbled softly beneath my tush. Dust shook loose from the Grotto's ceiling, and I pressed my back harder against the bars separating me from Mom, as if these slender bars of iron could protect me from a cave-in.

The trembling hadn't stopped since it'd begun, and the walls hadn't changed from their pulsing, scarlet light. If my theory was correct, the light was the fortress's clock, since there was no sense of day or night this deep. But the emergency lights had thrown everything out of order. I had no way of keeping time.

My guards had left us here alone. Not like I was a threat. I scratched at the Siren-silencing collar around my throat, pulled my elbows in close to my body, and hugged my bruised ribs.

Jared had attacked me to protect Colin.

I banged the back of my head against the bars, because if I thought too long or too hard about that...

"I really wish you'd wake up," I said to Mom. "It's dark in here and a little scary, and my ribs hurt, and you could make it all okay by waking up and talking to me."

I turned around so I could face her. She hadn't moved. Of course she hadn't.

Another blast from far above us shook the room.

"Dad died." I leaned into the bars, and the cold metal was almost comforting. "It was just a few days ago. He was a guardian—but I guess you knew that already. Anyways, he disobeyed the Council, trying to protect me."

I took a moment. The only moment I'd really taken since he'd been executed to process.

"He was a really good dad. Not perfect, like *at all*. But a really good dad. And he didn't have to be, you know. He could have just been my guardian."

Mom's finger twitched.

"He spent his last days trying to find and save you. So it'd be really great if you could wake up. He'd like that." Sniffles had taken over my voice, and I lay back.

It was a while before I could control myself again, and when I could, I kept talking.

It was going to be a long night. It sounded like bombs were trying to bring the underwater fortress down, and sleeping was not in my near future. So I told her everything. From finding her message on the toy box to how I discovered we were Sirens to how I fell in love.

I told her how I'd saved Demeter, that I had Siren cousins who were super weird—especially Tanzy—but lovable, and if she could just wake up, she'd meet them. Because together, we could find a way out of here. I knew it.

"One week, Mom. That's all he gave me. I've got one week to figure a way to get us all out of here."

Times like these, I wished I could switch powers with someone. Like Mom's powers of seeing into the future or Tanzy's powers to see how different decisions affected the threads of Fate.

My heart punched into my throat. I sat up.

I'd always planned to reach out to Tanzy if my surprise trip lasted any longer than a few hours.

I just hadn't planned on having such a short timeline to get her up to speed, on board, and ready to hatch my escape route.

Judging from the amount of tired grit in my eyes, I'd been awake most of the night. I wouldn't be left alone for too much longer, so I took a deep breath, centered my mind on Tanzy, and fell into her dreams.

Neon colors rained around me in a field of black flowers. Tanzy lay spread-eagle in the middle of the scene, popping drops of color as they came near her.

"Hey, Tanzy," I called out. "This place is like a trippy kaleidoscope."

She sat up. "Korrina?"

Her hair had loosened from its typical braid, and long wavy locks of light brown hair trailed behind her, mixing in with the flowers and raining colors.

"Glad to see you're somewhat conscious. Sometimes when I do this, the sleeping person is in so deep, they don't recognize I'm real." I reached out a hand and pulled her to a stand.

She shrugged. "I'm not most people."

"Truer words have never been spoken," I said solemnly. "We probably don't have much time, so I'll cut to the chase."

She raised her eyebrows, and her bright green eyes narrowed, as if she doubted that I could stay on point.

I totally could.

"I'm in Phorkys's fortress. The Grotto to be exact."

Her lips tightened, but she didn't interrupt.

"I went to save Jared, but...he's not really ready to be saved yet."

"I could have told you that," she said.

"I also found my mom. She's in some sort of coma in the cell next to mine. And also, we're being attacked."

She dipped her chin, her eyes wide. "And...? Spit it out, Korrina."

I sighed. "And I've been given one week to join up with

Phorkys or he's going to lock me up forever. So, I need a way out."

"Is that it?"

I nodded, then stopped. "Wait, no. They cut off Luke's finger, ground it up, and turned it into a charmed collar to silence my Siren song. And it *works*."

She went quiet as she took in everything I'd said and tapped her lip. "Amity's going to murder you, you know."

"I know."

"And then Neri. And then Cloud."

I nodded.

"Danica demanded to go last. Said she has a special torture just for you."

"It's 'cause they all love me."

Given the opportunity, it's best to reframe the situation.

She shook her head. "What's the plan?"

"Luke's getting close to Phorkys. We'll use his powers to make Phorkys powerless. While he's weakened, I take him out with my song and the scepter."

She pointed to her voice box. "And the collar around your throat?"

"I saw the creature that made it. I think I can convince her to help me. Or at the very least, force her to take it off."

"And you'll do all of this while locked in a dungeon?"

I cleared my throat. "No. I'm going to give Phorkys what he wants. It's the only way I can get close to him."

She yawned, and the dream shifted. The colors faded as she grew closer and closer to waking up.

"Your plan has about a one in a hundred chance of succeeding, and I'm only giving you that much of a success rate because there is something else toying with the horizon of my vision."

I crinkled my forehead. "And that is…?"

She rubbed between her eyes. "I don't know. I've never experienced anything like this. It's a presence, almost suffocating. I can't get too close. But I know this. Friend or foe, this presence is coming for you, really, really soon, and it may be the only way you live through to next week."

"Awesome," I said, my voice flat.

"Amity and I will work on a way to get you out of there."

"I've got that figured out too. Amity just needs to write an escape route into existence, but not until I give the signal. Any time before then, and Phorkys will come up with some way to keep me trapped here forever."

"I wouldn't exactly call that 'figured out,' Korrina." She finger-quoted her words and grabbed my hands. "Visit me tomorrow night, and I'll have an update for you. We're family. We won't leave you down there. No matter how much we all agree you deserve it."

"You love me. You really love me," I sang out, and Tanzy's dreamworld faded to black before I had a chance to ask how *they* were doing and what was going on in the human world.

I sank back into my body, and nausea rocketed through my system again. A groan escaped my lips as I tried not to hurl. Never had I ever experienced this after a dream walk. But I was two for two so far in dream walking and waking up with my mouth tasting like yesterday's breakfast.

I lay there for a moment, arguing with my body to move. Around my cell, the scarlet emergency lights had disappeared and the walls had taken on a good-morning hue. No more rumbles, it seemed.

But I had to get up, had to put my plan into action. There could be no rest for the insanely beautiful and super-sneaky. And modest.

I pep talked my body into action, only to find that the guard-room was occupied by not one, not two, but three thorned guards playing cards. My little attack must have put Colin on higher alert. Thanos was there, sitting slightly apart from the other two, his gaze fixated on my bars.

Near the door of my cell, someone had pushed in a cup of water and a plate of wormy green things. I picked one up, wiggled it in front of my nose.

Seaweed.

Ugh.

I held my nose and gulped down what I could. Despite how hopeless everything looked, I wasn't about to starve and make myself weak.

The vomity feeling began to fade. I emptied my cup and dragged it against the bars so that it went *rat-a-tat-tat-tat-tuh*. "Hey, guard-y, guard-y, guard-y. Sa-wing, guard-y, guard-y, guard-y," I heckled.

Not working. To have any chance at all of getting out of here, I had to actually get out of *here*. Bars did not work well with any of my plans.

"Hey, Curly, how about some coffee?" I called out. Naming them after the Three Stooges made them less scary.

One of them looked up, claiming his new name. Thorns bristled at the base of his neck. He didn't get up but pulled another card out of the deck and turned his attention back to his brothers.

There wasn't much difference between the three of them, except for their size and the intensity of their glowers. All three had pink-tinted flesh with hints of the ruby-red spikes poking out of their skin. Their black eyes glistened in the dim light of the Grotto, and their sledgehammer-sized hands made their playing cards look like confetti.

"Curly," I called again. "Yo momma's so ugly, she turned Medusa to stone."

"It's Crox," he growled, his voice a deep peal of thunder.

Thanos kicked him under the table, and Crox turned his back to me.

"Nice to meet you, Crox. And you big boy, you're Thanos, right?" It couldn't hurt to get to know my captors.

"Shut it, Siren," Thanos said.

Yeah, like that'd ever stopped me before. "Hey, third guy. What do I call you?"

He didn't look up. He didn't answer. The creature didn't even flinch.

"Silent Bob it is," I sighed, threw my cup against the back stone wall of my cell, flopped to the cushiony floor, and watched my mom sleep in the cell next to mine. Her feather-dusted ribs moved up and down, up and down, ever so slightly. It was almost peaceful.

A door creaked open down the hall, and something scented the air.

I sat up on my knees, my nose pointed up like a bunny sniffing for danger. But that scent. It was warm and home and safe and love all bundled up into…

A mug slid into view, steam curling from the open top.

"Coffee," I whispered. Tears formed in my eyes, and I couldn't bring myself to wipe them away.

Could it be real? Or was this a mirage? A dream? Was I going crazy?

"If this is crazy, I don't wanna be sane," I muttered and scrambled for the mug of all-things-good. I didn't care if it was full of chicory or rat poison. As long as it wasn't seaweed.

I curled my fingers around the warm porcelain, inhaled long and deep, and took my first sip of coffee in approximately sixty-three hours.

It was everything I'd dreamed and then some. Caffeine rushed into my veins like flood rains pouring into a dry riverbed. It scalded the back of my tongue, but I didn't care. This had to be some new kind of torture Colin had come up with. Give me a taste of heaven, then rip it away.

"You're going to give yourself throat cancer," a dry voice said, but I recognized that lack of humor. I knew that empty tone.

Intimately.

I slowly lowered my coffee mug, held it close to my chest, and studied this guy who'd rammed a stick into my ribs less than twenty-four hours before.

"Would you care?" I meant it to come out sarcastic and bitter, but it didn't.

Jared lowered to a crouch. "Very much so." He pushed a sweep of his hair out of his brown eyes, no trace of Siren Hunter red in them, pressed his lips together, then unlocked my cell.

I eyed him suspiciously and took another scalding sip. "Colin busy?" I asked.

Jared shook his head. "I want to show you something." He stood and walked out of sight, leaving my door wide open.

CHAPTER 10

JARED

She followed me.

I didn't look back to see—I vowed not to—but her presence was lightning, and it shocked me every time she was near.

Never did I expect to be leading her around this place. From what I could remember, I never led her anywhere.

I stopped at the Grotto's exit and waited for her to stand next to me. She may be Phorkys's prisoner, but she wasn't mine.

She reached my side, and my skin crackled from her nearness. I wanted to grab her in my arms, hold her close, tell her how sorry I was that I hurt her yesterday, that I couldn't listen to her when she'd first arrived, that I was not my own man.

But that would only put her in more danger. I'd be dead, and no one would be left to watch her back.

I grazed my elbow against her arm, hoping the contact would discharge some of the static between us.

She gasped. Her bright blue gaze punched my shoulder.

I clenched my jaw, stared straight ahead, though every cell in my cursed body was on fire. Her touch didn't dispel the buzz. Not. At. All. "Are you in pain?"

Her hand strayed to her right side. "No," she lied.

If she had her Siren song, she could heal herself. I'd not only helped silence her song but made her vulnerable in every way imaginable.

We made our way up a spiraling walkway. No steps here, as Phorkys's children did not always have legs, and we walked across paths that bent and curved like the waves that covered us miles above. The walls were smooth, and always a little slick, as if even a god that predated Pangaea wasn't powerful enough to keep the ocean contained.

Not that the recent attacks had made the place any less wet.

Made of stone, ancient coral, and bones of prehistoric sea monsters, Phorkys's fortress had a natural yet alien look to it. It blended perfectly into its surroundings on the ocean floor, and yet, it had the shape, the defenses, and the aura of a giant sea creature bent on destruction.

Korrina kept silent as we passed the same monsters who'd jeered her yesterday morning. She fiddled with her collar, a black chain with a magicked shell and Luke's finger, at her throat.

We reached the upper levels of the fortress, and the corridors were all but empty.

"Why today?"

My gaze jerked toward her, and I broke yet another vow.

I drank her in, and she filled me more completely than any feast. Her pale skin, her dark red curls, her crystalline eyes, the dark lashes that framed her moods, the curved lips that shaped her fire.

"Jared." My name on her lips was dessert. "Why today?"

I blinked, turned my gaze to the hallway before us. "I met with Phorkys."

She stopped walking.

I faced her. Somehow, she seemed smaller. Her face paled further. I wanted to see her under the sun.

"Is he going to kill me?" Her voice shrank. "Is that where you're taking me?"

"No, not at all." I grabbed her hand without thinking, without checking to see who was watching.

Someone was always watching.

She flinched, and it cracked something inside me, something fractured and hard and bloody.

I let her go, took a step back. "Phorkys does not want you dead. He wants you to join our cause."

She snorted. "Puh-lease. Tartarus will freeze before that happens."

I sucked in a breath, held it in my chest. "Don't doubt Phorkys's resolve. He will do anything to win this war. He will do everything he can for his children."

She had to see. This wasn't just a grab for power. Phorkys was fighting for the survival of his family. A family the world on both sides of the Veil viewed as nothing but monsters, because of what they looked like.

Power was funny like that. Those with power painted everyone else whatever color they wanted. And Phorkys, with his misshapen figure and banished status, had been painted as the father of monsters with a heart for destruction.

But he *was* a father.

And what some viewed as destruction, others viewed as creation.

Even monsters had fears, desires, needs, and hopes.

I kept walking. She followed, no longer at my side but a step behind.

"I won't hurt you again. I vow it," I said in a low voice, not looking at her. I did not make smart decisions when I looked at her for too long.

"It's hard to vow anything when you aren't in control of yourself," she whispered.

Her words hit me hard. I spun around, my hands in fists.

Anger coiled around the tight ball of fear in my stomach. "Your little stunt with Colin cannot happen again. It can't, okay, Korrina?"

Her eyes widened at my use of her name, the panic in my tone.

I hadn't meant to sound panicked.

She chewed on her bottom lip and at least had the decency to look abashed. "Is that why I'm out of my cell? They figured isolation in the dungeon wasn't working, so they're trying out a good cop approach?"

I shook my head. "Maybe. I don't know. You're out though. That's what matters. Don't screw it up." I pushed on a heavy wooden door, warped from age and moisture, and led her onto the crumbling parapet.

It was dark. The damaged edges of the fortress gleamed like broken teeth.

Bioluminescent fish flashed, and I imagined, as I did so often, that they weren't undersea creatures but distant stars.

Korrina squeaked.

"Are you okay?" I rushed to her, pushing aside how adorable that little noise was, escaping from her inescapable lips.

"It looks like we're in space," she said, her voice low, awed. She lifted her arms, walked closer to the broken edge. "To infinity and beyond," she whispered, then laughed to herself.

I shook my head. "You amaze me."

She cocked her hip, tilted her chin. "You mean, 'you're amazing.'"

"You still laugh. How can you still laugh?"

She moved closer. "I've seen darkness before, and this? This place is full of light." She reached down, linked her fingers through mine. "You're here. I'm here. My mother is alive."

She linked her fingers through my other hand, and I began to lose myself in her eyes. The lights of the deep reflected back at me, as if her eyes held an entire other world.

"The floors are comfortable." She rose up on her toes. "I'm out of my cell. And you brought me coffee. Just like you used to." She kissed the corner of my mouth, and something inside me remembered her. Remembered how we used to be. The small moment we had before everything changed.

Everything had changed.

It killed me, but I let go of her hands. Stepped back from her. It was safer for her this way. No one could know the depths of my heart and how much she filled every mile of every league.

"I brought you here to show you there is no escape. Phorkys has agreed to let you out of the Grotto. You'll be given a secured room, but even if you were to run free in the fortress, there is nowhere for you to go. You would never make it through the forcefield." I pointed to the shimmering bubble overhead. "And if you did, you'd never make it to the surface."

She pressed her lips together, tore her gaze from mine, and something hard crossed her expression.

"The only way to leave is by using Phorkys's power. And the only way you'll ever leave is by joining our cause." I turned and started walking toward the door.

She didn't.

"If you don't, you'll die here, Korrina. This is a fight you cannot win."

I left her alone on the parapet.

I needed her to see.

There was no freedom. Not here. There was no escape.

The sooner she accepted that, the safer she'd be.

Moments later, Korrina joined me inside. She was quiet, which for her was concerning.

I led her down the damaged hallways, rubble and debris still piled up in the corners. We'd lost twelve civilians. One was a child, and it tore at my gut at the waste—being in the wrong place at the wrong time was something I was vastly familiar with.

The wings of the fortress were living spaces for families and staff. Full-time soldiers lived in the central part of the fortress. That's where Korrina would be housed. In the middle of an army to make sure she didn't escape.

Luke skidded around a corner, a wild look in his eyes. Korrina stiffened at my side.

"Oh good. You're together."

I wasn't sure what to make of his tone, other than it made me want to sucker punch him. What he'd done in yesterday's fight was legal. Didn't mean I liked it. Or trusted him.

"We have a guest. You're to join Phorkys in the throne room immediately. Bring her." He thumbed at Korrina, then sped along the hallway as if on a mission.

I stole a look at Korrina, who had gone pale. I felt the same—Phorkys had that effect—but rolled back my shoulders and changed direction.

The closer we got to the throne room, the slower we seemed to go. Korrina grabbed my hand, and her mouth moved but no sound came out. A few seconds later, her words hit me. "Someone's messing with time."

I sloth-nodded, held onto her hand, and pulled her forward. We bent our heads and made our way forward as if fighting a strong headwind.

The throne room danced in light. We crossed the threshold, and the force of time let up.

I blinked, shook my head. Phorkys had set another throne next to his, and in it, sat the titaness Mnemosyne. I'd seen enough paintings, tapestries, and tributes to this ancient power to know who it was. I was not prepared, however, for her presence.

I dropped to my knee and bowed my head. Korrina stayed where she was, not bowing, but at least not advancing.

"Approach the throne, *Elpida*," Phorkys commanded, but his voice sounded as if it was coming through water.

Time slowed again, and I lifted my head.

Mnemosyne made eye contact.

Her eyes were an indescribable color, her face perfect and painful. She dipped her chin at me, and my mind flooded with images.

Images like what Luke's power had shown me, but more. I felt the magic of making Korrina laugh and the warmth of being surrounded by friends. Scents that were at once delicious and gut-twisting filled my nose.

I remembered my mother.

My fingers dug into my thigh. I gritted my teeth against the flood of memories. Untwisted tales, not at all what Colin had described of my life.

The memories pushed in harder. Siren Hunter poison burning my veins for the first time. Korrina's song lighting up the world and setting my mind free for mere moments while the poison worked its black magic.

Kissing her in those few moments before the transformation was complete, when things hadn't yet become clear. Watching her fall after I transformed, as if she were dead. Staying hidden in the trees until she stood once again.

Waving goodbye.

A low groan rumbled at the base of my throat, and I pushed back against Mnemosyne's power with all my strength. It wasn't enough.

"Let my *strategos* go," Phorkys snarled.

Mnemosyne made a small click at the back of her throat, and I fell back onto my heels, gasped for breath.

Mnemosyne, mother of time, memories, and tales, had made her presence known. I reached for Korrina. Grabbed empty air.

She'd left my side. Was stumbling toward the titaness as if she couldn't resist. As if Mnemosyne was singing a Siren song only Korrina could hear.

I scrambled to my feet, but there was no time to react. Time was no longer ours.

"Come to me, daughter, and tell me your story," Mnemosyne purred and grabbed Korrina's hand.

A brilliant blue light erupted from Korrina's body.

I'd seen her use the scepter before. I'd felt its power. Its ultimate might.

This was something more.

Korrina had become the scepter. No orb floated apart from her body. The power came from her, amplified, magnified. She glowed at every edge. A girl made of light.

I fell. My knees hit rock. The brilliance was too much, too weighted. It pressed me into the floor.

But someone was screaming. She kept screaming.

I crawled forward, to the throne, to the titaness, to the girl made of light. The girl screaming in pain.

My girl.

CHAPTER 11

KORRINA

Exquisite pain rocketed through my bones. The world turned blue, reborn in fire. Crystalline light poured from my pores, streamed beneath my fingertips. My hair floated like fiber optics, firing sparks from the ends.

I was screaming. I was in pain.

And yet, I didn't want it to end.

The power of the scepter was tangible enough to bite into. In this moment, I could control the world.

The woman on the throne next to Phorkys, impossibly tall, painfully perfect, held my hand. Her nails tightened against my wrist, and deep, inner knowing washed over me. This being was the scepter's mother, and only she had mastery over it.

She controlled the scepter.

She controlled me.

A body red-rover'd into our linked hands and wrenched me from her grasp. I fell to the ground, the pain rushed from my limbs, the light ceased, and I felt…empty.

Jared crashed into the wall behind us, yanking an ancient tapestry off the wall.

"What is the meaning of this?" Phorkys roared and towered over Jared.

Jared stood, brushed himself off, and pointed at the woman. "She comes here as a guest but acts as an enemy. She attacked me, took over the scepter, and controlled the Siren. She is a threat."

Phorkys pressed his lips together. Smiled like an adoring father. "Mnemosyne, allow me to introduce my *strategos*, my ever-protective champion."

She stood, and it seemed as if her limbs would never stop stretching. There was something about her that was *more*. Like a soul barely contained or a presence hiding its true form. She nodded at Jared, then turned the full force of her attention to me.

"This is the vessel," she murmured, her voice at once deep, rich, and musical.

My spine stiffened, and I got to my feet. "I am no vessel," I said, fists clenched at my sides.

Mnemosyne spread her lips, showed her teeth, and made a small sound at the back of her throat. Almost like a purr. "I see Melpomene's fire has not diminished through her line."

I started. "Wait. You're Mnemosyne."

She nodded her head, as if she were doing me a favor.

"You're a titaness. Mother of the Muses and grandmother of the Sirens. The scepter..."

"Is mine."

The room went silent.

Phorkys stood straighter. "It *was* yours. A gift given cannot be ungifted. And now that it is back within my dominion—"

"You invited me here to gloat, as is your proclivity," Mnemosyne finished.

Phorkys bristled, but Mnemosyne had already turned her attention back to me.

"He's correct, in part," the titaness said with a sigh. "When it became apparent that Phorkys had seduced my daughter Melpomene, I gifted Phorkys the scepter. I would not have my daughter birth monsters."

Phorkys clipped his claws. "My children are not monsters." This time, when Mnemosyne showed her teeth, it was anything but friendly. "*My* granddaughters are not monsters. *Your* children are."

"The gift of the scepter did not remove my blood from the Sirens' veins, Titaness, just as it did not make my seed buried within your daughter's womb vanish."

My world began to spin.

"But it removed your taint, your sting," she retorted.

"Hold up." I raised my hand. "What's going on?"

Did I have any sway here to ask questions? No, I did not.

That had never stopped me before.

Jared stepped up, filling the gap between the titaness and the primordial sea god. "Phorkys is the father of the Sirens. The titaness gifted him the scepter to keep their true parentage secret, so none would be able to look upon her offspring with distaste."

I looked deep into Phorkys's eyes and saw nothing but darkness. "You hunt your own children?" I whispered.

Beyond the fact that a super-duper long time ago he had a hand in creating my life, this was what struck me the hardest.

Because Phorkys hunted the Sirens, there were Siren Hunters.

Because Phorkys hunted the scepter, I never knew my mother.

Because Phorkys hunted me, Jared was no longer mine.

"They stole the scepter from me," Phorkys thundered, "insisting it was their inheritance. They are no longer my children. But you..." He paused, took a breath, and the malice fell from his expression. "You can change all of this. You have the scepter. You are the link that can end the feud. Allow yourself into my family, allow Mnemosyne's gift to return to its rightful owner, willingly, and the Sirens will be safe forevermore."

My heart battled in my throat, beating against the collar tight against my voice box. I couldn't, and yet…I couldn't not. My mother, my cousins, all the other Sirens that had died or suffered at Phorkys's whims. My entire race. There were so few of us left.

And with the Sirens safe, there'd be no need for Siren Hunters.

"Why is the titaness here?" Jared broke the silence, saving me from an impossible answer.

"Do not forget your place," Phorkys snarled and slapped Jared with a thunderous crack. He flew against the wall, slumped to the floor.

I darted toward him, but Phorkys threw up a claw, freezing me in my place. "The titaness is here at my bequest."

She nodded. "And I could not deny myself the opportunity to be so close to the scepter once more."

Jared slowly got to his feet, his expression bland, as if he were used to such treatment.

"I am here for the vessel." Mnemosyne's voice rose, and that hidden presence I'd sensed before began to reveal itself. She turned her gaze on me, and the rest of the room faded. "War breaks out among the gods, and it will have no end unless the scepter chooses a side. Already violence spills across the Veil and humanity suffers."

My stomach dropped, and worries circled my brain. "What's happening across the Veil?" My throat was dry, my voice a rasp.

Mnemosyne shook her head, not giving me an answer. "The scepter is forever tied to you, Korrina. You cannot exist without it, and it cannot exist without you. You will come with me, learn from me, and I will teach you to unlock the scepter's secrets."

"Not without first swearing allegiance to our family,"

Phorkys growled, snapped his claws, and Mnemosyne went still. "You forget whose roof you reside under, Titaness."

I looked at Jared, who looked as bewildered as I felt. Mnemosyne's eyes darted from side to side, but other than that frantic movement, she was a statue.

Phorkys circled the three of us. "Do you really believe that I would not have impregnated my home with defenses against *all* of my enemies? And you, Mnemosyne…the insult you delivered to me, to my children…you and your daughters acting as if you are better than us, just because your appearances are more approachable than ours." He stepped close to her, stretched until they were nose to nose, dropped his voice. "Your heart is just as wicked as mine."

He stepped back, and Mnemosyne's body relaxed. She sucked in a deep breath, but the look on her face was anything but cowed or fearful.

Titaness looked ready to rumble.

"You will stay as our guest," Phorkys said and took his seat on his throne. "You will teach the *Elpida* the secrets of the scepter. But the scepter will not be engaged until it fights for me."

Mnemosyne shook her head. "Then you face an endless war, and your children already suffer."

Phorkys stood. The room darkened. "You know nothing of what my children can endure. Perhaps while you are here, we may demonstrate to both of you the strength of our family. *Strategos*," Phorkys yelled, though Jared was less than six feet away, "show them to their rooms."

CHAPTER 12

KORRINA

Jared led us out of the throne room to a more polished part of the fortress. If he hadn't shown me how much ocean we were under, I would have guessed we were in a fancy palace on a sun-drenched hillside.

I looked up—way up—at the titaness matching her stride to mine. Mnemosyne was tall.

Intimidatingly tall. I doubt she would have even fit on a runway, though she definitely had the cheekbones to get her there.

Her gray eyes flicked to mine. "It is not polite to stare, Korrina."

I started to say something sarcastic but stopped. "You're the first mythical I've met who has called me by name."

The corner of her lips turned up. "Despite what I said during our unfortunate meeting with Crabby, you are more to me than just a vessel."

Jared and I both stopped walking. My eyes were saucers. They no longer felt like the fit inside my head.

"Crabby," I choked.

It was one thing for me to call him names. It was quite

another for a being more ancient than continents to call him a name.

Jared huffed. His face had turned tomato. "Do not disrespect my master. He is showing you great favor by allowing you to stay here." He started down the hallway again, leading us through palatial rooms and columned corridors.

"Allowing," Mnemosyne said with a snort and rolled her eyes.

Titaness. Rolled. Her. Eyes.

"Tell me, Jared, why do you follow him like a dog follows his owner?" She cocked her head, as if honestly trying to figure it out, rather than deliver a burn. "Do you truly believe Phorkys shows us favor? I doubt Korrina would love someone unintelligent, so what is his hold over you?"

My stomach jolted. "How did you—"

She gave me a puh-lease look.

Right. Titaness of Time, Memory, and Tales.

"I am Phorkys's Siren Hunter and his *strategos*. He has no hold over me. It is an honor to serve him." Jared's chin was high, and he quickened his steps.

"He was poisoned, turned into a Siren Hunter, and has totally forgotten who he was," I filled in.

Mnemosyne tsk-tsked. "That's not fair, Korrina, and you know that. He is remembering. You will help him. *I* will help him."

Jared didn't respond but placed his hand on a black stone plate outside a big door. A light etched around his fingers, and the door opened. "Your room, Titaness," he said and stepped to the side.

Maybe ignoring us was his coping mechanism.

"Why?" I asked Mnemosyne. "Why help us?"

She turned as she entered, and I caught a peek of her room. A fairytale princess would have been speechless.

"This war must be a true fight. Without you, without the

scepter, the fight will have no end. Aimless, pointless, with nothing accomplished or decided. Wars are cruel. Necessary, but cruel. The price of war must be worth the prize."

She softly shut the door, and Jared and I were left alone.

I huffed. As cool as Mnemosyne seemed, she still liked riddles.

Crossing my arms, I turned to Jared. "Where to now, Thalassa?"

He jerked a little at the sound of his last name. Had he forgotten that as well?

"I'll show you to your room," he said and turned down a sloping hallway.

"Yeah, about that"—I hurried to catch up with him—"I'm not leaving my mom in the dungeon by herself."

Jared looked at me without looking at me, his eyebrows doing a confused dance. "You'd rather go back to the Grotto than sleep in your own room?"

I shrugged. "She could be moved with me. But if not, the floors there are comfy. I'm not leaving my mom."

Jared stopped and pushed between his brows. "Phorkys does not allow cursed Sirens in his fortress. That she is allowed in the Grotto at all is a miracle."

I gave him a so-what look.

"And I've been commanded to take you to your new room. So that's what we are doing." He sounded tired, but also, unrelenting.

I planted my feet. Settled my hands on my hips. He'd never won a game of Who's More Stubborn since we met, pre-kindergarten.

"I will carry you over my shoulder if I have to," he threatened.

A grin spread across my face. "Promise?"

A hint of a long-absent dimple appeared on his cheek. His fists clenched again.

"Korrina, please. Please don't do this." He took a deep breath, checked around us, waited until we were alone, and leaned in. "If you insult him by denying a room in his home, I don't know that I can protect you." His voice went low. He held my gaze and stepped closer. His hand reached for my hair, and he brushed one of my curls with the back of his finger. "Please let me protect you."

His nearness sizzled against my skin, and every memory of every gravity-defying kiss flushed against my lips, trembled down my body, settled in my heart.

I nodded. "I can visit her whenever I want?"

He let out his breath, his hands slowly relaxed, and he stepped away. "Yes, that we can do."

"And maybe, maybe we can bribe Colin into moving her to a better room? One near mine?"

"If it were allowed, he would have moved her next to his room," Jared muttered, killing any hope of me getting Mom out of the Grotto.

We continued along, and Jared pointed out various landmarks along the way so I could orient myself. "We're south of the banquet hall" or "We're northeast of the Grotto."

It was sweet of him to help me get a sense of the place, but I understood directions like *turn left at the third Starbucks on the right*.

I finally patted his arm. He froze, like my touch had turned him to stone. "Things like north and south barely meant anything to me when I could see the sun."

He opened his mouth, closed it, didn't open it again, and I regretted saying anything at all.

We turned down yet another hallway, this one full of wooden doors on either side. He approached one at the very end of the hall, this one with French doors instead of a single slab of wood. The knobs were made of seashells, and the hinges looked like they were made of gold. Like Mnemosyne's room, this one had an identical black stone plate.

Jared placed his hand against the plate, and again, it glowed around his outstretched fingers.

"Your turn." He stepped away from the plate, nodding at me to mimic what he'd done.

I pushed my lips together, then copied what he'd done. The plate warmed against my hand, flashed twice, then cooled.

"This room is now calibrated to only open for you…and those with the right security clearances."

"Like a high-tech hotel key." I looked from my still-warm palm to the stone plate. "Never would've thought Phorkys would invest in technology," I muttered.

"You have no idea who Phorkys is," Jared said, his tone not snappy or sassy-pants, but matter-of-fact.

I didn't have a chance to respond because he pushed open the doors.

Floor-to-ceiling windows stretched on the opposite side of the room. In one corner, a pile of plush pillows and furry blankets begged me to run and jump into them. On the other side, a giant seashell—big enough to fit two people—held steaming water. A fire crackled in a hearth, the flames normal red and orange instead of Hunter green, and a dressing mirror and wardrobe completed the room.

I stepped inside, spun around.

"Is everyone's room like this?" If so, I could see why Phorkys inspired such loyalty.

Jared chuckled. "Not even close. But Mnemosyne is the equivalent of a visiting queen, and you are special to Phorkys."

"Phorkys picked out this room for me?" I asked, my tone all Doubting Korrina.

He toed the rug. "Not quite. He just asked me to make you feel more at home."

I liked this room even better. I walked over to the giant seashell and dipped my hand in the bath water.

"And where do you sleep?" I lifted my gaze and discovered he'd drifted closer. The buzzing in my stomach, the one that happened every time he was near, started again.

He checked over his shoulder toward the open doors, then picked up my hand and pressed a kiss to the tattoo on the inside of my wrist.

Oh sweet mother of coffee.

"I'll find you later." He spun on his heel before I could react, stepped into the hallway, and began to close the doors. "Oh, and Korrina?"

I ripped my gaze away from my wrist, which still burned from his lips. "Yeah-huh?"

"Keep these doors locked. Phorkys may have issued orders to not attack you, but that doesn't mean accidents don't happen." He shut the doors with a click, and the mechanical deadbolt turned as he locked the door for me—with his *right security clearance*—and just like that, I was left alone in a princess room in my worst enemy's home.

CHAPTER 13

KORRINA

I explored every inch of my new princess room, all while letting the last few hours percolate in my brain.

First, it was a really cool room. If I had to be a prisoner, this was the place to be.

Second, Jared kissed me, Jared kissed me, Jared kissed me. I stood in front of the huge standing mirror and did a shameless booty dance.

Third, a titaness had come looking for me. I still wasn't sure what her end goal was, but if she could help me figure out how to control the scepter, stop the gods' civil war, *and* help Jared, she was my new best friend.

Tanzy needed to know there'd been a slight change of plans. I was still going to wake Mom, help Jared, save Luke, and get them all out of here after taking Phorkys down.

But I wasn't leaving Mnemosyne until she taught me what she knew about my scepter.

With that in mind, I ignored Jared's strong suggestion to stay put and resolved to find Isamarine, the creature who'd made my chains. Because, first step first, I had to get this collar off.

And coffee.

Always coffee.

I peeked my head out of the massive door to my room. The hallway was empty, the lights were midday bright. My stomach growled.

The kitchen was as good a place as any to start. Surely there were kitchen servants there who could give me a snack and a clue to finding Isamarine.

The fortress was a repetitive collection of narrow hallways and sloping walkways. Thanks to Jared's directions, I had a small idea of which direction to walk. Or the direction I thought the kitchen would be. Somewhere near the banquet hall, unless this fortress designer was a complete idiot.

An hour later, I determined the fortress designer had been a complete idiot.

A creature with a few extra limbs and oversized ears passed with a look on its face that I wasn't sure how to interpret.

Never a bad time to make new friends. I reached out my hand. "Hi, I'm new here, and—"

It snarled, showed fangs. One of its extra hands gave me the finger.

"Never mind." I dropped my hand and hurried on.

Small talk was not a good idea.

I experimented on other creatures I came across. Angry face made the scary creatures laugh. Or snarl. Smiling made them sniff my hair.

"And I'm done trying to make new friends," I muttered, after escaping a beastly woman who had a fancy curl in the center of her forehead and calamari legs.

Finally, I saw a small, imp-like creature heading down the hall with a tray full of empty plates and bowls.

I stalked it.

It led me down a side hallway, so narrow that none of Phorkys's larger children could possibly fit inside. Did size mean power here? If the smallest creatures were servants, the largest were...what? It didn't seem as if anyone lived a life of leisure here. The entire place felt very much like a war camp, and not like a kingdom that felt safe.

I smelled the kitchen before I saw it.

The pungent aroma of steamed seaweed—a smell once smelled, never forgotten—permeated the air. But other scents too. Nice scents. Coffee scents.

I plunged forward without a thought to danger or to making up reasons to be there.

Coffee was always a reason.

The kitchen was saturated with white light. Pots boiled, steam escaped out of tilted lids, and freshly baked bread cooled on worn wood countertops. It was a mixture of old and new. A hint of medieval with a taste of Michelin.

A plate full of deliciousness spun out from the many hands of one of the chefs. "Order up," it called out.

I propped my hands on my hips. This was nothing like was they gave me in the Grotto.

"If you're going to take up space in my kitchen, you better make yourself useful," a little voice barked at my back.

I turned. Saw no one. Then looked down.

Isamarine twirled her chain at the end of her finger and looked me up and down.

"Your kitchen?" I put the emphasis on *your*, which in hindsight was not a good idea.

Her eyes sparked. "Yes, mine. Or mine when head chef is on a bender, which is pretty much all the time. Gorlon," her gaze darted to my left, and a monster who looked more Jabba than chef jerked his head up—"mop that sweat up. They want it spicy, but not *that* spicy." She refocused on me. "Back to you. Grab that plate. Follow me."

"But—"

She glared, and in those golden orbs, I saw my future as a Korrina-kebab.

I grabbed the plate.

She stacked three ready-to-serve plates on each of her arms and wove through the kitchen.

She wasn't the easiest thing to follow, being no bigger than a garden gnome, but I kept an eye on the tips of her bat wings and followed the movement of her bobbing head as she navigated the kitchen and led us into a smaller dining room.

The creatures here were in various types of work suits. Some had oxygen tanks on their backs, as if they'd just come in from working outside the forcefield. Others wore tool belts and the trappings of Mr. Fix-It. Sulfur and oil scented the air, and it was an odd mix with the aromas steaming up from the plate in my hands.

"That table. Apologize for it taking so long," Isamarine ordered then disappeared.

I looked from the plate in my hand to my new customer to every single escape route in the room.

The customer wasn't scary. What he was went beyond scary. Danica would have to invent a new word to describe him.

He had no face. Just an open maw full of rotating teeth, eyes where his chin should be, and T-Rex arms that had to be some leftover evolutionary thing that was no longer needed. Like wisdom teeth.

"I'm, uh, sorry this took so long." I placed the plate in front of him and slowly backed up.

His chin eyes narrowed. "You're new here."

His voice was nothing like I expected. I expected shrieking, grating, discordant tones, but what I got was a deep bass, comforting and kind.

"I hope Isa's treating you nice. She tends to throw newbs to the gorgons. Lucky for you, you got me, eh?" He reached out with a T-Rex arm and shook my hand. Not a greeting shake, but a we're-in-this-together hand wiggle.

"Lucky me," I squeaked.

"You need anything, you just ask for Ben. You got that?" He gave my hand a final shake, then let go and turned to his food.

I backed away. Heard chuckling. I turned, and this time, I looked down first.

Isa stood there, arms folded, grinning like she knew she was funny. "Isn't he the greatest?"

"You're part devil, aren't you?"

Her eyes sparked again, and her grin grew even bigger. "He wishes."

My stomach twisted into a knot. Crap. She was my people. That was going to make everything about this way harder.

"C'mon. I'm due a break and you look peckish." She waved me to the side of the room, led us back through the kitchen—where she grabbed various foods from various pots—to a small table in the back, out of the way of the not-so-ordered kitchen chaos.

She shoved the plate food at me and gestured for me to dig in. "I'm Isa, by the way."

"I know." I tapped the collar at my throat.

"Ah, that's why you look so familiar. Took part of my chain."

My eyes went wide, and I tried not to be hurt. *She* didn't recognize *me*? I was kinda a celebrity.

She held my gaze for a moment, stone-faced, then let out a giant laugh. "You should've seen the look on your face! Of course I know who you are. You're the *Elpida*." She made woo-woo hands. "We're all very impressed. What I want to know is what in the Styx are you doing in my kitchen."

I gulped down a bite of pastry. "Hungry," I said. "Coffee," I said.

"Bell in your room," she said and made a ding-a-ling gesture.

"Oh. Well, they don't have room bells where I come from."

"No, you have phones and room service. But they work the same. You ring, we serve. You do not come to the kitchen and forage. Understand?"

"Yes, ma'am," I muttered and shoved more food in my mouth. If she was about to kick me out, I was going to eat all I could first. I desperately scanned the room for a coffee pot.

"Phorkys warned us about you. Said you were wily."

I straightened. Didn't even bother to hide my grin.

"I can only assume you're here to learn about my chain around your neck." She intertwined her fingers and leaned forward.

My mouth was full again, so I threw out my hand, palm to the sky, in a *duh* gesture. She wasn't beating around the bush, so neither would I.

"I'll make you a deal. You wait tables for a shift, I'll tell you one thing about my chain. You can come as often as you'd like or not at all. But it's the only way I'll tell you anything."

"One fact for an entire shift? That's a little lopsided, don't you think?"

"Not if you're a terrible waitress. But I'm willing to take the chance. Lost half my staff to the attacks, either injured or reassigned to repairs." She picked a small cookie off my almost empty plate. "Besides, I have a feeling you need a distraction." She bit into the cookie, stood, and grabbed a new apron from a hook. "See you in a few hours."

She ta-ta waved and was about to disappear into the kitchen chaos.

"Wait. What are you?"

She twirled the end of her chain. "You may be a Siren, but I'm the one who drags sailors to their deaths."

CHAPTER 14

JARED

Korrina wasn't in her room. I shouldn't have been surprised, but I'd gotten used to having my commands obeyed. After spending ten minutes of knocking at her door like a fool, I'd finally walked in to make sure she was okay.

I slammed the doors behind me, startled a harpy in the hallway, and engaged the lock. "Sorry," I murmured and stomped off, my combat boots thudding more heavily than usual.

Korrina was in one of two places. Either the Grotto visiting her mother or the kitchen stealing snacks.

Mnemosyne's trick in the throne room had opened something in my brain, something chained shut since my transformation. Chained shut, but not sealed tight.

And now? Those bit and flickers of memories that had tortured me for the past year?

I remembered them all.

The kitchen was on the way to the Grotto, and while I walked, I tried to sort out my emotions. I was the *strategos*, and everything about who I was now was perfectly crafted to be the best. My mind was fine-tuned for battle tactics, my instincts for attack. My need for action fueled my need for war.

And yet...there was this other life. A whole other me. A me I'd been forced to unbecome.

I'd had no choice, and that settled wrongly in my gut.

If I'd had a choice, who would I have become?

Korrina exited the small hall leading to the kitchen, some twenty feet ahead of me. Her face looked paler than normal, and she absentmindedly tapped a cookie against her lips before biting into it and turning toward the corridor that led to the Grotto.

I caught up, slipped my hand under her elbow. "I thought I told you to stay in your room." It came out as a growl, and her blue-skies gaze slipped to mine, the black centers widening as if I'd scared her.

She raised her chin into the air, recovering. "You're not the boss of me," she said and yanked her elbow away.

I frowned. Korrina rarely recoiled from my touch. I guided her to the side of the corridor, where we'd be out of the main foot traffic. "What happened?"

A weighted sigh escaped her lips. "I just keep meeting creatures who are scarier than me, and..." She fidgeted with the collar at her throat.

I smiled. This, I could fix. "I know just what you need. Follow me." I took a few steps and realized her electric presence was slipping away from me. "Korrina?" I turned around. She hadn't moved.

Her hand found its way to her bruised ribs—ribs I'd bruised. She looked between the direction of the Grotto—of her mother—and me, as if unsure of herself, and once again, I was left struggling with the memories of her charging forward in spite of danger versus this girl who stood before me, silenced and uncertain.

She wasn't herself.

Of course, neither was I.

"Korrina, trust me. This will help."

She met my gaze, and something incredibly sad passed through her expression. "I'm trying."

I tossed Korrina two Kampur wraps and began wrapping my own hands. She let the white strips of cloth fall to the floor, raised an eyebrow, then twirled in a circle and surveyed the training room.

She'd been here once before but had been a little distracted.

I avoided looking at the spot on the floor where she'd popped into my world, where we'd kissed. Kissing wouldn't help her now.

No matter how much I wanted to.

I picked up her wraps again, grabbed her arm, and started wrapping her wrist and hand. "This is how you stop feeling helpless," I said and pressed my thumb into the center of her palm. Her nearness crackled against my skin. If I looked up, she'd be looking at me, and we'd both be lost. "Train. Get strong." I tucked the end of the wrap into itself, handed her the other wrap, and stepped away. Only when I was a safe distance from her did I dare meet her gaze.

Her cheeks were flushed, but she said not a word. Just took one end of the wrap, placed it between her teeth to hold the wrap tight, and copied my work.

Never thought I'd be jealous of a strip of cloth.

"I assume you've been trained in the basics?" she asked, tucking the end of the Kampur wrap into itself and falling back into a defensive stance.

A grimace shot across my face, and I shook my head. "Oh yeah, I've been through the basics."

"Good." She tied her hair into a knot. "Then I don't have to take it easy on you."

She lunged forward, a flurry of fierce fists.

I raised my arms, deflected her blows.

We'd fought before, but that had been different. So very different. Then, I hadn't known. I hadn't understood my feelings for her.

I hadn't believed how dangerous she could be.

I hadn't witnessed her pain.

I'd only wanted to inflict it.

She kicked into my ankle, and I collapsed like Achilles. "You're not fighting back," she huffed. "You want me to train, to be strong? Fight. Me."

Her eyes blazed, and the scepter shone through. Did she know? Did she understand how intertwined it was with who she was?

I leaped to my feet, grinned. "Have it your way." I lowered my shoulder and plowed into her.

She shot backward with a loud grunt, but I went with her, wrapped my arm around her waist, following her to the ground. I'd fight her, but I wouldn't allow her to hurt.

She didn't hesitate but punched my ribs as we went down, knocking my breath loose. I landed on top of her, pinned her wrists down, and the heat from her gaze blasted through me.

We froze.

Her breath came in pants. Mine matched her rhythm. A bead of sweat trickled from her temple, and I didn't think.

I licked it away.

Korrina drew back to look at me. "Did you really just do that?"

Heat flushed my cheeks, and I rolled off her. "Uh."

Rather than staying where she was, she crawled forward, her mane of hair falling around her face. "Do you make a habit of licking your enemies?" Her voice dropped. Good gods, she practically purred.

"You're not my enemy," I somehow managed to get out.

She sat back on her heels, tilted her head. "So we are making progress."

"Are you two done yet?" a voice called out from the other side of the room.

Korrina looked past my shoulder, narrowed her eyes. "Why? You want a turn at getting your rear kicked?"

I spun around, folded my arms, blocked Luke from Korrina.

He sauntered forward, too cocky for a guy who'd barely made his way back in. I didn't trust him. Not here, not with Phorkys. Definitely not with Korrina.

Korrina brushed past me, and I swear she grazed her arm against mine on purpose.

"Whatever that was, it was not a rear-kicking," Luke retorted.

They began to circle one another.

Korrina tossed her hair over her shoulder, shot me a searing side glance. "It's because Jared can't resist me. You on the other hand—"

Her leg shot out, and she hooked her foot around Luke's knee, brought him crashing to the ground. She gave him no time to react but jumped on top of him, pinned his arms down with her legs, and drove her forearm against his throat. Her hair cascaded down, blocking their faces from my view.

Pride, and a flash burn of jealousy, rocketed through my bones. She could take care of herself, but her being that near any other male brought out my Hunter.

Green flames erupted from my palms, and the crackle of power drew Korrina's and Luke's attention from each other to me. "Training's over," I growled, aware of what a d-bag I was being. Didn't care. Didn't trust the guy.

Didn't want anyone's hands on Korrina but mine.

Korrina got off him.

Luke raised his paws and backed off. "Our girl's a fighter. Glad to see she can throw down without her song."

"Pfft," she responded and blew the hair out of her face. "As if there was any doubt."

I clenched my jaw shut tight and called on every iota of willpower to tone down my magic, to not cave Luke's face in just because he used the word *our*. That would be an overreaction.

Worth it. But an overreaction.

"Thanks for the workout. Later kids." Luke sauntered out of the room, the same way he'd entered.

Korrina walked to my side, elbowed my folded arms. "Breathe, Jared."

I looked down at her, found her smirking. "I'm fine," I said.

"Uh-huh. Wanna lick me again?" Her tone, her lips, the dancing light in her eyes—they all said she was teasing.

"You have no idea." My voice dropped to a grumble, and the tease fell from her face.

She checked the room, made sure we were alone. "There will be no more licking the Siren, got it, Thalassa?" She flicked my arm and walked away.

"Not unless you ask for it," I called after her, and she sashayed her hips as she left me alone in the training room.

I cracked my knuckles, gave her a few seconds head start, then went after her.

No more licking. Didn't mean I'd let her out of my sight until I was sure she was safe.

CHAPTER 15

KORRINA

I let Jared think he'd left me safely in my room. I doubted his idea of safe activities included serving dinner to a bunch of monsters.

But Isa's offer was too enticing to pass up, and if I was going to get my first fact about the chain around my throat, I had to shower and get to my shift. Stat.

Besides, Luke was meeting me there. His whispered words after I'd knocked him to the ground? *I'm still here. We're still good.*

My insides felt like I'd been filled with helium. Jared was into me. Luke was on my side. Mnemosyne was going to teach me about the scepter.

Whoever said I had bad ideas should see me in action now.

I stepped out of the shower onto a heated floor—still surprised that the god of all things scary had amazing taste in bathrooms—and threw on a pair of black linen pants and a fitted, cream-colored shirt I found in the wardrobe. The pants were a little big, but the drawstrings cinched things right up.

My journey to the kitchen was much shorter this time around. I kept my head down, didn't attempt to make friends, and smelled yummy kitchen scents within minutes of leaving my room.

The kitchen was standing-room only. I slipped through a small gap between two large beasts and began the concert-shuffle to the front of the crowd. Isa had to know I'd shown up; otherwise, I wouldn't get my promised download.

"All right, miscreants!" Isa shouted somewhere in front of the gathered crowd of kitchen staff. "We've got a hungry room full of fangs. Let's get dinner out and serve our guests with all the attitude we can spare."

I pushed my way to the front as the staff bumped each other. The anticipation in the room grew thicker, as if they all knew what was coming. Finally, Isa finally came into view. Standing on an empty crate, she nodded at me, acknowledging I was present, and fixed her attention on the crowd.

"What do we want?" Isa screamed and punched her fist into the air.

"No one in the weeds!" everyone screamed back.

"How do we want it?" she screamed again.

"No deaths tonight!" they all screamed again.

I gulped.

"Let's get busy then. Dismissed!" Isa's voice had to be raw by now.

The crowd broke up with creatures hurrying to their stations in the kitchen and out the door to the dining room with trays.

"Korrina, grab a server's jacket. You're in the round section tonight. It's easy to find—only area of the room with round tables. They like to begin their meal with seaweed tea, and they do not like it cold." She whipped a dishrag at my batookus, spun on her heel, and left me on my own.

"Nothing like on-the-job training," I muttered, buttoned up my fancy serving jacket, and made my way to the drinks station. Hot tea kettles were at the ready, so I grabbed one, lifted my chin high, and waltzed into the dining room like I knew what I was doing.

The chaotic noise of the kitchen dimmed to a dull din in the dining room. I scanned the room, found my section, and headed over.

"What's up?" I addressed the table. For the most part, these creatures looked semi-human, which made them only semi-scary, if one chose not to focus on their extra appendages. "My name is Korrina, and I'll be your server this evening. Seaweed tea?" I lifted the pitcher and filled mugs of various shapes and sizes.

Either no one recognized me, or they'd been warned the *Elpida* would be serving them tonight. They avoided eye contact and continued their conversations as if I didn't exist.

Fine. With. Me.

"How 'bout some service over here?" someone called out from behind.

I turned and saw at least three more round tables, at one of which sat Luke.

I walked over, filled up the teacup of the creature next to Luke, and shook the kettle. Barely any left. I turned my back to the rest of his table, took his teacup, and slowly poured the little bit of remaining tea.

"Have you gotten close to him yet?" I murmured, not making eye contact, trying not to move my lips.

"No one gets in to see him." Luke covered his mouth so no one could see his lips move. "Colin's on the surface, and Phorkys hasn't been seen since he left."

"Isn't that weird?" The kettle was now empty, but I kept up my pouring motions.

"No, just makes it impossible to get close to him."

"I think he's had enough," Luke's neighbor grumbled.

I met the creature's dark gaze, shrugged. "All out. Have to get more." I knocked Luke's spoon off the table. He bent to pick it up, and so did I. "Make it possible," I hissed. "This doesn't work unless you short out his power."

Back in the kitchen, I grabbed a new kettle as Isa marched up. "Korrina, we need your food orders."

"Orders?" Panic seeped into my voice. "What orders? I'm not even done filling teacups."

Isa's face went murderous. "We're in the weeds," she yelled. "Who can take over the rookie's tables?"

"I gotchya, Boss," someone else called out and headed into the dining room.

"We have an important guest staying with us." Isa addressed me again.

"Yeah, I know." I spread out my arms.

She snorted, rolled her golden eyes. "Not you. The titanness. She's requested her meal and that you of all creatures serve it to her. Gods know why. Take her that plate over there. Don't screw it up."

BALANCING A TRAY FULL OF FOOD AND DRINK WAS EXACTLY AS hard as it appeared.

I knocked on Mnemosyne's door with my toe. A fairy-looking creature with horns and black wings passed and gave me a what's-wrong-with-you look. A few seconds later, the door opened, and the titaness hovered over my barely balanced tray, eyebrows raised.

"Once again, I'm reminded how blessed I am that I don't need to eat to survive." She sighed, extended her arm. "Just leave that in the hallway. Somehow you've managed to turn prime rib into a dubious-colored stew."

I set the tray down and pointed at myself. "Siren. Not server."

"I agree. Follow me."

Mnemosyne's room was imbued with light. White columns held up an expansive stone ceiling, and floor-to-ceiling doors opened onto a balcony carved from white, sparkling stone. Her view looked much like the view out of the rest of Phorkys's fortress windows, except that her side of the fortress looked onto an undersea coral garden teeming with bioluminescent creatures.

I walked onto the balcony and peered over the edge. "Wow."

Mnemosyne joined me. "Darkness can be breathtaking. But you've discovered that on your own, haven't you?"

My fingers tightened around the stone railing. "Ania," I whispered, somehow knowing Mnemosyne knew.

Her profile was sharp against the undersea light show, each line perfect, symmetrical. She made my hands itch for charcoal and canvas...things I'd been too long without. Maybe someday, when the world wasn't tearing itself apart, my art would find me again.

"Yes, your shadow side. Too often humans reject those darker parts of themselves, and in doing so, they are weakened. Only in our darkest moments may we be refined."

I nodded. "I can't hear her anymore. Something about this place is blocking her."

"Yup," she agreed. "You."

My stomach dropped, but Mnemosyne didn't give me a chance to respond.

"You've put her in a box, a box you've so tightly associated with your power, that you cannot hear her without also using your Siren voice."

I shook my head. "No, she's part of that power, she's—"

"Part of you," Mnemosyne interrupted. "Like you said in the throne room, you are more than just a vessel. You are more than just your power. More than just the scepter. And until you believe that, Phorkys wins."

I turned my back on the dark sea and stared into her

princess room. Of course I knew that. And I believed that. Didn't I?

"There's not been a moment of my life that hasn't been defined by my voice," I said. "How do I separate me from that?"

She placed her hand over mine. "You don't. You accept that you are more."

Her touch sent blue light through my veins until I looked like one of those bioluminescent creatures, glowing like starlight.

Her truth bombs were more than I could process right now. I shook her off.

"You said you'd teach me about the scepter. And I'm pretty sure the kitchen boss is wondering where I am by now."

She smiled. "You forget I am Time. You've been gone from your shift for mere minutes."

My jaw dropped, and I felt very, very human.

"But I agree," she continued. "There is only so much we can cover in this moment. To understand the scepter's secrets, you must first understand why it was formed." She strolled back inside, and I followed, close on her heels.

"You've heard stories of mothers lifting cars off a child in a moment of superhuman strength? Or a grandparent holding onto life until his grandchild arrived to say goodbye?"

I nodded. Of course I had. But these stories had nothing to do with the scepter.

"Humans are defined by time, by story, by memory. Time, because, for them, it ends. Story, because courage must be spoken. Memory, because paths are paved by those who went before."

"Okaaaay," I said, impatience not creeping into my voice. Not at all.

"Time ending too early can give a mother strength. The story of a grandparent's love for a grandchild can give courage to hold onto life, and the knowledge that they will be a treasured memory can allow them to let go."

She snapped her fingers, and scenes of what she'd just described unfolded, but our vantage point was distant and high.

"The gods experience none of this. They are powerful beings, but they do not feel beyond very extreme emotions. Anger. Pride. Lust. They do not feel more because they do not have an ending. They have no definition to their lives beyond the roles assigned to them."

The scene sped into the ocean and circled around a younger version of Phorkys, strong and handsome, the scepter at his side.

"And in the case of an obsolete, primordial god of monsters, whose role has been replaced by other gods—"

Time passed, the scepter vanished from his hands, and he became the god I knew today. Gnarled, old, scarred, with a deep bitterness that glinted in his gaze.

The scene faded, and Mnemosyne's room came back into view.

"That's what happened to him when the Sirens stole the scepter?"

She nodded. "The scepter captures the very essence of what makes humans human. It allows the bearer to experience human emotions, to know what it is like to have a beginning and an end, and through this, a god's power is amplified."

"No wonder he wants it back," I breathed.

"In Phorkys's hands, the scepter helped him birth monsters and breed terror and darkness." She picked up my hand, placed her palm to mine, and a blue light radiated between our palms. "But because of who you are, the scepter heals. Hope heals, as does time, story, and even memory. Through you, those core pieces that define humans are amplified. Only you can allow that to be corrupted."

She broke contact, and I was back in the hallway, staring at

Mnemosyne's closed door. The unintended stew at my feet was still steaming, and the black-winged fairy was still giving me the stink eye.

I returned to the kitchen to finish my shift, while Mnemosyne's words peppered my brain.

Phorkys may control my voice.

But I controlled my power.

CHAPTER 16

KORRINA

The dinner shift wrapped up with tired cheers for Isa and annoyed grimaces for me. The kitchen no longer smelled yummy but instead an odd mix of sweat, seaweed, and dessert.

I washed my hands, dried them on my server's jacket, and surveyed the waitstaff's buffet at the back of the kitchen. Comprised of leftovers from the cookpots, I had my pick of every dish on the menu.

"A job with benefits," I muttered and started loading up my plate.

Someone snorted behind me. Already, I'd grown familiar with that snort.

Without taking my eyes off the lukewarm food, I said, "Get ready to dish, Miss."

"I'm fairly certain you haven't earned any share of information."

I turned and met Isa's murderous gaze, hands on her tiny hips, vibrating as if she were a stick of dynamite about to explode.

"That wasn't our deal." I picked a piece of meat off my plate and popped it into my mouth. My stomach growled, loudly and appreciatively. "I came, I gave out food, I get deets."

She huffed, gestured for me to follow her, and led me back to what I was coming to think of as *our spot*.

"My chain regenerates," she said, before I'd even sat down. "Come back tomorrow if you want to know more."

She made to leave.

I put out my foot, balanced my plate in my hand—I'd improved my technique through the course of the dinner service—and waggled a finger. "Nope. I already knew that. You have to give me new information. Otherwise, I put those wiles you keep talking about to use in your kitchen."

Her gaze darted around the kitchen, as if assessing just how much damage I could do. She sat down.

I joined her and popped another piece of food into my mouth in triumph.

"You already know that my chain regenerates and that I am the force that drags a shipwrecked sailor into the depths."

"And that you use your chain to do so," I jumped in, not wanting her to use that as my quote-unquote fact.

She nodded. "Each link of my chain holds a small essence of the life that the ocean has stolen. It weighs me down even as it drags others to the depths."

I fiddled with the chain at my neck, chills running the length of my spine. "There are dead people around my neck?"

"Essence of dead people," she corrected.

"That's not better."

Her lips twitched to the side. "My power operates much like Newton's law of motion," she said, as if that explained things.

I thumbed at myself. "Haven't graduated high school." Nor had I been in school in the past year. Getting my GED was top of my list after my world went back to normal.

If it ever went back to normal.

She pressed her lips together, as if gathering patience. "An object in motion stays in motion. At least until an unbalanced force acts upon the object. So as long as humans and mythicals keep drowning in the ocean, my chain remains eternal. My power is fueled by the force of previous deaths."

I crinkled my eyebrows. "So what unbalanced force could disrupt your power?"

She grinned. "You'll need to come back for another shift for that answer. And"—she shook her finger in my face—"not get stuck in the weeds."

I STUMBLED BACK TO MY ROOM, MY FEET TIRED, MY ARMS TIRED, my brain tired.

Rumors had circulated the dining room as I'd tripped my way through dinner service. Colin was on the surface—I knew that—and word was that the assault on the fortress wasn't a glancing blow from another battle, but targeted. An attempt to take out Phorkys before he joined the war.

Sides were being picked, and Phorkys was expected to fight alongside Hades. Between Phorkys's monster children and Hades's underworld powers, they could make a scary dent in any opposing force.

I sidestepped an ogre flexing in the hall outside my room. She looked like one of Luke's cousins. An oversized creature with the ability to turn fat into muscle, to bulk up and go from huggable to Hulk-able in mere seconds.

She stared me down as I pressed my hand to the black pad by my door. It lit up under my palm, my door unlocked, and I scooted inside before the ogre decided we needed a girl's night.

Mnemosyne's and Isa's words kept circling my brain. If I controlled the scepter, with or without my song, was it a force that could unbalance Isa's power long enough to get this collar off my neck?

I eyed my fluffy pillows piled in the corner, sighed—"Soon, my loves, soon"—and settled myself in the middle of the room. A quick twinge of I-don't-wanna-hurl flew through my brain, but I pushed it to the side. I could handle a little nausea if that was the price of dream walking. A few deep breaths later, I'd connected with Tanzy.

She wasn't asleep, and her headspace was foggy and muffled. Distantly, her voice came through the haze. "Hold on, hold on. You can't just step inside my head and expect me to be waiting."

The space she held me in slowly cleared, and Tanzy stood in front of me, arms crossed, looking irritated.

"I thought you could only step inside someone's dreams," she said.

I shrugged. "Me too, but you're a psychic, so I figure some part of you is always dreaming."

Her expression lit up. "Never thought of it that way, but yes, that makes sense."

"How are things going up there?" I wanted an update on my friends before we got sidetracked with all-things-Phorkys.

Her lips pursed to the side, as if debating what she should tell me and what she shouldn't. "The weather has gone crazy. Hurricanes in the Atlantic, tsunamis in the Pacific, tornados everywhere. Meteorites are falling. Not little shooting star ones —the kinds that leave craters."

"Not good," I said.

"Understatement." She let out a breath. "Attacks from actual mythicals have been low. So far, most are completely unaware that this craziness is caused by anything other than climate change. But our sightings of mythicals have been ratcheting up. Amity's building a force of mythical refugees on this side of the Veil—those that don't want to harm humans and need to escape the coming war."

"What about those that do want to cause harm?"

"Neri, Cloud, and Dave-plus-the-gun take care of those." She made a slitting motion across her throat. "Danica found some obscure reference that a combination of iron and ebony can hurt mythicals. So she made a bunch of bullets for Sully."

"Dave's still acting like his shotgun is a person?" I rolled my eyes.

"When he's not making out with Amity, yes. He's a good guy. Great part of the team."

I hummed. Dave was not who I'd have picked to be part of our team, but Amity loved him and he loved her. "I'll give him another chance," I muttered.

Tanzy smiled and patted my arm. "Good girl. Now, what's going on down there? Are you ready for us to pull you out yet?"

I shook my head and gave her the titaness-Luke-new-job updates. "So basically, I can't leave yet."

She nodded. "Obviously."

"If Danica's done wanting to murder me, can you ask her to do some research on a mythical? This one is responsible for sailor drownings. The chain she wears around her waist holds the essence of the drowned."

"Creepy," she said.

"Understatement," I said. "I need Danica to find some sort of force that could unbalance her power. I think it'll help me get this collar off."

"Danica's super busy keeping tabs on all the news sites, traffic cams, and conspiracy chatrooms to keep up with the mythical sightings, but I'm sure she'll make this a priority. We need you back, Korrina. Soon."

My stomach twisted, and the corners of my eyes burned. I'd left them without warning, knowing I'd have to beg for forgiveness. And still, they were willing to work with me, to help me come back.

Tanzy's world faded as I sank back into my body, and my stomach balled into a hard knot. Waves of clammy gonna-spew rolled through me. I jammed my knees into my stomach, the pressure doing exactly nothing to alleviate the sensation.

C'mon, Korrina. Pull it together.

Could something in Phorkys's fortress be messing with my dream walking?

I shoved my knuckles into my mouth, knowing my next step would be more than my stomach could handle, but I'd deal with that later. I breathed deep and fell into another dream walk.

The Void swallowed me whole.

THE VOID SLIPPED OVER MY SPIRIT, AND THE ABSENCE OF SOUND thundered past.

Ania waited.

"How's Mom?" I thought at her, grateful that I had no stomach here—therefore, no nausea.

Ania shook her head, her silver eyes dimmed. *She needs you. She doesn't have much time.*

Ania gripped my spirit and pulled me through the Void. Something like a shot of adrenaline coursed through me, scaring away the heaviness in my spirit.

Without light, speed and distance were hard to judge, but it felt as if we were moving fast enough to break the sound barrier.

If soundwaves existed here.

Despite our pace, lost souls began to chase us, dark shadows barely visible in the black backdrop of the Void. In the distance, a faint silver flame glowed.

Only...

Ania slowed down. The flame hadn't grown any brighter, but we were here. This flame wasn't faint because it was distant.

It was about to go out.

Spirits darted in and out like carrion birds attacking a carcass. Her flame flickered.

I was not allowing this to happen. Mom had run away before, but I wouldn't, couldn't let her this time.

I twisted my spirit into Ania's. Light grew around us, our two dyad halves combining into one strong whole. Spirits scattered. Mom's flame cowered.

Before she could escape, we threw ourselves on her, around her, encased her in our supernova.

She was a ball of pain, weak and quiet. *His scars bind…it hurts…*

"Who's scars, Mom? Colin's?" Was she somehow bound to Colin's scar? Is that why she'd been stuck in the Void, unable to fully transform?

She didn't answer.

"You are not allowed to die on me." I pushed my light into her like paddles on a defibrillator, and life pulsed back into her spirit. "You have"— *more light*, Ania coached—"to wake —*more love*, she sang—"up!"

Colors erupted from our combined spirits, wrapped around Mom, and exploded outward. The Void lit up, as it only had once before, but it hadn't been this bright or for this long.

Large rocks floated in the Void—which made the name counterintuitive—like miniature planets caught in orbit. Structures glinted in our glow, and dark spirits danced around them, some having human form, most not.

They gathered, sped toward us.

You must go, Korrina, Ania shouted. *I don't know that I will be able to meet you again.*

Her sorrow spilled into my soul, and I twisted myself tighter with her. Mnemosyne had said I was the only one blocking Ania. She was tied to me, not my song. She was part of *me*.

"No Siren left behind!" I yelled, grabbed hold of both Mom and Ania, and sent us hurtling back to the physical world.

My spirit crashed into my body, settled into my chest, and I blinked open my eyes. The nausea was back. Violently back. I made it to the toilet and reintroduced myself to my last meal. Maybe Mnemosyne would have a theory on why I was suddenly allergic to dream walking.

"Ania, are you with me?" I gasped, once my meet-and-greet with the toilet was over.

The darkness in me smiled.

I smiled back, bounced my legs to get the blood flowing back to my feet, and brushed my teeth. Mom was not okay, and what I just did to her...

A red light flashed in the corner of my room.

Bam, bam, bam.

I peeked out the door peeper. Jared stood on the other side, ramming his fist into my door. I flung it open.

His eyes were brown, wide, panicked. He held out his hand. "It's your mother. Something's wrong."

CHAPTER 17

KORRINA

The hallways blurred by, the walls a soft violet as if something wasn't terribly wrong. The pounding of our feet against stone nailed in Jared's words. *Something's wrong, something's wrong, something's wrong.* Despite Jared's hand warming mine, his words had sent ice crashing through my veins and my mind into a tailspin.

What had I done?

What you had to, Ania whispered, all dark comfort.

"I don't remember the Grotto being so far," I panted. "Did it move?" It hadn't taken this long when I was being walked down as a prisoner…and now we were running.

Jared shot me a sideways glance, squeezed my hand. I didn't have it in me to smile at him, but I held on tighter, matched my pace to his.

What would all his monstrous underlings think of him holding my hand?

Why didn't he care?

The Grotto's gates appeared before us, ajar as if someone had already rushed through. Here, the red emergency lights pulsed, rocketing up my blood pressure.

Jared tugged at me, but I'd stopped. One more step, and that *something's wrong* would become real.

"Korrina?"

I shook my hand loose from his, straightened my shoulders, and walked through the gates of the Grotto alone.

Jared wasn't far behind.

Ahead, the guard room was empty. But down the corridor, next to my old cell, not so much.

Thanos, Crox, and Silent Bob hovered at the door to Mom's cell, blocking my view. Jared held me back from pushing through them.

"Let me do this part," he muttered.

Mischief and Mayhem had taught me that those best suited for a particular job should be the one to do it. In this case, Jared's position as *strategos* would get us in that cell faster than me playing the daughter card.

"Why did you sound the alarm?" His voice had grown deeper, louder. He projected to the back of the room and then some.

Crox flinched, dipped his head to Jared in a show of respect. "*Strategos*. We thought it was one of her normal fits, and with Colin at the surface we didn't think there was anything we could do, so—"

"I didn't ask for story time. I asked why you sounded the alarm."

Crox didn't answer. He exchanged glances with Thanos, who dipped his head in agreement. In unison, they stepped away from the door.

Jared gasped, and I didn't care anymore. Didn't care about his position or need to keep me safe. I pushed past him, stumbled to a stop.

My mom lay on the floor. I dropped to my knees, pressed my hand to my mouth, and everything inside went numb.

She'd transformed.

Her arms had disappeared. Silvery-white feathers covered her torso and spread down to scaly bird legs. Her talons clenched, and in the only human part of her left, her lips contorted in agony. Small whimpers rumbled from her closed mouth. Still, she slept.

I hadn't wakened her. All I'd done was give the curse power so her transformation could complete.

She was still in the Void. Her soul was still dying.

"Mom?" I reached out, but Jared pulled me back.

"No one touches her until Colin arrives." His tone was all *strategos*, but the soft grip on my shoulder was all Jared.

I nodded. She seemed fragile, somehow less alive than Molpe and the others, an ancient statue that might crumble at any moment.

I kneeled next to her, careful not to step on her wings or her tangled curls, and bent close to her ear. "I'm sorry," I whispered. "So very—"

"What have you done?" A harsh voice rang out through the prison cell.

I jerked back and met Colin's violent gaze.

The scar on his cheek shone white with fury. His face had gone red, and the violet in his eyes was quickly turning scarlet.

"I—"

"Get away from her." Green fire arced out of his palm. I scrambled backward, but there was no avoiding his magic.

Siren Hunter fire popped up all around me, creating a shield, and deflected Colin's attack. Jared's hands were raised, and his eyes had gone Hunter red, but he wasn't attacking me.

He was defending me.

"She is innocent," Jared growled. "She wasn't even here when this happened."

The guards nodded their agreement, though why they were defending me was a mystery.

Or maybe they weren't defending me. Maybe they were supporting Jared.

Choosing Jared over Colin.

"Who was then? You three—" Colin flung his fire toward them, stopping it just before it impacted with their faces.

"She had a fit," Silent Bob gasped, finally scared into speaking, his voice higher pitched than I'd expected. "We didn't think anything of it."

Colin narrowed his eyes and snapped his hand closed, and the fire plummeted into Silent Bob's eye. He screamed, covered his face, dropped to his knees, and the scent of seared flesh smoked through the room.

"Didn't think anything of it?" Colin repeated. "Her medicine could have prevented this."

My heart jumped in my chest. *I didn't do this?*

Thanos and Crox exchanged glances, picked up their fallen comrade, and backed out of the room.

Jared cleared his throat. "With all due respect, her medicine simply numbs the pain and keeps her asleep. I'm not sure—"

"Then what, *Strategos*? What caused this? What else has changed? She's been this way for seventeen years." Colin's gaze narrowed, traveled the room, landed on me.

I felt sick. It wasn't her medicine.

Colin pointed at me. "You. It's you."

He advanced. Jared mirrored him. I stayed where I was, crouched in a defensive position that could easily shift to attack.

Not that I was any match for Hunter fire without my Siren power.

"You're the only thing in this situation that has changed. Since you came here this fortress has been attacked"—he held up one finger—"the Betrayer returned"—two fingers—"my *strategos* has lost his head"—he jerked his head at Jared—"a titaness shows up"—four fingers—"and now, Raelynn."

Five fingers. Full hand. Fire sparked from the center.

"Circumstantial evidence," I said and thanked Cloud and Mischief and Mayhem once again. Who would have thought that a high school prank gang could teach such valuable life skills?

"Enough to convict," he said, voice quiet, fire bright.

"Phorkys wants her alive," Jared said, the only voice of reason in the room.

Colin whipped toward him. "You have no idea what Phorkys wants," he hissed, and his scar grew even more livid. Fire lashed out of his hands, wrapped around Jared, pinned his arms. And once again, came for me.

Scars bind, Ania whispered.

Mom moaned.

I held my arms in front of my face. "I can wake her," I yelled.

Colin froze.

"But if you kill me, that'll make it a little difficult," I said, lowering my arms.

He waited.

"The scepter heals. Once I learn how, it'll heal her, I'm sure of it." Little did Colin know, I already knew that scepter trick. But something like this? Healing Mom? I couldn't just blast out blue scepter light. And right now, I couldn't blast out any light with my song collared.

Colin leaned in, dropped his hands. His fire vanished. "Learn fast."

CHAPTER 18

JARED

I pulled at Korrina's hand as soon as Colin turned to tend to Raelynn. She didn't budge.

"He'll take good care of her," I said under my breath. "He has since it happened."

I didn't have to explain *it*. She knew. The moment Colin chose Phorkys over Raelynn.

The moment he'd never forgiven himself for, though I doubted Korrina saw it that way.

She finally let out a sigh, nodded, and followed me out of Raelynn's cell.

"Will he still care for her now that she's…like that?" Korrina asked.

I shook my head. "He's cared for her too long to just dispose of her now that she's changed. That kind of love—"

"Obsession," Korrina corrected.

"Whatever. It lasts. It doesn't go away just because someone's appearance has changed. Would you care for me less if I lost an arm?"

She snorted. "Of course not. Though I may come up with some new nicknames for you."

I grinned. "Fine with me."

She paused. "What if I went bald?"

I tilted my head, imagined her without hair. "Hot."

She rolled her eyes and elbowed me. "So you finally admit it."

I shot her a sideways glance as we left the Grotto. "Admit what."

"That you luuuuuurve me."

My heart all but stopped. My veins burned. "I'm incapable of love, Korrina. Do not confuse any of this"—I gestured between us—"for that."

Hurt colored her cheeks, and I hated it. I hated every shade of pink she went. I hated every minute I had to convince her that what I felt for her meant nothing.

But if she knew how I truly felt, she'd never leave me here. And sometime soon, she'd have to.

Korrina stayed silent at my side, until we turned past the throne room. "Where are we going?"

"You promised Colin you could heal your mom. He doesn't take promises lightly." I stopped in front of the titaness's door. "Train. Save your mom. Otherwise, Colin is going to kill you."

All the color my words had slapped into her cheeks paled. "But Phorkys—"

"Colin will kill you and accept whatever punishment Phorkys commands. Colin is the most dangerous creature here besides Phorkys, and you promised him a miracle. He will get a miracle."

I knocked on the door, waited until Mnemosyne let Korrina in, and left her there. Painful as it was to leave her side, it was even more agony leaving her when I'd just shoved a knife into her heart and twisted it.

I pressed the pain down until it was a tight knot behind my ribs. I didn't have room for this kind of emotion. Phorkys demanded obedience, full use of my wits, the power he gave me.

He demanded I win Korrina over to him.

Colin laying on threats would not help that mission succeed.

I waited in the war room for Colin, moving through the mind-clearing exercises of tai chi. My muscles relaxed, though my thoughts were more stubborn. It might be hours before Colin left Raelynn and met me here, but I needed his debrief from the surface, and I needed to buy Korrina more time.

The door scraped open, and Colin walked in. Thanos followed, his carapace already healed from our fight night. As head of the guards, and in war times infantry, he'd need Colin's debrief as well.

Exhaustion had crept into Colin's face, and he looked old. The gray in his hair showed more prominently, the lines on his face were etched more deeply.

He sighed, placed his hands on the glossy black table in the center of the room. At his fingertips, a map appeared with 3D images of the gods and their armies. "Hera, Aphrodite, Ares, Hermes, and Dionysus have all declared for Hades." Hades's forces, as well as the gods who had sided with him, turned black. "Athena, Hestia, Apollo, and Artemis have sided with Demeter." Their forces turned red. "Hephaestus refuses to take a side, as does Poseidon. Zeus maintains that he must stay out of the conflict as the self-named king of the gods." Those spots on the map turned gray.

Thanos leaned in, studying the map.

My mind clicked along, finding the pieces Colin laid out and rearranging them into different scenarios. "Which one attacked us?"

"Apollo. Artemis." Colin gestured, and those two figurines turned toward our part of the ocean.

"So they've chosen our side for us," I muttered and narrowed my eyes at the board. In the background, Thanos growled, but my focus had tunneled in, the room had faded, and the prophetic sounds of fighting filled my mind.

"We would never join with Demeter"—Colin's fist clenched—"and they know it."

I nodded, acknowledging his distant words. "What about the demigods and minor gods?" I circled the table, surveyed all angles.

"Sticking to their loyalties. No surprises." Colin stepped back, crossed his arms, and let me muse.

"But easily swayed…"

Colin's eyes slitted. "Perhaps. What are you thinking, *Strategos*?"

"Whether Demeter or Hades wins this conflict is of no consequence to us." I paced the room. Thoughts flowed better when I moved. "What matters are the weaknesses we discover."

Colin stepped back, remained silent. Thanos flexed, his carapace bulged.

We knew our mission. And it was not a fight against a god.

It was a takeover of the entire mythical world. As quietly as possible.

We'd be in power before the rest of them understood what had happened.

"Phorkys planted the seeds for this fight long ago. Now, we must be as weeds. We appear as one with Hades, but always, we play against him." I placed my palms against the table, and Phorkys's many, many children popped up all over the map. "We use our forces to strangle his roots, while crowding out the other side on the surface."

"So we declare for Hades," Thanos said.

I nodded. "With our fingers crossed behind our backs."

We made plans long into the night. Plans for negotiations with Hades, for the declaration of war against Demeter, for all the nuances it took to double-cross the gods.

The halls were quiet when we exited the war room. Thanos bid us goodnight, but Colin held me back.

"You care too much for the *Elpida*. Gossip has infiltrated the Horde about you and her."

I bowed my head. There was no denying it. Not anymore. Flashes of me grabbing her hand and not letting go until we reached her mother invaded my mind. All I'd cared about was getting Korrina to her mother in time. I didn't know if her mother was waking up or dying. All I knew was that Korrina needed to be there, and I had to be the one to get her there, to be there for her.

"If the Horde believes we care for our enemies," Colin continued, "it makes us weak."

Weak.

My blood boiled into my throat. He might as well have said disrespected.

"As you care for Raelynn?" I said, slowly, carefully, not out of caution, but so that he caught every single word.

"That's different," he snapped, seemed to grow in size.

"Explain how? You've kept her as a pet for seventeen years, you've made your feelings for her well known, and yet, you still command the respect of the Horde. How is my caring for Korrina any different?"

Colin leaned in. "Because I'm not skipping through the hallways holding hands with her. Because I keep her locked in a cage. Because I have not been ordered to flip her allegiance."

My jaw locked. He wasn't wrong.

"Do not mistake your position for being invincible, *Strategos*. We survived without you for a millenia, and we can survive without you again."

He left. And those doubts that had been whispering since Korrina arrived, since Mnemosyne performed her memory trick, began to roar.

CHAPTER 19

KORRINA

Elegant fingers appeared in front of my face and snapped. "Focus, Korrina. You are wasting my time, and as the creator of time, that is quite the feat."

I shook my head and tried to re-center on Mnemosyne's instructions, instead of Jared's words. So many words. Too many words. Crushing words.

I fell dramatically to her floor and laid out on the plush rug in the middle of her suite.

"What have I been telling you?" she prodded.

"The scepter amplifies human emotions," I recited as I stared at her painted ceiling and tried to push down the emptiness inside that threatened to swallow me whole. Between Jared and my mom, it was too much. "It needs fuel in order to work, like a rocket needs jet fuel. The stronger the fuel, the stronger the scepter."

"Good," she said. "So what do you feed it?"

I shrugged. "So far, the scepter has fed on my life force and my song. Option A almost killed me, and Option B has been taken off the table." I dug my finger at my neck, the collar just loose enough to not make me feel like I was choking.

"So now you must find something else to feed it." She fell back on the chaise lounge at the foot of her bed, a graceful giantess, and tucked her bare feet under her rump.

I snorted. "Think it likes coffee? 'Cause that, I can do."

"Magical objects require a sacrifice. You must give a part of yourself. Otherwise, the magic has no meaning. The trick is to give something you have in great supply that also does no damage when it is diminished."

"How about a broken heart?" I was jesting, but Mnemosyne perked.

She tapped her lip. "You have experienced a lot of loss lately." No sympathy coated her words. Instead, she regarded me like a scientist regards a rat.

I propped up on my elbows.

She unfolded herself from the chaise and circled me on the rug as if studying me from every angle. "It could work," she muttered.

I sat up all the way and crisscrossed my legs, grateful for the distraction Mnemosyne provided. If not for the Titaness of Time giving me magic tips, I'd be in my room, filling that giant seashell tub with chocolate ice cream and tears.

She sat in front of me, copied my pose, and folded her hands under her chin. Even sitting down, she was three feet taller than me. She reached for my hands, flipped them palms up, then rested her hands below mine. Not touching, but almost.

"Ania will help you with this—it is good you brought her back with you."

I swallowed, nodded. At least I'd done one thing right.

Mnemosyne stared into my eyes, her own an ever-changing mix of stars and glaciers. "I want you to sink into that heartbreak, and push it toward your center. Imagine it flowing into the scepter."

I snort-laughed. "Easy peasy. I've done nothing but swim through heartbreak for a year. What's another lap?"

Mnemosyne's eyes softened, but not enough to let me off the hook.

I sighed, closed my eyes against the sudden burn of tears, and envisioned the scepter. Ania appeared in my mind's eye, head bowed, a flow of scarlet energy floating through her circled hands. Not an aura, but a river. It fed into one side of her hands from some place inside of me I couldn't determine, and it flowed out the other side, toward the scepter, like stardust flowing into a black hole.

"Careful not to send too much," Mnemosyne cautioned. "Your greatest strength is your emotions, even the hard ones. We want to give the scepter only enough to fuel it. It should take the edge off your pain, no more."

I nodded. Ania looked relieved. The scepter burned brighter. The light beyond my closed eyelids changed, took on a blue hue. I peeked open one eye, then the other.

Blue light flowed from the center of my palms. It wasn't the orb I was used to seeing, nor the fully-formed scepter I'd managed to bring out a time or two. Feeding the scepter emotions instead of my song wasn't nearly as powerful. But it *was* something.

And I didn't have to use my song or my soul to do it.

Mnemosyne smiled.

To my surprise, I smiled back. My heart no longer burned like my ribs had caught fire. I no longer felt like I had a giant hole in my middle.

"Better?" she asked.

"Better," I agreed. I could still feel the hurt, but it wasn't so blinding. "I am going to have a much healthier relationship with the scepter from now on."

Mnemosyne frowned. "Be careful of feeding it too often or too much. Ridding yourself of emotional highs and lows can become addictive, and then you'll be no better off than the gods."

I'll help her, Ania said.

Mnemosyne bowed her head. "Thank you, Ania."

"You can hear her?"

She thumbed at herself. "Titaness of Memory, Time, and Tales. Gives me insight to just about everything." She gave me an I-know-I'm-amazing smirk.

"Cool," I said. "So you know what I did to my mom in the Void and why dream walking now makes me upchuck."

She shook her head. "I know almost nothing of the Void. In a place without time or memory or tales, my power sees very little, but we'll get to that in a moment. Your dream walking..." She trailed off, as if confused.

"Makes me upchuck." I mimed the motions, so there could be no confusion.

"I see." She curled her upper lip into a that's-gross snarl. "Power must feed. Your dream walking abilities usually feed on your song or the scepter, but since both are blocked, it is likely feeding on you. I imagine you're experiencing something akin to altitude sickness. The vomitus is your body's way of adjusting."

I crinkled my nose. "Lovely."

She dipped her head, regally. "And now, tell me your story of the Void."

I gave her the CliffsNotes, ending with, "So I think the scars my mother gave Colin are what has sealed her in the Void. She's somewhere between life and death, and when I pushed my power into her, she completed her Siren transformation."

Mnemosyne nodded along with me. "And you told Colin you could heal her with the scepter."

I nodded.

"But you think you need to heal him in order to heal her."

I nodded again.

She shrugged. "Worth a shot. You already know how to heal

using the scepter, and now, with some practice, you can use it on command."

My mouth gaped open. "Worth a shot? What happened to you being all time, memory, tales?" I made my voice sound like an all-powerful genie.

"My power lies in understanding the past. The future is for the Fates."

"Lotta help you are," I muttered.

She threw a pillow at me. "Practice what I've taught you. Tomorrow, we'll delve deeper."

I saluted and got to my feet, but Mnemosyne remained sitting. "Before you leave, there are two things you need to consider. First, healing Colin's scars may not wake your mother. It may kill her instead. Those scars could be the only thing tying her to life."

I pressed my lips together and considered her words. "What she's living is not life. It's torture."

Mnemosyne nodded. "Second, I cannot see Colin's past."

My forehead crinkled. "What does that mean?"

"Either someone has been messing with time and memory—my memory specifically, which I don't think I need to explain how impossible a task that would be—or…" She worried her lip between her teeth.

My heart sped up. "Or?" I prodded.

"Or Colin doesn't have a past."

"That's not possible."

"Neither option is possible. Tread carefully, Korrina. Whatever you decide."

CHAPTER 20

KORRINA

My personal Siren was named Sleep. She called to me, luring me to bed, where she could take over my mind and manipulate me out of what I needed to do.

That was how the old historians had portrayed the Sirens.

I just couldn't give into her yet, because I owed my best friend a psychic phone call. And yeah, Danica was worth the probable pavement pizza. She might even forgive me faster if she saw the punishment for my dream walk.

I dragged some pillows into the bathroom—easy access for aftereffect—settled in, and prayed Danica had given into her sleep Siren. So far, it seemed as if my hours matched their time zone, but who knew how time actually flowed in the mythical world versus the human world.

Her presence surrounded my dream walking self, all sarcasm and heart dripped in thick eyeliner. The walls of her dream took shape, and I found myself back in high school, walking the empty hallways of Prospect Prep.

Danica's mind was more structured than I'd imagined it would be, though with her genius aptitude for dissecting and analyzing, I shouldn't have been surprised. The dream version of Prospect Preparatory Academy was pristine, as if it had never been touched by a thousand high schoolers' sneakers. I wandered through the locker area, the amphitheater, even climbed the steps to the forbidden attic where I'd met Neri and discovered I was a Siren.

Danica was nowhere to be found. It was if she knew I was here and was deliberately avoiding me.

I stopped in front of her locker and stomped my foot. "Danica Maryanne Andrews, I swear by all things holy if you do not show your face right now, I will tell everyone your middle name."

"You wouldn't." Her voice popped up at my back, and I whipped around.

Her dream self had no makeup on. Her hair was a natural light brown, and it fell down in soft waves around her face. She looked…young. Fragile.

Except for the I-will-murder-you look in her eyes.

"I'm sorry I left."

She folded her arms and stared me down with an expression that was pure Danica.

"And I'm sorry I pulled you and Cloud into this mess, made it a bigger mess, and then didn't help with any of the cleanup."

Her expression got scarier. "You think that's why I'm mad? Because you helped start a civil war between the gods and then abandoned us?"

I shrugged. "I mean, isn't that enough?"

She rolled her eyes. "Korrina, as long as I've known you, you've been making giant messes. Messes are just part of being your friend. I'm mad because—no, I'm not mad. I'm hurt. Really, really hurt." Her lips pressed together. "Why didn't you tell me? Why didn't you trust me?"

My heart plopped into my stomach. Mad I could handle. Mad I deserved.

But hurting Danica?

I blinked back tears and held out my hands. "I thought you'd stop me."

"I sure as hell would have tried," she snapped, huffed. "But once we'd talked it through, I would have trusted *you* to know what you were doing. I'd have had your back. Like I *always* do." Her fists clenched, and the hoop of silver threaded through her bottom lip wobbled.

My hands fell to my sides. My shoulders sagged. "You're right. I should have trusted you. All of you." I flung my hand out, gesturing past Danica's dream world to the rest of the team I'd betrayed. "I'm so sorry."

She sniffled and wiped at her nose with the base of her hand. "Say it again."

"I'm...sorry?"

"No. The part where you said I was right."

I laughed, but she only lifted an eyebrow.

"You are the empress of being right," I said, with as much seriousness as I could muster.

"Damn right I am." She stepped forward and flung her arms around my neck. "Never, ever, ever do this again. Deal?"

I squeezed her tight. "Deal."

"How's it going with Jared?"

"Not, um, good," I choked out and told her everything. After we went through the typical we-don't-need-'em pep talk, I sank to the floor. "I'm starting to doubt I can save him."

Danica sat with me and held my hand. "If anyone can, it's you. He's forgotten who he is, but Korrina..." She waited until I looked at her. "From everything you just told me, that boy loves you more than life itself. He may not know how to break free of whatever hold Phorkys has on him but he loves you, no matter what he says."

I nodded, mainly to change the subject. I wasn't sure what I believed yet. "Anyways...have you found out anything about that creature I asked you to research?"

She cracked her knuckles. "Mythology is fascinating...especially now that I know it's real. Okay, so there wasn't anything specific about this creature, but I did discover all these examples of unbalanced forces in the mythical world." She held up a finger. "Things are supposed to be balanced, like light versus dark, chaos versus order, good versus evil. But because the gods are imperfect, power easily becomes unbalanced. For example, too much chaos disrupts order. That one's easy. But too much good?"

I nodded along with her. "Exactly. How can you have too much good?"

"It's like having all light and no darkness. You can't discern the light if you don't have darkness to compare it to. Likewise, too much good just becomes a different type of evil—kinda like eating too much candy makes you vomit."

"Or too much coffee makes your hands shake."

She snorted. "Yeah. We *have* to have those opposing forces to be able to see one side or the other. Make sense?"

"So the opposing force to death by drowning...?"

"Peace."

"Peace?"

"Peace."

"Peaceful life?"

"Peaceful death," she clarified. "Can't stop death, but my theory is this creature gets her kahunas from the trauma of the death, not death itself. So if you were to find a way to put a lot of traumatized spirits to rest in peace..."

I jumped to my feet. "It could break the chain! You are a freaking genius!"

She polished her nails on her shoulder. "I know."

The tardy bell began to sound through her dream version of Prospect Prep. She yawned. "That's my wake-up call. I've got watch duty. Be careful, okay? I want to hear you call me the empress of right in person."

She and her dream faded before I could respond. But when I got back to my body, I found I was already smiling. Right before my date with Mr. Porcelain.

~

IT WAS A RESTLESS NIGHT OF INDECISION ABOUT WHETHER I should visit Mom in the Void again. Ania felt I should sleep on it. I wasn't sure if that was just the coward's way out or wisdom from my darker half. Either way, she won.

I spent the night not sleeping, but distracting myself from Mom with practice calling out the scepter. I fed it small doses of worry, grief, sadness—all the emotions I had in extreme surplus.

By the time the buttery yellow lights in the walls announced morning, I'd taken the edge off all the debilitating feelings and I'd managed to reproduce the glowing orb of the scepter. Still not a fully formed scepter, but powerful nonetheless.

It'd been over a year since I'd pulled out the true form of the scepter. It'd almost killed me, but it'd also healed the tear in the Veil, stopped Phorkys's attack on the human world, and healed Jared from the Siren Hunter's poison—if only for a second.

What if I got really good at powering the scepter? Like so good it didn't almost kill me but made me stronger?

What if I could call out the scepter's true form and heal not just my mom, but also Jared?

Those were the questions that kept me working all night.

Those were the questions that would keep me going each day.

I would not rest until those what ifs were why nots.

I yawned and gave in to the need for caffeine. I fluffed my hair in the mirror, growled at the bags under my eyes, and headed for the kitchen.

"Pancakes and bacon and coffee, oh my," I muttered when I arrived and beelined for the coffee station.

An apron slapped me in the face.

I spun on my heels, made my before-caffeine face.

Isa was scarier. "If you wanted to eat, you'd have rung the bell in your room. You're here, you work. Even you can't screw up refilling coffee mugs."

"But…coffee," I begged.

She snapped her fingers, and a server appeared with an itsy-bitsy cup of coffee.

"It's espresso. Faster caffeine injection and healthier too. Drink up, let's go." She turned on her tiny heel and waltzed through the kitchen.

I took a sip and about gagged. "This is not coffee."

"You get used to it," the server smirked. He was a coral-inspired creature, with growths all over his body and an elongated purple face. But non-threatening. Kind, even. "Trick is to toss it back before you can smell it and remind yourself that coffee can be drunk anytime of the day."

I grinned, held my nose, and drained the tiny cup. "Thanks," I said. "I'm Korrina."

He chuckled. "Yeah, I know." And walked off like I was taboo.

"Not the place to make friends," I reminded myself.

"Korrina!" Isa yelled. "Breakfast means the scary horde of the deep are breaking their fast. Get out of my kitchen and start pouring coffee before one of them eats us!"

I grabbed a coffee pot, petted it for only a second before a towel stung my backside, and rushed out of the kitchen to fill waiting coffee mugs and avoid monster morning breath.

By the end of my shift, all I wanted was to pee and to curl up in a dark hole with a coffee bean plant. I'd chew the beans if I had to.

The kitchen quieted as servers wrapped up, as tables cleared, as the cleaning staff began to clean the dining room.

Isa waited at our table. "I've got lunch service to prep so we're making this quick."

I tilted my head. "Why aren't you running this kitchen?"

She stopped. Her mouth hung open, and I spotted tiny fangs glistening inside.

"I mean, you already run it. So why aren't you head chef?"

She let out a breath and thumbed over her shoulder at the still-sleeping-it-off head chef. "He got here first. And if you haven't noticed, not many females are in positions of authority in this place."

I had noticed.

I reached out and covered her hand with mine. "Ask for a promotion. I'd bet the last pot of coffee on earth that the kitchen staff would back you up."

She yanked her hand out from mine and changed the subject. "Payment time." She pushed out from the table and stood, as if greatly offended that I thought she deserved more. "Any god whose power is tied to the sea or to death may cut my chain."

"Well, duh," I retorted.

Isa shrugged. "Fact's a fact. See you later." She ta-ta'd her fingertips in the air and disappeared into the bowels of the kitchen.

I huffed. "Stop sticking your nose where it doesn't belong," I muttered and headed out of the kitchen in search of other distractions.

Distractions like ex-boyfriends turned evil Siren Hunters turned something in between.

CHAPTER 21

JARED

Steam floated up from hot rocks in a fog of white, and my muscles began to relax. Through the night, I'd tested and proven my theory that no amount of punishing exercise could banish Korrina's face from my mind.

Other guards relaxed in the steam around me, most with a towel around their waist, some not. I was very careful to maintain eye contact. Many of Phorkys's children were not just well-endowed, but overly so.

The door whooshed open, and a rush of cool air swirled the steam around the sauna, momentarily clearing the air to reveal a girl with her hand covering her eyes and her face framed with tendrils of escaped red curls piled high atop her head.

"Korrina?" I choked.

"Hey dudes," she called out cheerily. "Might want to cover up some of those packages. You are in the presence of a lady."

The guards scrambled for their towels, a wash rag, anything, because Korrina waltzed in like she belonged and uncovered her eyes.

Wearing nothing but a towel.

Tucked between her breasts, the edge of the white cloth

barely went to mid-thigh. She stepped over feet and tails, muttering, "Excuse me. Pardon me. *Excusez-moi*," before stopping in front of my seat and squeezing herself on the bench between me and one of Thanos's guards.

"Well, isn't this cozy," she said, leaned her head back against the cushioned head rest, and stretched out her feet.

"Korrina," I sputtered. "You can't be in here."

She peeked open one blue eye. "Seems I can," she said and closed her eye again.

Some of the guards shot me glares before leaving, others just got up and left. Not a one saluted or asked to be dismissed.

Colin was right. I was losing my edge.

And without it, I had no way to keep Korrina safe.

The door slammed shut behind the last of the guards, and we were alone. She sat up, as if it had been her plan all along, and poked my rib. I jerked back, smothered a smile. Siren Hunters were not ticklish.

She smirked and scooted closer. "I remember when you thought a six-pack meant taping the plastic rings from a six-pack of soda cans to your stomach."

I sucked my stomach in, blamed the heat in my cheeks on the sauna, and put a few inches between us. "You're really ruining my street cred with the Horde, you know. You could at least pretend to be afraid of me in public."

"Like you pretend to be afraid of me in private?" Her voice dropped, slowed, went all husky, and she somehow closed the distance between us without moving.

Or maybe I moved.

"I'm not afraid of you." My words went hoarse. "Water, I need water." I stood quickly, grabbed my water bottle, turned around. And bumped into her.

"You're lying." She took my water and squirted some into her mouth. "About more than this, I think."

I couldn't take my eyes off her. Her curves barely hidden by the small towel, the curls tightening around her face in the steam, the shine of her skin. I grabbed her waist, pulled her close, and she fitted herself against my stomach.

It'd be too easy to give in to her. Too easy to nibble the side of her neck, to kiss her until she lost her breath. Too easy to lose myself. To lose my mission.

I leaned close to her ear, breathed her in—I could allow myself that one small pleasure at least—and lowered my voice. "I don't lie."

I stepped away, didn't stop even when I was at the exit. "When you get done in here, I have something to show you. I'll meet you in the training room."

And I kept walking, because if I didn't, I'd go back in there and show her what a horrible liar I'd become.

I paced in front of the locker room, waiting for Korrina, Colin's words rolling around my mind as if they were prayer beads. *Flip her allegiance...*

The order burned in my veins, a demand I could not deny. My bones were infused with Phorkys's power, and I could not ignore his commands, just as I could not ignore the need for air.

But I also could not place Korrina in harm's way. Not again. Not anymore. Not now that I knew.

I loved her.

And there was no way to reconcile the two. I had two masters, and they were at war.

But if I could help them understand each other...

Korrina entered the training room, fully clothed once again, but I could never unsee her wearing nothing but a scrap of cloth and glistening skin. Her hair was still piled on top of her head, and the curls at the base of her neck were still damp from the sauna room steam. She looked like a goddess.

I shoved my hand inside my pocket, determined not to touch her. Perhaps I could kill off the rumors, but not if I confirmed every rogue word.

"I get the impression that you think Phorkys is a monster."

She snorted.

I led her out of the room and down a corridor I only walked in the dead of night, when everyone else was asleep.

"Monsters are created by those who write history. Rarely do conquerors depict their enemies as good and noble."

"You want me to believe that Phorkys is good and noble?" Disbelief dripped down her every vowel.

"No, because he isn't. But he is a good father and a steadfast protector of his family, and if you are ever going to see Phorkys and his children as anything other than monsters, that's the first thing you must understand." I stopped in front of a glass-lined wall.

Behind the glass, babies slept.

Miniature-sized harpies sucked on pacifiers in their cribs. Little balls of sleeping ogres twitched in their sleep. Other creatures, some humanoid, some not, all tiny, were in various stages of nap, play, or feeding time.

Across the room, Luke's mother waved hello, and I dipped my head back in respect. She was the only one who knew I came here. Maybe she even knew why.

"They. Are. Adorable," Korrina squealed.

I hid my smile and entered the nursery.

"You've brought a friend," Luke's mother said, her voice low so as to not disturb the sleeping babies. Her words settled in my chest, and a sense of being almost home overwhelmed my senses.

Maybe it was her...the reason I came.

"Lydia, this is Korrina. Korrina, this is—"

Lydia stepped forward, tears shining in her eyes, and clasped her hands around Korrina's. "The *Elpida*. I've heard many a tale of you from my son."

Korrina darted a glance at me.

"This is Luke's mother," I clarified.

Her eyes went wide, and a grin flashed across her face. "Your son is quite the troublemaker. It's nice to meet you."

Lydia smiled. "I've heard the same of you, my dear." She let Korrina go and stepped back to give us access to the nursery. "You know the rules, *Strategos*."

"Yes, ma'am." I led Korrina into the nursery's interior.

Korrina huffed. "Yeah, *her* rules you follow."

"Wash your hands," I ordered then handed Korrina a mask. "With so many different species of infants in here, we have to be very cautious about the spread of germs."

She nodded, scrubbed her hands, and donned her mask. When she was done, I picked up one of the griffin triplets and placed it in her arms, along with a bottle.

I grabbed the other two and led the way to the rocking chairs. "Little known fact, baby griffins must be rocked while feeding, so that their milk settles in their stomachs."

Korrina hadn't followed me. Instead, she stood in the middle of the nursery where I'd put the griffin into her arms, eyes wide, and I imagined her jaw had dropped open under her mask. "You help rock and feed babies so they don't get upset tummies?"

I shrugged, tried to look tough. "Helps the Horde."

She narrowed her eyes. "Huh," she said, then settled in the rocking chair next to mine.

We sat there, feeding the griffins their bottles and rocking them back and forth, and there was something oddly intimate about being here, with her, taking care of innocents, with her.

For a moment, I could trick myself into believing a life with her could be real.

CHAPTER 22

KORRINA

My emotions were all aflutter. I'd fallen harder for Jared in the past five minutes than I had...ever.

The guy was cuddling twin baby lions with wings like they were his most important mission.

Swoon...

I shook my head, blinked, remembered his words.

Not love.

I'd been feeding the scepter my worry and my heartbreak all night long, and I still felt I could stuff the scepter full. Seeking out Jared was not the smartest move to protect my heart.

But I hadn't come here to protect my heart.

I'd come here to save his.

I swallowed and broke the silence. "How often do you come here?"

That sounded like a bad pick-up line, Ania said.

Shut it, I shot back.

Jared's brown eyes met mine. "Every night."

I felt my own eyes pop open wide.

He shrugged. "I don't sleep well. Haven't since..." He went red and concentrated harder on his rhythmic rocking.

"Since...?" I prodded.

"The desert." If possible, he turned even more red.

"Sedona?" My heart kicked up a few notches.

A week ago, the Council of the Gods had sent me to Sedona to find Tanzy before the Puppeteer did. Turned out, Demeter *was* the Puppeteer, had gone dark-side, crazy goddess, and was picking off modern-day Sirens to use them to stop Persephone from going back to the Underworld.

We'd gotten to Tanzy before Demeter had, but Jared had gotten there too.

Not on Phorkys's orders, but his own.

Jared bit his lip, stared straight ahead. "When I—we—"

"Had a hot make-out session and got caught by a bunch of priests?"

Across the room, Lydia snorted, then went back to pretending she couldn't hear anything.

Jared went silent, and I regretted my less-than-subtle phrasing.

"Sorry," I lowered my voice. "You haven't slept since we kissed?"

"Not...well. I started coming here after I first arrived, sometimes in the mornings, most of the time at night. After the insomnia started, I found this was the only thing that could calm my mind enough to let me sleep."

"Rocking babies," I clarified.

"Rocking babies," he confirmed.

"Hawt," I said. "Just in case you didn't know."

A trace of Jared's old smile, the one with the dimples and the shy tilt of his lips, teased his mouth. "I didn't bring you here to talk about that. I brought you here because I needed you to see."

I looked around the room. "To see babies?"

One of Jared's griffins got done with its bottle, and Jared placed it on the table next to his rocking chair, then tucked the griffin close to his chest. The little beastie snored softly and cuddled in, like it knew it was safe.

"To see the picture from a different perspective."

I stopped rocking. My griffin snarled against my chest, and Jared toed the edge of my rocker to remind me to keep moving. The griffin settled, snuggled, and went back to drinking its milk.

Gazing down at the tiny griffin in my arms, I had an inkling of what he meant. "Conquerors depict the defeated as the monsters and themselves as the heroes." I used his words from earlier, but added to them.

Jared didn't respond but kept rocking, letting me work through the parallel.

The nursery was filled with so-called monsters, and I'd fought many of their adult-sized relations. Fought them, defeated them, sent them back through the Veil, all without ever once considering what their life must look like. Without thinking through what had driven them to the human side of the Veil in the first place.

Because they were monsters. And monsters were bad.

I, of all people, should have questioned that line of thinking. Especially given that I was half mythical myself.

But it was Amity who had questioned the company line. Who had discovered most of those displaced creatures in the human world weren't bad but looking for a safe place to live.

My griffin finished its bottle, hiccupped, and fell asleep. Lydia came over, took it from my arms, and placed it in a nearby cradle while Jared did the same with his two. My arms were tired, but delightfully so, and warm from the griffin infant's little body.

I followed Jared out of the nursery. Peace had wrapped itself around my mind, and the pain stabbing at my heart had numbed. I didn't want to chase it away, but I had very few good choices.

"If Phorkys were in power again," I said, "how far would he go to protect his family?" I understood what Jared wanted me to see—and I'd be lying if I said it didn't make me see Phorkys as slightly less monstrous—but a good father did not a good being make.

Jared peered down at me and let out a slow, deep breath. "How far would you go to protect yours?"

A sarcastic laugh escaped my throat, and I held out my hands in a see-what-I-did gesture. "Obviously, too far."

Jared blinked, and something in his eyes warmed. "You see me as family?"

My throat tightened. "Something like that." I walked back the way we'd come, and Jared matched me stride for stride. "Is there a scenario in which Phorkys's children and the rest of the mythicals live in peace? And leave humans out of the equation?"

Jared scoffed. "No. I don't think you quite understand, Korrina. It is not Phorkys and his children who have alienated themselves from the rest of the mythicals. It is the rest of the mythicals who have placed them underfoot and stomped down."

"His word against theirs," I said, but the way Mnemosyne had treated Phorkys when she arrived, how she'd treated him in the past, stole my conviction.

"Think of it this way," Jared said. "In Mischief and Mayhem, we protected the misfits and pranked the misbehaving popular, right?"

I nodded, but since when did Jared remember his life *before*?

Jared shrugged. "Phorkys and the Horde are the misfits. The rest of the mythicals are the misbehaving popular."

I stopped walking. He'd yanked not the rug, but the floorboards out from under my feet.

"Phorkys's power was stolen," he continued. "His domain diminished, his kingdom's boundaries shrunk, and with each new limitation on the Horde, we have less to eat. Less room to roam. The Horde is not living free. We are in a cage."

"And you think I've been helping the misbehaving popular every step of the way," I finished.

He didn't respond.

Had I been helping the popular gods beat down the already downtrodden? I hadn't given it much thought. Gods were gods, and I did my best to stay out of their way, though rarely succeeded.

Phorkys hadn't endeared himself to the Sirens. Certainly not to me. And his mission to only serve his family instead of the greater good? Not one I could support.

I kept these thoughts to myself. Jared wanted me to see Phorkys as more than a nightmarish beast. He succeeded. I did.

We left the nursery area. Jared had made one thing clear—the Horde, and those super sweet babies, did not deserve to pay for the sins of the father.

Fact was, this father was still a monster, still alive, and still very deserving.

But before I could deliver Phorkys's comeuppance...

"I'm going to see my mom," I announced.

He stopped and gave me that look. All raised eyebrows and waiting for more.

After a year of getting used to him treating me as a stranger, this thing where he knew me, like *knew me* knew me, was disconcerting. I wasn't sure when it had happened or what had triggered it, but something inside him had changed.

"I'm going to try to heal her," I finished.

He pressed his lips together. "There better not be any trying, because Colin will hear of this. You heal her, or you wait until you're ready."

"I've been practicing. I can do this. But Colin has to be there."

Jared folded his arms and all but blocked my way forward. "Why?"

I sighed, but Jared had to be on board. "I think they're

connected somehow, through the scars she gave him. I think if I heal him, I'll heal her."

"You think." The heated protectiveness for his master radiated from him in waves.

I jerked my head up and down. "I'm like ninety-percent sure."

His eyes went red. Scarlet, bloody, Hunter red. "You want me to allow you to use the scepter on Colin, because you say it may heal your mother? Isn't it just as likely to incinerate him, so you can escape?"

They didn't call him *Strategos* for nothing.

"If I did that, I'd be risking my mother and you, with no guarantee for escape," I pointed out.

His lips worked to the side. His shoulders relaxed, his arms uncrossed, and he held out his hand in a you-shall-pass gesture, but his eyes held on to a dark hue of Siren Hunter red. "I'll send word to Colin and meet you in the Grotto. And Korrina"—he paused, met my gaze—"be sure you're ready for this. If you fail, I'm not sure I can keep you safe."

I grabbed his hand, squeezed it, and with very little effort, pulled the glowing blue orb of the scepter out of my chest and let it float between us. A mix of heartbreak, love, and hope is what I fed it this time, not that I had much hope to spare, but for Jared, with Jared, I wanted the scepter to be fed from my heart, not my pain.

He gasped and, with his free hand, reached for the orb. His fingers grazed the blue light, played with it as if it were dancing flames, and the red in his eyes disappeared. His face softened, his ever-tense muscles relaxed, and the wonder I used to witness in his eyes when we'd experience something new together—like a shooting star or a magician in Prospect Park—came back.

He came back.

A scuffle erupted at the end of the hall. Jared's hand dropped from the scepter's light, and he put distance between us, his eyes scanning the corridor as if ashamed to be seen with me.

I closed off my connection to the scepter and let it float back into my chest. "I can do this," I reiterated, my tone grim, firm. "Have Colin meet me in the Grotto. Tell him I'm ready to save my mother and make him pretty once again."

CHAPTER 23

KORRINA

Thanos, Crox, and Not-so-silent Bob waited at the entrance to the Grotto. Not-so-silent Bob wore an eye patch over his left eye.

"Hey guys," I said, from a distance. "Just here to visit my mom."

Thanos's eyes narrowed, and he slammed his spear onto the ground. "Denied entrance without escort."

"Seriously?" I held out my hands, the picture of innocence. "What kind of damage do you think I could do?"

Granted, now that I could semi-use the scepter, I had a powerful weapon on my hands…if I knew how to use it for things other than to heal. So far, I'd never commanded the scepter. I'd just let it do its thang at my own expense. But they didn't need to know any of that.

Loud footsteps echoed down the stone corridor. I turned, muscles clenched, as Colin appeared around the corner, Jared at his side. The guard I'd taken down in the throne room, the one with a hard shell for skin, followed the two Hunters.

Between those three and the two stone guards at my back, I

felt like a fly caught between a fly swatter and a Venus flytrap with nowhere to run.

Colin stopped in front of me, bent his face close to mine. "If this is a joke, I will kill you."

I nodded, but he wasn't done.

"If this is a trap, I will kill you. If this is an attempt to escape, I will kill you. If this fails, I will kill you." He pointed at the locked gate behind the two guards. "If you pass that door, more than likely, I'm going to—"

"Kill me," I finished and patted his arm. "Don't worry, bud. This will be over quick, and if you're a good boy, maybe you'll get a lollipop."

I strode toward the gate before Colin could kill me on the spot. Behind me, scuffling sounds and Jared's low voice kept Colin in check. Crox looked over my shoulder, waited for the go-ahead, and then unlocked the door and stepped aside.

Mom's cell pulled me forward like a magnet, and the voices and other creatures faded into the background.

Mnemosyne's acidic words floated through my brain, and my stomach curdled its contents. My hands were slick as I wrapped them around the bars of Mom's cage and studied her new form.

Healing Colin's scars would either save my mother, kill her, or do nothing and Colin would kill me as promised. But whatever I had done to her in the Void, it'd set this in motion—I had to see it through. Mom could not stay as she was, trapped between life and death, her soul slowly consumed by lost spirits over the years.

I couldn't imagine many worse tortures.

Colin inserted a key into the locked cell door, turned it with a loud click, and swung it open with a theatrical flair.

I mean, sure, the next few moments could determine all our destinies. And sure, I hadn't forgotten Mnemosyne's warning that she couldn't see Colin's past life. But still, Colin was being a little melodramatic.

He entered Mom's cage and sat on the floor next to her head, the only human part of her left. I joined him and completed our circle of three. We could have been a family, if not for Phorkys turning Colin into a Hunter. My whole life would have been so different, but I had no time to spare for pointless musings.

Colin gestured. Thanos grabbed Jared and held a knife to his throat. Jared sucked in a breath, held himself very still.

"What are you doing?" I lunged for Jared, but Colin threw up a hand and Silent Bob stuck out his foot, took me down to the ground.

"Insurance," he said. "Anything goes wrong, Thanos will slit his throat."

I bristled, scrambled to my feet. "That wasn't our deal. I'm the one getting killed, remember?"

He leaned forward, bared his teeth. "I don't make deals outside of family, and you, despite my blood in your veins, are not family."

My pulse shuddered in my throat, and a buzzing, electric current coursed through my chest, delivering a staccato beat of adrenaline to my system. *Not Jared, not Jared, not Jared.*

I took a shaky breath. "Hold her foot, please. The one that gave you the scar."

Colin raised an eyebrow in response, stretching out the scarred lines of his face. I wasn't in the mood to explain myself, but he made it clear he wasn't moving without a reason. "It can't hurt. If you two really are connected, doesn't it make sense to reconnect with the part of her that damaged you?"

He scooted down next to her foot and took her clawed toes in his hand. I didn't bother hiding my revulsion. I hated every time he touched her, hated knowing how many times he'd touched her over the years. It was extremely wrong to touch someone when they were unconscious or hadn't given consent. In Mom's case, it was wrong-squared.

Let's just get this over with, Ania growled.

I closed my eyes and concentrated on Mom, on all the complex emotions I had surrounding her. How betrayed I felt that she'd agreed to attach the scepter to my soul when I was an infant. How she'd sealed my fate before I took my first breath. How, even though it wasn't her fault, she hadn't been there my entire life.

All those complex feelings boiled down to one concentrated sediment of emotion.

I was angry.

And I had an abundance of anger to feed a ravenous scepter.

The room took on a dark blue hue. I opened my eyes, and the blue orb floated in front of me, unsteady—as if it were thinking of changing shape or dissolving.

I fed it more. My hair lifted from my shoulders. My gaze slid to Colin, to his hand holding onto Mom's body, to the fire in his eyes, to the scars that had ripped open his face.

In the past, when I'd used the scepter's healing powers, I'd let its light gently fall on those harmed.

Not. This. Time.

Everything in me boiled. I pushed it all into the scepter's energy and flung it at Colin.

Distantly, I registered Ania telling me to pull back, but the force of the scepter, of my anger, drowned her out.

The orb met Colin's skin, and he cried out as if being burned alive. Mom twitched, her foot jerked under his hand, but he held on tighter despite screaming as if his skin was melting off.

It wasn't. Yet.

Feeding the scepter hadn't taken the edge off my anger.

It had amplified it.

I gritted my teeth. It would be easy, too easy to let the orb destabilize, to incinerate him, to rid both sides of the Veil of his acidic presence once and for all.

"Korrina!" Jared called out, and something in his voice broke the barrier I'd created. Blood trickled down Jared's neck, Thanos holding true to his orders.

Too much, Korrina. You're killing him, Ania's voice came through again. Louder. More intent.

I narrowed my eyes, kept my concentration, but pulled back on the dark undertones of the tempest inside my chest. I couldn't keep looking at Colin and heal him, and as much as I wanted Mom to wake up, the anger swirling inside was self-feeding, and she was caught up in the loop.

So I turned to Jared. Jared, with the knife at his throat, who seemed more concerned about me than the blade that could end his life. Jared, whose eyes were clear brown, whose expression I understood, recognized, felt deep inside. An expression only created when watching someone you love turn into a monster.

I blinked, took a deep breath, and fed the scepter an apology. Then I dug deep and relocated the feeling I was known for, called by. Hope.

Colin's screams diminished at my back. Jared's focus left my face, slid over my shoulder, and his jaw dropped. The guard dropped his blade and bowed at the waist.

I spun around. Blue energy swirled around Colin and made him look distorted, as if he was no longer human-shaped. I called the scepter back. The energy left his body, and he was Colin-shaped once more.

Colin-shaped with no scars. Cold relief flooded my veins, closely followed by something that felt a lot like buyer's remorse.

He reached up to his face, felt his smooth cheek, and his gaze snapped to me. "Was all that necessary?"

"No beauty without pain," I quipped, but my sarcasm game was off.

Mom stirred then groaned. Colin whipped around and knelt by her shoulder, careful to avoid her wings. He held her medicine at the ready.

Every muscle in my body tightened, my breath trapped deep in my lungs, but she didn't scream, she didn't convulse, she didn't writhe.

She opened her eyes, found me across the room, and smiled.

CHAPTER 24

JARED

The guards ushered us from Raelynn's cell, and I allowed myself to be poked and prodded out of the Grotto.

Korrina fought every inch of the way. I couldn't blame her. She'd just awoken a mother she'd never met, except in her dreams, and almost killed her birth father in the process. We were both lucky to get out of there alive.

And what she'd done to Colin…

I couldn't deny what I'd seen inside the scepter's energy, wrapped around the body I'd fought alongside, looked up to, shared my secrets. But I also couldn't accept what I'd seen, wasn't ready for all that it meant.

The gates of the Grotto slammed shut and locked behind us. I grabbed Korrina's arm and pulled her into a seldom used room, really more of a cave, located in the oldest part of the fortress. Water trickled down the roughhewn walls. A darkened and sooty torch was bolted to the back wall, awaiting a match. Puddles of water pooled on the floor, and a fine layer of slick moss covered the stone-like carpet. I'd learned where to step, where to not, and where to pass through the stone to the hidden passage.

In the dim light, Korrina had gone pale. I switched my hand from her arm to her palm and clutched her fingers tight. Her hand was limp, clammy, non-responsive. When she'd used the scepter before, it had tried to kill her.

This time, she was walking, which was a definite improvement, but it had to have taken a toll.

"Are you okay?" I whispered as I led her in a winding pattern to the back of the cave.

She didn't respond. Her hand trembled in mine. My battlefield medic training kicked in, and I recognized her symptoms. The urgency to find a fire to warm her, blankets to drape her in, and something to heat her from the inside out quickened.

But first, I needed to get us out of sight.

With my free hand, I felt for the break in the stone. Constructed to look like one solid slab, the wall was really two massive pieces of rock set slightly off from one another, with a narrow opening hidden in plain sight.

I pulled Korrina inside along with me. The cool stone pressed in on us from either side, and she gasped.

"Almost through," I murmured.

This passage had not been designed with most of Phorkys's children in mind, and I wondered who had created it, used it, and if it was for secrecy or refuge.

We broke free of the stone and entered another cave. Best I could tell, this room was at the very edge of the fortress, furthest from Phorkys's power, and from here, I'd slipped through the Veil to the human world in secret.

The air was stale. A solemn presence was in residence, as if a god had been worshipped here long ago. It had the feel of the ruins of an ancient temple or church, and if I breathed deeply enough, I could almost smell incense.

"What is this place?" Korrina asked, her voice crumbling on the edges.

"Sanctuary," I responded without thinking and turned to her.

"Phorkys's power is weak here, so we should be safe. I know you've just been through a lot, but I must ask you to go through a little more."

Her blue eyes met mine, full of trust and love. Trust I hadn't earned. Love I didn't deserve.

"You're you again," she whispered, and her hand went to my cheek, her thumb rubbed over the stubble I hadn't shaved.

I covered her hand with mine and leaned into her. "Not quite, but my previous life has grown clearer since you arrived, and the life I'm living now seems murky."

"Probably doesn't help that Colin threatened to kill you just now."

A low laugh rumbled at the back of my throat. "No, it doesn't." I traced the curves of her face. "I'm afraid you're going into shock. May I hold you, try to warm you?"

"Yes, please." She snuggled into my chest.

Her scent washed over me, a mixture of home and places exotic. I held her close, rubbed her arms, let my body heat combine with hers. After a few minutes, she stopped shivering, her muscles relaxed, and she lifted her face, rose up on her tiptoes.

I couldn't resist her. Had never been able to. She was a Siren, but my Siren, and the fire in my veins stilled with that acceptance. Her nature and mine warred, but my heart belonged to her and no other creature could claim it.

My lips met hers, and despite the collar around her throat, I heard her song. She wrapped her arms around my neck, pressed into me, and if we had been nothing but two souls, we'd have combined into one. I deepened our kiss, tangled my fingers in her hair, tried to tell her through touch that I didn't want to let her go, that nothing about my life made sense without her.

Our bodies lifted from the ground, exposed all my lies.

I loved this girl. And now she knew.

She pulled back, her lips separated from mine, and I felt abandoned somehow.

"Will you leave with me when it's time?" Her eyes searched mine, and we touched the ground.

I traced her cheek. "If I can," I lied. "But in case I can't, will you do something for me?"

Her gaze grew serious as she awaited my request.

"Allow me to bind myself to you. With a blood oath."

She shook her head. "We are already tied together. Our hearts are linked."

I nodded. I'd figured as much. It was how she'd found me, how I could feel where she was. "Phorkys still commands my blood, my power, and my actions. He is my master. I'm asking you to be my mistress. To give me a chance at fighting his control."

She looked torn.

"It may be the only way I can break free of his grasp and leave with you when the time comes." I lied once again, but she wouldn't be able to refuse this request.

Things had changed. I knew with certainty that she'd leave me here, knew I'd probably never see her again, and I needed to tie myself to her light so I didn't lose myself completely to the God of the Deep.

Her teeth worried at her lip, but she nodded.

I pulled out a blade, not my Hunter knife but one filched from the weapons room. Small and coral-handled, it was the least threatening blade in the entire cache.

But the point was sharp.

I dug it into my palm, until a bead of black blood welled up, then handed the blade to her. She repeated my motion and held her own red-smeared palm to mine. We pressed our hands together. As soon as my blood met hers, a bright blue light flashed between us, battled against the power in my veins. Pain followed closely behind, searing, blinding, and my breath hissed between my teeth. I forced my eyes to stay open, forced my hand to keep clasping Korrina's, forced all my focus on her face.

"Jared Thalassa, do you swear yourself to me?" I started to answer, but she shook her head. "Do you swear that your mind, heart, body, and soul will choose me over all other masters?"

Smart girl to include that. No wonder I loved her.

And if she made this oath stronger than the hold Phorkys had over me, could it break the curse? A whirlwind of anticipation whipped at my ribs.

"I swear it," I gasped, gripped her hand hard, and prepared to let go, but she held on.

"This oath can only be enforced as long as Phorkys has you under his control. Once you are free of the Siren Hunter curse, you will also be free of this blood oath. This I swear to you," she said, her focus unblinking.

I brought our linked hands to my mouth and kissed the back of her hand. Her skin was warm, no longer clammy. We broke contact, breathless, blood-smeared.

Her eyes were a brighter blue than I'd ever seen, and it almost allowed me to forget the fire coursing through my body. This pain was different than the Hunter flames. Intense yet bearable. It was the difference between getting a sunburn after a day at the lake and being thrown into the fire every time I used my power.

"You okay?" she asked.

I nodded, smiled. I didn't know how this would affect my power, and I hoped Phorkys wouldn't be able to see a change, but yes. For now. "Very okay."

CHAPTER 25

KORRINA

Jared and I left separately from the secret room and to be perfectly honest, I was dizzy. Dizzy from waking Mom, healing Colin, kissing Jared, combining his blood and mine.

But especially dizzy from the kiss.

It was a really good kiss.

I rubbed at the cut on my palm, already closing up. Nothing about blood oaths sat right with me. It was suffocating, having your free will limited.

And I'd just allowed Jared to do it to himself. With my help. He was bound to me.

I wandered the fortress in a haze, not sure what to do with myself, where to go, or if any of the choices I'd made since coming here had been good ones.

Someone yanked me into a side hall.

Dad's training echoed in my head. *Punch first, questions later.* I balled my fist and swung.

"Oof," someone grunted and huddled around his middle. "Geez, babe. Are you ever going to greet me with a hug?"

"You ever going to not irritate me?" I retorted but held out my hand to help Luke stand straight. My fingers closed over his missing one, and my stomach folded in half. I held onto his hand a second longer than necessary. "Sorry for punching you."

He rubbed his belly. "No sneaking up on you. Lesson learned," he squeaked, then checked over his shoulder.

I checked as well. We were not supposed to be on friendly terms.

"The Horde has already heard of your healing Colin and waking Raelynn. I'm surprised Jared let you out of his sight. Now that you can use the scepter—"

"I'm a walking weapon," I finished.

He nodded, his lips a thin line, and lowered his voice. "Phorkys will soon declare for Hades in this war."

I felt like I'd been the one sucker-punched. "How do you know this?"

Luke shrugged. "I'm the messenger boy. I listen."

I pressed my lips together. If Luke knew, then Jared knew. He should have said something. Why didn't he say something?

"Usually this kind of announcement takes place in the throne room," Luke continued, unaware of the full impact of his words. "Attendance mandatory. Everyone shows up." He grabbed my hand. "Everyone," he emphasized.

I blinked, refocused, realized what he was saying.

"Phorkys?" I breathed.

"This may be our only chance. Have you figured out how to get that collar off?"

"Working on it," I muttered. Even though I no longer needed my Siren song to use the scepter, my song would make the scepter much more powerful, and I had a feeling we'd need every ounce of magic mojo we could gather. "I'll work faster. Any ideas when this announcement is taking place?"

He lifted his shoulders, shook his head. "Now that you've displayed the scepter's power, Phorkys will want to move quick to show Hades that he's on the Underworld's side and has a powerful weapon to offer."

"Me." I harrumphed. "Even though he has no guarantee I'll fight for him?"

"He has you here. That's enough. Phorkys has ways of making creatures do what he wants, and honestly, Korrina?" He paused. "He has more than enough on you to control you for the rest of your life."

A stone formed at the base of my ribs, blocking my air. "Jared. Mom." Their names sounded like a hammer pounding in nails. Yeah, Phorkys had leverage.

Tasks whirled around my head and began to sort themselves into priorities. "I'll get our escape route put into place. You figure out how to get up on that throne stage thing so you're close enough to grab Phorkys."

He nodded but hesitated as if he wasn't sure if he should say what he was thinking. His gaze traveled down to my fist. "If you don't find a way to break that collar, I'm not sure you'll be able to leave here, no matter how foolproof your escape route."

Dread thrummed a song in my gut, deep, low, and resonant. Footsteps came closer, and Luke mouthed "Go" before turning the other direction and sprinting down the hall.

I kept to the shadows, avoiding others, and headed for Mnemosyne's room. If everything that Luke said came true, a titaness's help could come in handy.

Mnemosyne opened her door like she'd been expecting me and ushered me inside. The lights in the room were low. A cloth trailed out of a bucket of ice near the bed. I took a closer look at the titaness. She pinched the brim of her nose, her fathomless eyes mere slits.

"Are you okay?" I asked.

"I'm having what humans call a migraine." She rubbed at a spot over her left eyebrow.

"Didn't know titanesses could get those."

"Neither did I," she muttered.

Her room was a bit of a disaster. A silk robe was piled on the floor, her bed unmade, clothes strewn all around the room. The remnants of a midnight snack sat cold on the table. She kicked an abandoned slipper out of the way. "Please ignore the mess. What happened?"

"Don't you already know?"

She lifted her hand from her forehead and glared. "I want to hear *you* tell the tale."

Right. She ate stories for sustenance. I started from the beginning and ended with the wrench Luke had thrown.

Her expression became graver and graver. "He may not be wrong. What have you discovered about the collar?"

"I need to calm a bunch of restless spirits to break the chain, but it's not like there's a back door to the Underworld somewhere in the fortress." I gestured dramatically.

She raised an eyebrow. "Korrina," she said. Slowly. Patiently. As if speaking to someone whose mental capacities had been impaired. "Where else have you found a lot of restless spirits?"

I drew a blank.

"Lost souls?" she prodded. "Perhaps lost souls who like to feed on living souls?"

"Oh. My. Gawd." Even Ania dropped her jaw.

"'Oh my Titaness' works just as well. I'd also accept 'goddess,' but it doesn't have quite the same ring." She twitched her mouth, then got serious again. "Use the scepter. Start small. See if it has a measurable impact. If it does, wait until the right moment to break the chain."

I nodded. Once the chain broke, Isa would know. She may feel a soul or two being calmed, but a thousand? Ten thousand? A million?

It'd be a sucker punch to her power.

"You've also learned that different emotion affects the scepter's performance," she stated.

"Anger turns it into a weapon."

She held up a finger and sashayed it, before returning to massaging her temple. "Not just anger, but a need to cause pain. One of the most important things to understand about the scepter is how closely it is tied to who you are."

"That's clear as mud," I snarked.

"The scepter heals because you are the *Elpida*. Healing is its strongest, most natural power. But you are also Ania. Sorrow. And you feel a great range of other emotions. Each of these will impact how the scepter behaves. Go forward slowly. Test what you feed it. Measure the results."

She guided me back to her door, her large hand covering most of my back.

"Wait. What else do you have to teach me about the scepter? You mentioned secrets. What are they?"

Her lips moved, not quite into a smile, but into something infinitely sadder. "Those are buried deep and are different for every wielder. Some can only be discovered after years of introspection. Others will be happened upon by accident, but only for those who have a listening mind and an open heart."

"So you're not going to tell me." I folded my arms and tried not to budge, but titanesses are *really* strong.

She let out a soft, pained laugh. "Go now, Korrina. Continue along your path. And...be careful. Colin's tale fades from my mind, as if it never existed," she muttered, so low I almost didn't catch her words.

CHAPTER 26

KORRINA

I left Mnemosyne's room with no less dread than I'd walked in with. If Luke was right, the little bit of freedom I'd enjoyed since leaving the Grotto was about to be axed. If Mnemosyne was right—and if the first ever titan migraine was a portent of what was to come—things were about to get a whole lot worse.

My time here was drawing to an end...whatever end that may be. I needed to kick my plans into a faster gear.

Luke knew Phorkys's plans.

Jared most certainly knew Phorkys's plans. And despite our blood oath, he hadn't told me what they were. What else was he hiding?

My hands turned into fists. I loved that boy. Loved him but didn't trust him and had a very hard time holding those two truths simultaneously. Until the curse was broken, for Siren and Siren Hunter alike, Jared was not worthy of trust.

Despite exhaustion pulling at my every limb, joint, and bone as if it was a rip current, I started my search in the training room.

You need sleep, Ania whispered.

If I sleep now, I could be dead by morning. If I didn't have a way out of here by the time Phorkys declared for Hades, I was as good as dead.

But if I didn't find some weakness in Phorkys's plans, some way to stop his Horde, everyone I'd left behind was as good as dead.

I circled into the bowels of the fortress. The air grew cold, and more of the armed Horde roamed the hallways. The training room was dark, empty, and I had no idea where Jared slept. This relationship was a bit unbalanced. He had a key to my room, and I didn't even know where his was.

I stopped one of the soldiers in the hallway. "Excuse me?"

He turned, and the snake head growing from his neck hissed.

I swallowed. *Show no fear.* "I'm looking for Jared's—the *strategos's* room."

A smile curled at his scaled lips, and the snake at his neck flicked its tongue. "I bet you are." The words curdled out of his mouth, and a shiver ran up my spine.

"Leave her be," a voice growled out behind me.

The soldier gulped and hurried on his way. I really did *not* want to see what would scare a guy with a snake neck tumor.

"I got you, kiddo," the voice said again. I vaguely recognized it.

I turned and met a giant slug that was nothing more than a mouth with rotating teeth, his chin eyes full of concern. He tapped his fingertips together, which barely reached, thanks to his short arms.

"Hi, Ben," I squeaked.

"How can I help you, my dear?" His voice came from behind the rows upon rows of teeth, and somehow, *somehow,* I felt safer with him here.

Not safe, but saf-*er.*

"I'm looking for the *strategos*. I thought maybe he'd be in his room?"

Ben checked the walls, which pulsed a deep orange hue. "We can check, but at this time of night he's usually in the war room. Not that we plebeians are allowed in there." He chuckled—a metallic rasping noise—like we were the same.

I followed Ben down the hall, avoiding his slime trail, until he stopped in front of an unassuming door.

"He doesn't have a special room?" I was sure, given Jared's status, that he'd have a room like mine, somewhere way above the soldiers and monsters.

Ben shrugged. "He insisted on this room once he arrived. Said he wanted to be closer to his men. I liked that about him."

Of course he did plunked into my mind and tinged against my heart. Because even when he wasn't my Jared, he was.

Standing at the door, I was nervous all of a sudden. My hands jittered, and my nerves buzzed. A peek inside his room would be a peek inside who he'd been for the past year. A peek into what he'd been through.

I took a breath and knocked.

Silence.

I tried again.

Ben cleared his...throat? Did he have a throat? Was he all throat? "Like I said, bet he's in the war room debriefing the *polemarchos*."

"*Polemarchos?*" I repeated, trying to copy Ben's inflections.

His fingers wiggled as if he were coming up for another word. "Colin. *Polemarchos*. Lord of War. If the *strategos* is our highest military rank, then *polemarchos* is his boss."

I had a hard time seeing Colin as lord of anything, but whatever. "Mind giving me directions to the war room?"

Ben's layers of skin shrugged. "Sure, but you can't go in. Guess it does no harm to wait outside though. War room is just left of the throne room, down a side hall. Can't miss it." He waved and slugged down the hall.

Left of the throne room. Where Jared had entered from the day I was brought before the throne. The day I got my collar. Only he hadn't come from the side hallway.

There was another door.

If there were two entrances, I may just have a chance.

I STUCK TO THE SHADOWS AND MADE MY WAY UP THE WINDING corridors to the main floor of the fortress. A pressing need to discover Jared's and Phorkys's secrets overwhelmed any hesitation that maybe this wasn't the best plan.

Everything rode on me figuring out a weakness, any weakness, that we could exploit. Jared knew what it was, but he couldn't tell me thanks to Phorkys's power running through his veins.

Sneakery was my only option.

I made record time to the throne room. Mnemosyne's room was just down the hall, and I'd had no idea that the room that housed all Phorkys's big plans was so close.

Guided by Ben's directions, I crept to a small, side hallway that snaked into throbbing darkness. The walls pulsed a gentle orange, the only light in the corridor, and it wasn't welcoming.

Jared was somewhere down there, maybe.

Secrets were definitely down there.

But also, that was the most obvious entrance and offered no hiding places. I needed to scout the other entrance from inside the throne room.

The main hall was empty, so I tested the black onyx doors. They were made out of solid stone. Of course they didn't budge.

A twist of panic spiked through my chest. I didn't have time to figure out how to pry the doors open. Someone could walk past at any moment, and probably wouldn't like me sneaking into the throne room.

But...

I closed my eyes and concentrated on the center scepter's power. Could the scepter move an object like a heavy stone door?

I fed the scepter my desperation to get through these doors and remain undiscovered. The edge of my *hurry, hurry, hurry* softened, a blue light flared against my closed eyelids and vanished, and a sensation of *something* moved through my bones. Fuzzy, tingly, foreign.

The feeling vanished...as did the doors under my hand.

I opened my eyes. I was in the empty throne room.

Not standing outside with the doors open, but inside, the doors shut behind me. Like they'd never moved.

"What just happened?" I whispered to Ania.

I'm...not sure. Confusion filled her hushed voice.

I moved quickly and scooted to the left wall. Tapestries hung from the tall ceiling, and I crept behind one. Mustiness and mildew cloistered around my nose, made it difficult to breathe.

Had the scepter moved *me* instead of the doors? Was that possible?

Something to explore later. Right now, I was hiding behind an old rug and about as invisible as a toddler hiding behind curtains.

I pressed into the wall, moved my feet. The door Jared had plowed through was near the front of the room, where I needed to be. The war room. The planning room. The brain stem of the fortress.

As I moved, stone changed to wood, and a metal door handle pressed against my wrist. Low voices came from the other side, too low to recognize or understand.

The voices were a quiet hum at the back of my skull, spiking and dropping in volume, and I was close to falling asleep standing up when another door slammed shut, vibrating the wall and the door next to my ear.

I listened, but nothing came from the war room other than silence. I tried the handle.

It moved under my hand, unlocked.

I silently thanked Cloud and Mischief and Mayhem once again for honing my instincts. This door was assumed secure, thanks to the unmovable throne room doors.

I pushed it open and slid inside.

CHAPTER 27

JARED

I felt her. Near enough to make my blood buzz. Too near.
Colin had hurried through our debrief, making it the shortest meeting I'd had since being inducted into Phorkys's family, no doubt in a rush to get back to Raelynn, though he'd said not a word about her. All business, short responses, little interest in our war, our plans, our strategies.

The door slammed shut behind him, but I remained.

I *knew* Korrina. I'd remembered the way her mind constantly moved, how she could always find the deeper meaning running through her current circumstances, and how that motivated her to make decisions others found questionable.

Like now.

She wouldn't escape from this place without first discovering Phorkys's plans and what she and the others were up against.

And this was where my oath to her raged against my vow to Phorkys. This was the test I knew would come.

I stepped into the secret room behind the serpentine bust of Echidna, hidden from the rest of the war room and magically warded to act as a two-way mirror. I could see in, could listen in, but no one in the war room could see or hear me.

Korrina slipped in through the throne room entrance. Because, of course, she'd figured out how to get those impossible doors open.

She crept to the table, dragged her fingers across the glossy black surface, lifted her gaze, and stared straight into my soul.

The air vibrated.

She couldn't see me. But she felt me. As I felt her.

She bit her lip, wrinkled her forehead, then continued her inspection of the room. A few minutes later, she thrust her hands to her hips and huffed.

The war room was plain, empty, and its secrets were not easily uncovered.

She turned, stared at the polished black surface of the war table, and I witnessed that infuriating, smart brain of hers figure it out. Her blue eyes widened, her mouth parted, and I caught a glimpse of her delicate tongue, touching the back of her teeth.

Gods, she was beautiful.

She placed her palm on the table, and a red line traced the edges of her hand. Not authorized.

Only Colin and myself were.

She needed me.

Her hand clenched around the palm she'd cut. The oath between us sung in my veins, and I could feel her warring with using the oath, forcing me to come to her, to give her what she needed.

"Jared," she whispered, and the stinging in my veins grew more intense. She gasped, let her hand relax, and dropped her head.

The oath relaxed. The pressure weakened.

I walked out of my hiding place and into the war room.

CHAPTER 28

KORRINA

Jared stepped out of the wall behind Echidna's statue.

Guilt surged through my system, hot and nauseating. "Did I just—did you—the oath—"

He shook his head with a grimace. "I came out before you could." He thumbed over his shoulder. "Secret room."

"This place has a lot of secret rooms," I said, even as cold relief flooded through me. His choice brought him here...not mine.

"Happens when a place is a few eons old." He looked from me to the table and let out a heavy sigh. "Why do you always make me make hard choices?"

It was only then that I read the agony in his expression. He knew what I wanted—the oath called to him regardless of what I'd intended—and it warred with who he was under Phorkys's control.

He reached out his hand and hovered it over the table. His hand trembled. Sweat gathered above his lip. Nothing happened. He groaned, his biceps flexed, and he pushed his hand down with his other hand.

His arm didn't budge.

"I'm not strong enough to fight this on my own," he gasped. "You have to help."

I nodded and placed my hand on his. Green fire glowed around his palms, and I jerked away.

"Use the oath," he hissed. "Without it, I will not be able to hold the Hunter back." Even as he was telling me what to do, his voice changed, deepened, filled with malice.

I swallowed. I was a threat to Phorkys, and he was Phorkys's defender and protector.

This is why he'd sworn allegiance to me.

"Jared Thalassa"—I squeezed the freshly closed wound on my hand—"who do you answer to?"

His expression was pinched and pained, but he gritted out, "You, Korrina. I answer to you."

How I wish he'd said himself.

"Then please, place your hand on the table and show me what Phorkys has planned."

Jared roared, a tearing sound filled with both pain and relief. The green fire that etched his skin disappeared, and he slammed his hand onto the table.

Maps of the mythical and human worlds appeared in a hologram-type image, with figures of gods, goddesses, and their armies. And monsters. Phorkys's children filled the empty spaces. More than I'd expected. More than I could count.

Even in the human world.

Especially in the human world.

I leaned in to study it closer, but the maps disappeared. The table faded to black. A thump hit the floor.

I spun on my heel. "Jared?"

I dropped to my knees, next to his fallen body. He'd crumpled, landed at an odd angle. His shoulders jerked. His head lifted up, smacked into the ground, again, again.

Seizure.

I pulled his head into my lap, tried to hold his head still.

What were you supposed to do for someone having a seizure? Give them something to bite down on? Leave them alone?

"Jared? Jared?" No response.

Black blood ran from his nose, slow at first, then faster. His head jerked more violently, and it was all I could do to keep him from cracking open his skull against the stone floor.

Panic pummeled my brain. Why had I allowed him to make this oath?

Each second stretched like pulled putty...putty that could break at any moment. I watched him helplessly. Thoughts swirled in my head, but none of them had any answer of how to fix the boy I loved.

His fits slowed.

Hope flickered inside me. *C'mon, Jared.*

Breath whispered between his lips, just barely, and his eyes darted beneath his eyelids. Still, he stayed unconscious.

Ania's cold presence swelled, chased the warmth from my fingertips.

Who could I go to for help? Mnemosyne wasn't allowed out of her room. There was no telling where Luke was. I had no idea how to get back to the nursery to Luke's mother. Isa was more likely to finish the job than help.

Not to mention that we could not be discovered in here. Not together.

And if I left this room, I may never get back in.

"Jared, please. Wake up." I dropped my forehead to his, willed him to be okay.

Low voices seeped into the room—from the hallway or from the throne room, I couldn't tell. We were out of time and had no other options.

I didn't know if the scepter would heal him or if it would bring out his inner Hunter. I didn't know if using the scepter would alert Phorkys to its presence.

Didn't have a choice.

I dug deep, fed the scepter my love for Jared—I had a never-ending supply—and my need to see him healed. Completely, fully healed.

A warm trickling tickled the inside of my chest, and blue light glowed around me. It wasn't the orb, but a soft light that seeped through my pores. As if somehow, I'd merged the scepter's power with my bones. My hair floated up, weightless, and danced around my face.

I cupped Jared's cheeks, leaned in, and kissed his lips.

Light surged through me and into him. An electric current, forceful, unstoppable, yet gentle, healing. I fed it more—more love, more healing, and memories of Jared as he used to be, free and happy.

I shared it all with him.

A snap cracked through the air, and I jerked back. The light between us shifted to a brighter blue. Jared gasped. Color returned to his face.

"Korrina?" He groaned and propped up on his elbow.

I slid my arm around his back, helped him sit all the way up. "Hey, handsome." I scanned his face, his eyes. I was no doctor, but he certainly looked better. "No more blood oaths for you." I wagged my finger at him, but I was serious. No way, not ever again.

"I passed out?"

I nodded. "Pretty sure whatever hold Phorkys has on you doesn't like the oath you made with me."

He wiped at his nose, and dark, ruby red blood smeared his hand. I tore off a piece of my white shirt and handed it to him.

"Also, you had a nosebleed, but no other injuries," I reassured him. "At least, not that I can see."

For a moment, he did nothing but stare at the blood on his hand.

"What?" I asked. "My shirt isn't that dirty."

He blinked, came back to himself, and took the white scrap

of cloth. "We have to get you out of here. Colin is notified every time the table is used."

I nodded and helped him stand. He was steady on his feet, but I kept my arm around him.

He scrubbed at the blood on his hand, wiped up his face. "All clean?"

"Like a baby's butt."

"Please never again compare my face to a baby's butt."

"Please never again pass out on me."

He hugged me close. "Deal."

CHAPTER 29

JARED

The Siren Hunter poison that creeped through my veins was incurable. There was no antidote, no curse breaker, no way to escape its claws.

I placed my hand on the small of Korrina's back and guided her through the throne room. The doors were attuned to my magic and my skin, so opening them shouldn't be an issue. Except.

My blood was red.

No longer black, but red.

What had she done to me? What did it mean?

The endless number of possible outcomes flew at me with the precision of a sharp shooter, pointed and deadly. Under Phorkys, I had become a different creature. So much so that my blood reflected the transformation.

If I was reverting back to human...

How could I keep her safe?

"Jared?" Korrina prodded at me, and the throne room came back into focus.

How many times had I told my men that a distracted soldier was a dead soldier?

"Thought I heard something." I couldn't tell her the real reason I was distracted. It would give her hope. Hope that would keep her here, keep her in Phorkys's grasp.

I placed my hand against the door, and green outlined my fingers. The doors unlocked with a dull thud, and all I needed now was a small push of my magic to open them wide.

The frosty-cold edges of my fire were as familiar to me as the lines in my palms. But something in my fire had dimmed, as if my power had been banked. Still there, but embers and ash instead of an inferno.

I gritted my teeth, thought of my enemy…but instead of Korrina's face, it was Colin's.

Sparks flickered to my fingers, along with the bitter pain that always accompanied the flames. It wasn't much.

It was enough.

The doors creaked open. I checked the hallway to make sure it was empty, and once all was deemed safe, Korrina slipped through.

I waited a full minute before following her out of the throne room and shutting the door behind me. A full minute where I allowed that sharp shooter of deadly endings to hit me with all the consequences of the oath I'd made to Korrina. I tracked every path, strategized all the possibilities.

Not a single outcome left me alive.

I'd just have to follow the ones that kept her breathing.

CHAPTER 30

KORRINA

The pile of pillows in the corner of my room begged me to join them, but I had souls to save, a chain to break, and a war to win. Plus, Jared's seizing body haunted my every blink, so sleep was not an actual option.

I filled the giant seashell bathtub and positioned a trash can by the side to catch my dream walk unmentionables. I undressed, piled my hair on top of my head, and stepped into the steaming bubbles. Going into the Void had never truly scared me before. But now that I'd seen what was trapped there? Now that I knew lost souls fed off the living?

Zombie ghost apocalypse.

I shivered, despite the warm water covering me from toes to chin. My feet floated to the top of the water, my arms buoyed by the bubbles, the tattoo on my wrist partially obscured by the suds, and I allowed myself for a moment to feel weightless. Free of all the things.

For a moment, I pretended I was any other almost-eighteen-year-old girl who took bubble baths, wore fruity body spray, and had fun with her friends.

And painted. I missed painting. I missed who I used to be when I could still be…normal.

I shut my eyes tight.

Time to go, Ania whispered.

"I know," I groaned and sank deeper into the bubbles in rebellion. Just one more minute. I counted to sixty, deep breaths in, long breaths out, and found my calm.

Then I propped my head up with a towel, leaned back, and fell into the Void.

Coming here had gotten easier with practice. The sensation of bodylessness, being fully spirit, had not. The knowledge that a world existed here, formations and ruins with spirits who may or may not know who or what they were floating about, made it scary.

Nothing wasn't nothing. The Void wasn't a void. It was a trap.

And to break my own prison, I needed to set these scary souls free.

Spirits fluttered to my sphere of light. Soon, they'd snap in and steal my light, like a thousand biting flies.

I needed to channel my inner Venus flytrap.

My spirit was a flame, a steady spark that burned bright in the darkness. I made it shimmy. A lost spirit ventured close.

What is your plan? Ania asked, all doubtful.

"Catch and release," I retorted. My life force was the bait.

The spirit darted in, and as its touch made stinging contact, I pushed my light into it. Much as I had Mom.

My light dimmed, but the spirit fluffed up, glowed faintly, took on the more defined shape of a peg-legged pirate. Awareness sparked into his eyes. Which promptly widened with fear. He looked around, screamed, and fled into the darkness.

Well, you woke him, but he's still trapped, Ania commented. *And terrified.*

"Thank you, Captain Obvious."

More spirits crowded in, and a feeding frenzy began on my soul. Pieces of myself floated away.

Got any other ideas?

The only experience I'd had in the Void was flinging my life force around willy-nilly. So no, I had no other ideas, except…

"Retreat."

STANDING NAKED IN FRONT OF THE SINK, I SCRUBBED AT THE BACK of my tongue with my toothbrush and got rid of the aftertaste of Void, vomit, and ghosts. Pirate ghosts. I shook my head, scrubbed harder.

A click sounded through the room. The handle of my door turned, and my heart went next level. Someone was coming in.

No time to throw on clothes. I darted back to the tub and slipped in. My chin touched the surface of the lukewarm bath water, and I swished the few remaining bubbles to cover my lady parts. The water took on a blue hue as I readied the scepter. I might be naked, but I wasn't vulnerable.

Jared walked in, a hand covering his eyes, and closed the door quickly behind him. "Korrina, are you decent?"

I rested my chin on the edge of the bath shell, made sure I was covered, and fixed my gaze on the spot his dimple would appear.

"Totally decent," I said, and his hand dropped from his eyes.

He looked around the room until he found me, obviously naked in the bathtub, his eyes widening and a smirk—and the predictable dimple—leaped onto his sexy, stubbled face.

"Not. Decent," he croaked.

I grinned and huffed. "Turn around. I'll get dressed."

Despite my Korrina-may-care tone, I really hoped he didn't sneak a peek. If and when Jared and I ever got to that place, I wanted it to be special and romantic. Not a peepshow in an enemy's fortress.

I wrapped and tucked a fluffy towel around all my goodies, made sure he was still turned around, and stepped out of the bath. "Okay, I'm covered up."

"Dressed. Clothes. Please," he said, without moving.

"You sound like you're in distress," I taunted. "I wonder why?"

He groaned. I giggled, hurried behind the changing wall, threw on my clothes, and crossed the room to where he stood, very, very glad I had prioritized brushing my teeth.

"Better?" I asked.

He let out a deep breath and turned slowly to face me. "Better is not the word I'd use." The words rasped out of his throat, as if he'd been too long without water.

There was no warning. His arm slipped around my waist, and he pulled me against him, hard. His mouth found mine, and these were not the sweet, breathless kisses of earlier.

They were primal.

Everything in me rose up to meet him, to drink in his need, to fill him with my own. His tongue slipped against mine, his hands roved, at once gentle and demanding. I dug my fingers into his hair, pulled him closer, as if we could somehow merge, be one body. He picked me up, threw my legs around his waist. Somehow we'd turned around. The wall pressed into my spine, his kisses slowed, found my throat, and all thoughts stopped. There was just Jared, his kisses, and an undeniable line we'd crossed.

Didn't care. I wanted him. I wanted all of him. I pulled his face to mine, buried myself in his kisses, his scent, his taste.

A flashing yellow light pricked through my awareness. Jared's mouth paused on mine, his breaths rapid, deep. Seconds later, Colin's voice echoed through my room from a hidden speaker.

"The Horde will convene directly after breakfast," he announced. "War comes, brethren. Sleep well."

Jared released his grip on my tush, and I slid down until my feet touched the floor. He leaned his forehead against mine and cursed, sharp and harsh. The word fell like a stone, plunked into my gut.

"My time's up, isn't it?" I whispered.

He swallowed, and I was close enough to witness his body tell the truth. "I came here because I figured how to get you in to see your mom. But if the Gathering is in the morning..." He cursed again and turned away, his hands tight fists at his sides. "Tell me you have an escape plan."

"I have an escape plan," I said dutifully. Sure, it only worked if I could break the collar, but technically, I had a plan. "But I have to see my mom first."

Jared lifted his face to the ceiling, took a deep breath, and turned around. A red glow left his eyes, and I wasn't sure how to interpret it. Had kissing me brought out his Hunter?

"Meet me at the entrance to the kitchen, when the lights fade to deep blue. Try not to let anyone see you, and Korrina?" He waited until he was sure he had my full attention. "No matter what happens, promise me you'll leave this place as soon as you get the chance."

I hid my hand behind my back, crossed my fingers, and said, "I promise."

I would do my best to do as he asked, but I'd finally, *finally*, learned that when it came to my life, there were no guarantees.

CHAPTER 31

KORRINA

I had hours to kill before it was time to meet Jared, and it made me antsy. The deep blue hour was the quietest part of the night in the fortress. A reverse golden hour that found every beastly creature fast asleep.

You have tasks to complete, Ania reminded me. *And you must find time to sleep.*

Right. Because walking-dead Korrina was of no use to anyone.

I contacted Tanzy. Let her know the plan and timeframe. She waved her hand at me, said she and Amity were on it, then *she* ended our dream walk session.

That girl was seriously impressive.

A yawn engulfed my whole world, made my ears pop. "Wake me up at the deep blue hour," I muttered to Ania and crawled into the pillow fort in the corner of my room.

Her satisfied smile curled at the back of my brain. *Sleep well, Elpida.*

I was too tired to be annoyed at her use of my title.

A blink later, Ania was yelling, *Wake up, Korrina. You've almost missed your date.*

Sure enough, the walls pulsed a deep blue, calming and rhythmic, a stark contrast to the hummingbird heartbeats trapped in my throat.

"Why didn't you wake me before?" I flew out of bed feet first and became a flurry of flinging clothes.

I tried. Her tone was as exasperated as if she'd slapped her forehead.

Despite my hurried panic to not miss the meeting time, I did feel better. More alert, less fog-headed. Naps were miracle-workers.

I pulled my hair out of its tangled bun, fluffed my crimped waves, and snuck out of my bedroom.

This was it. I wouldn't be coming back here—one way or another. Thank goodness I'd traveled light.

The door clicked shut behind me, and the dark hallway stretched out before me. I crept into the sleeping fortress.

My path would take me by the throne room. I edged my way down servant corridors that ran parallel to the main thoroughfare, following Jared's instructions. He was in charge of this mission, and that meant I would follow his orders to a T.

Well, almost all his orders.

Voices bounced from the main hallway, and I guessed I was near Mnemosyne's room. I took the next intersecting path and pressed my back to the wall, where I could monitor what was going on. I didn't have time for interruptions, but this was the shortest path to the kitchen.

Mnemosyne towered over four guards, who stood around her like the points of a compass. But something wasn't right.

Her head lolled on her neck, lazy and unsupported. Her hands were clasped at her waist, and a thin, gossamer string of gold glistened in a knot around her elegant bones.

The guards led her past my hiding spot, and her head swayed until she met my gaze.

Her fathomless eyes were cloudy, milky. "Trust no one," she

mouthed, then allowed herself to be guided away—to the Grotto, out of the fortress, I wasn't sure.

The not knowing made me feel unsettled. But her lack of fight downright terrified me. *Not good, not good*, my heart seemed to say with each hard thump.

She was no longer a guest.

I stayed put until they disappeared around the corner, heading not to the Grotto but upward. The only thing above this level were the broken parapets. There was nothing out there except for very wide, very empty, very deep, very heavy ocean. Surely they wouldn't…

I froze, just long enough for all my muscles to tighten and then launch me down the hall after them.

Mid-leap, Jared stepped in my path, wrapped his arms around my waist, and held me fast.

"She's a titan. She'll live." His lips moved against my hair.

"But—"

"She is a titan," he said slower. "She *will* live. You cannot save everybody, and not everybody needs saving."

I stood there a moment longer, staring over his shoulder after the empty hallway, and something sick settled deep into my insides. Would I ever see her again? And more importantly, was Jared right—would she be okay?

He tightened his grip around my waist. "Come on. Our window is almost up." And then he flung me through a stone wall and into a single-file corridor.

Only it wasn't solid stone. Of course it wasn't. "Is everything in this place an illusion?"

Jared shrugged. "Our architects are smart with a sense of humor. Many of this fortress's secrets hide in plain sight."

He'd said *our*. Not Phorkys's. *Our*.

He squished past me, snagged my hand, and gave my fingertips a light squeeze. "You've really left us no time to spare. We'll have to run."

"Ugh," I moaned but sprinted after him.

The hidden corridor curved down at a severe angle, so much so that by the time Jared slowed, I wasn't even winded.

"They should plan marathons on ramps like this. Or skate-a-thons! I'd totally do one then."

He gave me a dubious look, then... "Who's *they*?"

I shrugged. "People who plan things."

He rolled his eyes, but it was a you're-cute-but-ridiculous eye roll. Those, I didn't mind. He led us around a corner, then placed a finger to his lips. "Colin uses this passage, though he's never here in the deep hour."

A shiver of relief wound its way around my spine. I didn't know why. Colin had been watching my mom sleep for almost eighteen years. But something about him sneaking into her room when all was dark and everyone was asleep was next-level creepster.

Jared reached out, touched what I thought was solid stone, and pinched it to the side. Fabric designed to match the neighboring stone walls wrinkled and let him peek through. "Cloth on this side, stone on the other," he explained.

"Magic is so cool," I whispered back, my mind already whirring with all the possibilities of using such a material in a mixed-media piece.

He gestured me closer. "All clear. You have just enough time to tell Raelynn the escape plan, show her this route, and get out. No longer. The guards will wake soon." As if to prove his point, the next flash of time-telling color faded from deep blue to a bluish-purple. Jared parted the curtain, and I slipped through into Mom's cell.

She was awake.

Her bright blue eyes, mirrors of my own, blinked at me, not unlike a bird's. Not crazed by the curse though, so that was a bonus. Her hair flowed around her shoulders, somehow smoother than mine currently was, though she had no hair products or brush. And her smile. That was mine too.

All similarities stopped there.

Her rust-colored hair rested against a cascade of white feathers, like blood on snow. She held out a wing—my fault—and enveloped me in a soft, warm hug, one that had nothing to do with a mother's embrace and everything to do with being as comfy as a downy blanket.

"Only together can we do what you must. Fall with me."

My spirit slipped away from my body with hers, and for the second time tonight, I fell into the Void.

CHAPTER 32

KORRINA

Darkness slid over us like ice. But not emptiness. Now that I knew what hid in the dark, I felt as if I was in an abandoned city with a long-gone power grid. Built by whom, I could only guess. Surely not the spirits themselves. They seemed unaware that they existed, but still, now that I knew what to look for, I could see them congregating on distant islands that floated in nothingness.

How had Mom existed here for so long without completely losing her mind? Coming back here had to be harder than hard.

I searched for her flame, a silver slash of light in the darkness.

"I'm always amazed at how brightly you shine here," my mother's voice hit me from behind.

Not thoughts. Voice.

I spun around, my own spirit flame dancing around in a wide arc of light.

She floated before me, fully-bodied as her human self, before the curse ever touched her.

My spirit radiated shock. "Mom?" my thoughts shouted at her. "How do you have a body?"

She grinned. "This is how I survived for so long. I had to learn to create a barrier between myself and the spirits. It wore down eventually, but it will protect you for as long as you need to be here. That is, as long as you don't get trapped." The *like me* was implied.

"Show me," I thought at her, even as Jared's warning—we had no time—pounded through my memory. But already, spirits were darting toward me, about to go into a feeding frenzy. And I had to break free of my collar, or no escape, however well planned, would succeed.

She held out her hands, and her mouth took on a sorrowed shape. "You need your song."

The first spirit dove in, siphoned away a bit of my flame.

"Collared at the moment." Pain sparked bright, even as my flame dimmed.

"I know." She wrapped her arms around me, using her body as a shield. "You've learned to push the scepter's healing into others. Now you must learn to offer it instead."

"Offer it? Who wouldn't want to be healed?" Another spirit snuck in, sucked a piece of me away.

"Most," she said. "To be healed is to confront one's dreams. Because once healed, there are no excuses left for not chasing them."

On a certain level, I understood that fear. I dreamed of healing Jared, of healing the Sirens and reversing the curse, of defeating Phorkys…scary. Because what would life look like if it all came true? If I wasn't the *Elpida*, who would I be then?

Another spirit approached.

"All we can ever do is better," she whispered and let me go.

Spirits had formed a crowd. And no matter my intentions—to protect myself or to heal them—I couldn't throw the scepter's power or my life force at them.

I had to offer. They had to accept.

I reached inward, found the cool blue orb of the scepter's

power, and pulled it to the surface of my spirit. My aura spread wide, blue and silver with smalls wisps of purple. The silver flame of my spirit remained in the center. If the spirits wanted to feed on me, they'd have to get through an energy field of healing first.

The spirits shied away, darted outside the reach of the light, but slowly, one at a time, they began to come forward.

The first reached the light, a shadow of a flame, and reached for it. Blue light poured into the spirit, slow and steady, allowing the spirit to take as much as it wanted.

For an instant, the soul took on the shape of man wearing a captain's hat. He sighed, smiled, and disappeared with a wink of light.

More came. Some accepted. Few remembered themselves and were brave enough to free themselves of the Void.

But are they enough to break the chain? Ania asked, ever the half-empty glass. *We must return.*

"Mom, we have to go," I thought at her. My blue aura wavered. The spirits paused.

She glanced between me and the spirits, who were growing braver with each healing sip of the scepter's power. "We can't. There are so many of them."

More came, more drank, more chose to be healed.

My aura started to turn more purple. And the lost souls weren't zapping me at all.

Korrina, Ania pushed.

"Mom, we'll come back." I shut it down. My aura snapped away, and the darkness seeped in. The spirits wavered at the missing barrier, before floating toward my vulnerable and tasty spirit.

"But they need help." Tears shone like tiny silver flames in her eyes.

"We won't be able to help them if we don't leave now," I said, as gently as I could.

Mom reached out a hand to the spirits. I covered her like I had before, flame covering body, and despite her protests, pulled us back to our bodies.

∽

RETURNING FROM THE VOID WAS NEVER A PLEASANT EXPERIENCE. A body weighed a lot, though it's not something you'd notice unless your spirit took a vacation and then returned. But this time was extra.

Extra loud, extra panicky, extra out-of-time.

The lights flashed a light blue, and footsteps stomped closer and closer.

Jared stood at the edge of the curtain, and his eyes were brown orbs being swallowed by a darkening red glow. He mouthed, "Hide," and shoved the curtain closed. It fell into place, and the transition from fabric to stone was seamless and just in time. I took him at his word and ducked behind Mom's bulky bird body, just as Thanos, Crox, and Silent Bob rounded the corner.

Mom's eyes flicked from Jared's hiding spot to the guards. She spread her wings wide, giving me more of a chance to remain hidden. It wasn't a perfect cover, but unless the guards looked closely, I doubted they would I-Spy a Korrina.

Then I saw it. The chain. My collar.

Lying broken on the floor just out of reach, one of the links shattered into silver dust.

My hand flew to my throat, and for the first time in days, air brushed against the skin at my neck. My song simmered to the surface, begging to be used after so long of being blocked. It was a tickle at the back of my throat, one that would not be ignored.

I stepped out from behind Mom, reached deep, found my Siren center, and sang to the guards the notes I'd learned long ago. A song of control, of power, the first song any Siren learns to sing and the one I'd tried so hard to silence.

Now, I knew that sometimes childhood lullabies were exactly what was needed.

One by one, six eyelids grew heavy, and their thorny chins dropped to their chests.

"This is not the Siren you are looking for," I monotoned and waved my hand like a Jedi.

Silent Bob raised his head, a smirk on his prickly face. "Oh, I think she is."

A sick sensation thrashed against my insides, and from somewhere in the recesses of my memory, Phorkys's words came back with a gut punch. *Do you really believe that I would not have impregnated my home with defenses against* all *of my enemies?*

Mom threw me a panicked look, clenched her sharp talons.

The guards entered her cell. The hidden entrance was rock hard at my back.

She reared back, clawed her talons in the air, barely missed swiping Silent Bob's patch off his eye. Thanos grabbed her from one side, Silent Bob the other, and they forced her to the ground. I dove for the huddle, but Crox simply put his hand on my head, held my kicks and punches away from him at arm's length, and helped the other two subdue Mom.

"Korrina," she gasped, her face pressed into the floor. "Colin's scars are healed. Phorkys is free. Your dad—"

Thanos pulled a needle from his pocket, took the cap off with his teeth, and plunged it deep into her neck. Her body collapsed, boneless, on the floor.

The guards turned their attention to me, grabbed my arms, hauled me out of the cell, and all the while, Jared's reddened eyes haunted my thoughts.

Had Jared known my Siren song wouldn't work on the guards?

Had he betrayed me?

CHAPTER 33

JARED

The fabric of the hidden entrance brushed against the back of my heel.

Stone.

That was what I had become inside.

Once one thing and now another, forged by intense heat, unbearable pressure. I'd welcomed it.

I didn't think stone could feel. That rock, hardened by centuries of bully gravity, could be anything but impervious.

I felt every compressed inch.

I shoved my hands into my pockets and left Korrina to her fate. The empty vial of Demon Lace—the drug Luke had poisoned me and Danica and Tula with in another lifetime, the cause of my Hunter—brushed against my fingertips. This time, I knew what the vial's contents would do.

This time, I'd chosen my fate.

The hidden corridor behind me, I made my way to the war room. Colin would want an update. Phorkys must be told.

One of the Horde passed by, waved, as if we were equals. My lips parted over my teeth, and a feral, guttural sound graveled at the back of my throat. No more.

I was done bowing to rumors, to allowing the Horde to think anything other than what I allowed them to think.

Fire leaped to my fingertips. The burn was agony. I pulled more. More power, more fire, more pain. Sent a stream flooding toward the peon who'd dared address me.

The fire touched him, but his cries of agony were no match for mine. Fresh Hunter poison burned through my veins, fighting the oath I'd made to Korrina. My blood warred, and for all my talents, for all my accolades as Phorkys's *strategos*, I didn't know which side would win.

Stone. Stand firm. Push out thoughts of her, leave nothing.

Madness crept into my mind—or had it always existed?—revealed by the familiar strains of poison crawling through my blood. Any thought driven by emotion dissipated.

The war room door was cool under my fingertips, the cries of the Horde brethren who'd dared be familiar with me faint, and I was out of time to regret what had been done.

There was no other way.

Colin waited.

My breath stuck in my chest, but I dropped to my knee. "Master," I acknowledged.

He dipped his chin. "Is your mission complete?" he asked, his voice strong, fathomless.

"Her heart is mine," I confirmed. "And what is mine is yours. She will do as you say."

"The scepter belongs to us, once again." Not a creature alive could miss the triumph in his grating tone.

I bowed my head, fixed my gaze on the ground, told myself again that this was the only way.

She hadn't known it was coming. Hadn't known I'd led her into a trap.

And she'd never believe I'd had no choice.

CHAPTER 34

KORRINA

A drum beat in time to the breakfast-yellow pulses of light in my cell's walls. This wasn't like the prison I'd had before, with its cushy floors and open floorplan.

I was in a padded room. One etched with ancient symbols that predated Greek, symbols I could only assume existed to muzzle magic. Because that's exactly what my power was. Muzzled.

I had no idea what had happened to Mom. After the guards had knocked her out, they'd dragged me in here, deep in the Grotto, with not a word among the three of them.

As if they'd known exactly what to do.

For the thousandth time in the past hour, I squeezed my eyes shut and shook my head, as if I could shake loose the horrible thoughts clinging to my brain.

Tears burned my eyelashes. Jared. He was the only common denominator. I may not have finished high school, but I understood that principle. Add motive plus betrayal plus recent history, and you get three-fifths Jared.

It was that two-fifths I was still debating.

Because the blood oath was real.

Our kisses were real.

Floating in the air? Yeah. Real.

How could he love me and betray me at the same time? How could I hold those two conflicting truths and make sense of anything?

More immediately, how was I going to get out of this cell?

I punched at the pillowed walls, but Phorkys had taken padded room to a new level. It was like he'd turned the Marshmallow Man into a cube.

"I want to see her," a faint voice filtered through the mattress-thick walls.

Something clicked, and a panel in the wall turned translucent.

On the other side stood Isa, wearing a stained apron and wielding a serving spoon like a sword. It had to be breakfast service time—what was she doing here?

"Leave us," she barked at Silent Bob.

I dropped to my knees so we could be eye-level and placed my hand against the glass.

Unlike the movies, Isa did not place her palm on the other side.

"You did it," she said, her mouth cemented into a grimace.

I played innocent. "I know not of what you speak."

"Can it, Korrina," she hissed. "I know you broke the chain. I felt it. I *feel* it." She thumped her chest with her fist. Tiny. But effective.

"It wasn't *that* many souls," I said, going for a there-there tone.

She closed her eyes, gritted her teeth, and sucked in a huge amount of air before slowly letting it go. I totally recognized that move. When someone was trying to *not* lose their sanity. Hadn't used it much myself, but had been on the receiving end far too many times to count.

"The only reason..." She held up a finger and opened her

eyes, though the glare in them made me wish she'd shut them tight once again. "The only reason I have not gone to Phorkys with this yet is"—she took another deep breath—"you were right."

I lurched forward. It wasn't often I'd heard those words, and they were almost better than the sound of percolating coffee.

"Of course I was," I recovered. "About what?"

Isa took another deep breath, and I'd be lying if I said I didn't enjoy her struggle. "I asked for the promotion. I'm the new head chef." Her eyes shone with what I thought were happy tears, but maybe they were just the cries of the lost souls she'd collected.

My face burst into a smile, and I pressed both hands against the transparent wall. "You deserve it. I'm really happy for you."

She shook her head, and her lips curved up. "Thing is, I believe you honestly are." She sucked in another breath, fortified her shoulders. "After the Horde gathers this morning, I will meet with Phorkys and let him know the integrity of my chain has been compromised."

"After?"

She nodded. "After. Please don't make me regret it." She placed her hand against the glass, the expanse of her fingers barely filling my palm. "Good luck, Korrina. I sincerely hope I never see you again."

Isa left. The wall turned opaque. Helplessness seeped into my bones, heavy and depressive. I sank to the floor, buried my face in my knees, and waited. There was nothing else to be done.

Korrina...

"No pep talk, Ania," I snapped. "I'd like to wallow in silence, please."

To her credit, she went quiet.

For a few seconds.

You're out of time. Wallow later.

"And what exactly would you have me do? I'm in a padded

cell with no way out. They're going to bring me before the Horde. They know I can use my song, and they have found some way to protect themselves from it. I'm fresh out of plans" I could practically hear her mulling.

Luke. He's the ace up your sleeve.

"True," I grudged.

Assuming he was at least telling the truth about his intentions.

And your friends.

I let out a breath. And my friends.

We still had a chance to take Phorkys out. A smaller chance than we'd had before—and that wasn't saying much—but it was still there.

A sliver of hope.

All I'd ever needed.

CHAPTER 35

KORRINA

It wasn't long before they came for me. A line of light etched out a door, close to where Isa had held her Korrina peep show. The door swung open and revealed a contingent of guards, some humanoid, others not, all with fresh tattoos pricked into their bodies, the skin under the ink pink and raw.

Tattoos that matched the sigils inside my padded cell.

Great. Well, that explained how Thanos, Crox, and Silent Bob had resisted my song earlier.

"Hey, guys. Are all you here for little ol' me?" I popped my hip and readied my song. It was time to test the strength of those tattoos.

The contingent parted as if they'd been ripped down the middle, and through the gaggle of guards was Jared.

A sharp sickness bored through my chest, left a burning trail of acid in its destruction. Everything slowed, stilled, and he moved toward me as if caught in Mnemosyne's time trap.

I'd expected them.

I hadn't expected him.

I'd hoped…

I'd hoped.

A cruel grin marred his lips, and a darkness that hadn't been there before radiated from him. His gaze locked onto me and reddened.

Words toyed with the tip of my tongue. Questions, demands for an explanation, but I knew better. I'd seen this before.

"Was any of it real?" My words fell like shards of glass.

"What do you think?" And that cruel smile curled impossibly upward.

My shoulders fell, my heart emptied, my song died.

Jared's grip found a familiar place above my elbow. He held tight, not hurting me, but letting me know he was serious. The guards spread out around us until I was in a secured cocoon.

Nothing felt real. My feet didn't feel mine, my arms felt detached, and Jared's touch was ice cold. If he was here, with reddened eyes and a murderous grin, I couldn't fight. There would be no heroic rescue, no sneaking into the throne room and gaining back an element of surprise. No point in fighting my way out at all.

We passed the hallway to Mom's cell, and instead of the tips of her wings, the door stood open, her jail empty.

"Where's my mom?"

No one answered. No one looked at me. They didn't even act like they'd heard me.

"Where did you take her?" My voice had gone shrill, panicked.

Jared tightened his grip and pushed my stumbling feet forward, through the open door of the Grotto.

I had to know where Mom was. If she wasn't where she was supposed to be, I couldn't get her out. Tanzy and Amity would open an escape hatch, and who knew what would come through.

The floors sloped ever upward. The silence thickened. We reached the lower levels, where the training room and Jared's room were located. A loud *boom* shook through the walls, and the entire fortress shivered.

Our little gang froze. The guards had the decency to look wide-eyed at Jared.

"Continue," he ordered, as if nothing had happened.

"Are we under attack again?" I asked, since no one else had the balls.

Jared's mouth was a thin line. "No. We have guests who enjoy a grand entrance."

Moments later, we approached the black, polished doors to the throne room. They were flung against the walls, and the Horde spilled out into the corridor, unusually quiet.

They noticed us and parted to make a path, all without a sound.

The Gathering had begun.

Like the first time I'd traipsed through here, I made my way through a sea of enemies. Only this time, I recognized them. I knew them. I'd connected with them.

Ben, the terrifying slug with the kind heart. Isa, small but packed full of dynamite. Lydia, overflowing with compassion and love for the babies she cared for. They weren't a teeming crowd of nightmarish monsters anymore. They were individuals who, in a different life, could have been my friends.

Yet, not a single one made eye contact.

I looked for Luke as we drifted through the room, but couldn't find him. He had to be here, or all was lost.

Phorkys sat on his throne of conquered enemies. His gray beard curled down to his knees, but instead of clawed hands and a serpent tail, he wore a man's body.

I looked around to see if anyone else seemed surprised by the change in their god, but all eyes were focused on the front. On Phorkys.

On Phorkys's guests.

Cold breathed from the dais, from the God of the Underworld himself. As dangerously hot as ever, his smooth, silver-white hair, waist-length, and those black marble eyes that seemed to see everything. Persephone stood a step behind him, not the powerful Goddess of Spring I'd gotten to know, but the Queen of the Underworld, somehow more diminished with a darker aura. She'd lost her tan, her hair had been bleached of color, and a crown of bones sat heavily on her head.

It'd only been a few days since I last saw the happy couple, but it felt like much, much longer.

We approached the dais. Jared bowed, then took the steps with zero hesitation and settled into his place beside Phorkys, Colin oddly missing from the scene. I darted my gaze around the room, but my birth father was nowhere in sight.

Crox, Thanos, and Silent Bob fanned out behind me, providing a barrier between me and the Horde.

Hades began to laugh, a sound that clicked at the back of his throat like winter-cold trees, frozen and bare.

"This"—he said, pointing at me—"this is what has caused all the trouble?"

We were soooooo not going to be friends.

Phorkys waited for Hades to control himself, tapping a finger on the edge of his throne. Persephone's gaze darted from her husband to me, frantic, as if she knew exactly where this manic laughter was leading.

"My name is Korrina," I said, with all the oomph I could manage. "And I've met you before, though you probably don't remember."

He quit laughing. "Oh?" And raised a perfect eyebrow.

I made a peace sign—same gesture I'd forced a skeleton hand into in his potion room, when I'd stolen his priceless, once-in-a-century oath breaker. "Look familiar?"

"You." His voice dropped low, crawled through the room. The temperature fell to a haunting chill, and I sensed the Horde shudder at my back. "I hope the effort was worth the enemy you've made."

I shrugged, which dropped the temperature even further.

His eyes formed dark slits, and I knew he was trying to scare the power of the Underworld into me, but his scare tactics were wasted. I'd fed the scepter most of my fear, and Jared had killed whatever emotion had been left.

Hades bared his teeth, whipped to Phorkys. "We are here to receive your tribute and consider your forces. Stop with the showmanship, old man."

A hit-and-run glint flashed in Phorkys's eyes, easily missed, entirely unmistakable, and it was that look, that flash of fury, that finally struck terror into my bones.

"Old man, am I?" He rasped, pushed himself from his throne to his feet. His long, wiry beard fell from his face. His skin softened, turned flesh-covered, smoothed. The features of his face narrowed, lengthened. And those ancient eyes…

They turned violet with a tinge of red. Familiar.

The Horde behind me finally moved, gasped, but I couldn't breathe.

The god I'd known as Phorkys was gone. Instead, Colin stood before the throne.

Phorkys was Colin.

Colin was Phorkys.

Colin was my father, which meant…

The room swayed. Phorkys was my father.

All the things Mom had been trying to say hit me like pinpricks of blinding light in a lightless room. Colin's scars were healed. Phorkys was free.

Colin kept his focus on Hades. "This Siren is your tribute. However there will be no consideration of my family. You are here to witness our power and fall to your knees with gratitude."

Shadows in the room darkened from gray to black. I shot a

glance at Jared, whose expression was as composed as ever. He avoided looking at me, and that by itself poked the hardest question through—had Jared known?

"Children"—Colin turned to the Horde at my back—"show Hades your might."

I whipped around and found Luke at the edge of the macabre Where's Waldo scene. His gaze met mine and held it, then he gave a slight nod and melted back into the crowd.

The Horde seemed to take a collective breath, then transformed.

The giant sinkhole in my stomach widened.

I'd only thought I'd met monsters.

They became unrecognizable. Huge, teeming, frothing, a room filled with horrors my mind couldn't accept. My guards, who were already scary enough, grew extra spikes and fangs. Ben towered above the Horde, his layers of teeth rotating like a grinder. Lydia's violet eyes, so much like Luke's, glowed and her nails lengthened. Isa fluttered in the air near Ben, an oily substance dripping from the jagged tips of her wings, her chain wrapped around her arm like a professional gladiator.

Phorkys, still wearing his Colin skin, ripped away at his shirt. On his upper bicep was a tattoo. One that looked strikingly similar to the ones my guards wore, to the sigils painted in my holding cell. Only this one was larger, much larger, raised as if it had been burned into his skin, and it glowed.

His hand transformed back into a claw, and he scratched at the tattoo with a roar.

The Horde echoed his volume, and one by one, faster than I could keep up, that same tattoo appeared over their skin. Protecting them all. Not from Hades.

From me.

Jared's words hit me in the back. *Phorkys is first and foremost a father. And a father protects his children.*

Hades and Persephone clapped at the show, and Hades's

metallic eyes glinted with the advantage that Phorkys's children gave him. I didn't need to be a mind reader to know his thoughts. They would be anyone's thoughts who saw the Horde's display.

Whoever controlled the Horde would win this war.

CHAPTER 36

KORRINA

The cacophony in the throne room was almost more than my not-human ears could take.

Not. Human.

'Cause if my dad wasn't human and my mom wasn't human...

Process later, Ania cautioned.

Yup. Stuffing that in a box, I agreed.

I scanned the room. The Horde was nearing chaotic, and an overload of creature testosterone infected the air. I found Luke, nodded, and he inched forward, moving along the edge of the Horde, nearing the throne with every step.

My guards were too caught up in the addictive scent of mayhem. Phorkys-slash-Colin stood wide-legged, all proud papa. All not-watching-his-feet.

Luke dove forward, wrapped his hands around Phorkys's bare ankles, and before anyone could react, I drew a breath and let out a scepter-song scream.

The sound pierced the room. Almost inaudible yet utterly undeniable. The bones of every creature in the room trembled, and I felt every clickity-clack as if they were my own.

The scepter was full, content. I'd fed it slivers of emotion for days now, a little bit at a time, filling its seemingly bottomless stomach. My power, combined with the scepter's power, rang strong, stronger than ever before. The harmonies threaded through me, touched the strands of my DNA, and infused themselves with every coarse thread. Blue light blasted from my pores, a constant exchange of burning, healing so that all that remained was a euphoric mix of adrenaline and power.

Ania wove her dark self into my light and cast shadows in all the places my light could not reach.

No one was left untouched. Hades and Persephone grasped at one another, intertwined their arms, and covered each other's ears. Jared's eyes flashed red, his hands fisted at his sides, and green fire clouded out from his enclosed fists.

The Horde dropped to their knees, diminished.

Diminished, but not defeated.

Phorkys scratched again at the symbol branded on his arm, and the Horde got back to their feet, fluttered in the air, flicked their tails. He sucked in a deep breath, only it wasn't so much a breath as a collapsing of the fortress with his inhale, and a restoration with his exhale. His skin popped red spikes, and he morphed into some combination of the two creatures I known —Colin, my father, and Phorkys, the god who demanded the impossible.

He threw Luke off the dais with little more than a flick of his thorned finger, as if Luke were nothing more than a biting gnat. As if Luke didn't have the power to silence gods. Luke crumpled at the foot of the stairs.

Blood rushed out of my head, and a frostbitten sense of failure set in.

Split-seconds.

That's all it had taken.

Split-seconds, and the scene at my feet had been painted inside my brain, an image that would last forever, a reminder of the moment we could have ended the war before blood was shed. And I'd failed.

Phorkys with his familiar Colin eyes and his scarless Colin mouth looked up, met my gaze, and smiled.

My head was dead weight atop a straw body. I couldn't move, but my thoughts grew, and grew, and grew.

Phorkys had planned for this all along. He'd wanted me to demonstrate my power, and so I had. I'd shown Hades and Phorkys that I was stronger than an enchanted Horde—if for only a few seconds—and Phorkys had me in his grasp. With me and the Horde at his fingertips, no force could stand against him. Hades would be unnecessary. His forces would be unnecessary. Hades was no longer the driving force behind this war.

But the God of the Deep, with his Horde, with his infamous Siren, with his scepter, would be unstoppable.

I had to get out of here.

Jared began to clap. Slow, steady, sarcastic.

Phorkys-Colin grinned, joined him, and soon, the entire room thudded in a rhythmic thunder, no longer an applause, but a demand for more. More power, more chaos, more control.

Hades pushed Persephone behind him, but she darted out of his way, took her place by his side once more, and gripped his hand, her intent clear. No matter what was coming, they'd face it together. She had a serious case of Stockholm syndrome.

"Step forward, Siren," Phorkys commanded.

I crossed my arms, stood my ground, even as my heart fluttered erratically in my throat. "Don't you mean, Daughter? Sorry, Daddy-O. Not in the mood to blindly obey."

Phorkys just grinned his Colin-smile and jerked his head up. "Bring her out."

Two creatures left their place at the foot of the dais, opened the side door that led into the war room, and drug out a large golden cage.

With my mother stuffed inside.

"How about now?" he asked.

My palms grew sweaty against my folded arms, and my hands slipped to my sides. Luke had warned me Phorkys would use Mom to force me to do his will. I'd taken the warning seriously, but I'd also thought we'd be long gone before Phorkys had the chance.

My throat felt coated in sandpaper. "What do you want?"

Phorkys walked behind Hades and Persephone, clapped them each on the shoulder, as if they were old golfing buddies. "These two have such grand plans." He squeezed their shoulders and gave them a little shake.

Hades eyes narrowed, and dark smoke trailed out of his mouth and nostrils, as if he was so angry his insides were on fire. Persephone jerked her shoulder against Phorkys's grip, and he let them go.

"My plans are also grand. Sing us a song, Siren. A song that will bend this adoring couple's minds to my desires."

"No," I said.

"Your stubbornness does not disappoint." Phorkys walked across the dais toward my unconscious mother. "*Strategos*, your blade." He held out his hand. Jared snapped to attention, handed it over without hesitation.

Phorkys made sure I was watching, then morphed his face into Colin's features.

"Of all my children, you have been the only one who was unintended. Did you know this?"

I shook my head, focused on deep breaths, remaining calm.

"Raelynn was a dalliance, or she was supposed to be. But she became much more. A funnel for revenge against Mnemosyne, grandmother of the original Sirens. I suppose it was a bit too *Greek tragedy* to seduce one of my lineage, but it couldn't be helped. They had the scepter. I needed it back."

"Ew." I wrinkled my nose. Great. So not only was my father a freak, but I was the product of some twisted incestuous game.

Phorkys nodded but picked up Raelynn's hand through the cage. "I agree. What I didn't foresee was you. Or that the Sirens would hide such a weapon within you. Or the fire within Raelynn to protect you. You...our little complication." He kissed her fingertips, the blade resting lazily at his side.

"Again. Ew."

His eyes flashed. Behind him, Jared shifted from one foot to the other. Luke began to stir at the base of the throne steps.

"The power of Raelynn's song at the moment of her transformation transferred to my body through the wound she delivered. It all had to have been timed just right. The transformation, the combination of Demeter's power delivered through the blade, and the Siren power delivered through Raelynn's just-birthed talons. And the consequence? It limited me."

My heart struck a chord, low and dissonant, and the vibration rattled through my gut. "Limited you?"

"Yes. Diminished my power. Locked me into only two forms —my human body and an old, decrepit god. But you, with that healing power of yours, with the scepter's power buried in your soul, you delivered me from my imprisonment. You unlocked my power, reversed what your mother had sacrificed. All those years of her using her life force to keep me locked away, and you undid it in a matter of a few days."

The beating in my chest struck my ribs, again, again, and a scaled sickness slithered through my stomach. "And now, you're unleashed," I finished for him, kept my tone bored.

His eyes flashed. His hand tightened around Jared's blade.

During Phorkys's tirade, Hades had left Persephone's side and had crept close.

Phorkys flung open Mom's cage, pulled her out, and shoved the knife against her neck. Her head lolled in my direction, and she peeked open one eye, connected her gaze with mine, then went back to playing faint.

She was conscious.

"What wouldn't you do for family? What wouldn't I do for family? We are one and the same, Korrina. This way, you get what you want, your family safe and sound"—he nudged her chin up, nestled the knife snug against her throat—"and I get what I want—respect for my children. Merge the God of the Dead's desires with mine. Or else, Raelynn dies."

Hades was only a few steps away. He wasn't an ally, but right now, he was our best hope at killing Phorkys and escaping.

I let tears spring to my eyes and nodded. Phorkys's grin flashed triumph. I took a deep breath, fell into a momentary meditative state, and sent Tanzy the signal. It wasn't quite a dream walk, so I hoped I wouldn't puke all over Phorkys's claws. I had no time to deal with upchuck. Tanzy and Amity had to combine their powers and sing their song, but I still had to move fast.

Hades lunged. Phorkys thrust out his arm and caught Hades by the throat. Mom struggled, wiggled out of Phorkys's grasp, pushed her wings down and rose into the air. I ran forward to Luke and sang a song of control, but not the one Phorkys wanted me to sing. Mine. And aimed not at Hades, but Jared.

Chaos erupted.

Creatures surged forward to protect their master from Hades's attack. Persephone beat at Phorkys's arm. Hades used his own dark power and flung a black rope around Phorkys's neck.

All background. I kept my focus on Jared and sang to his blood. Mom landed next to us and gripped Luke's arm in her talon. Jared neared us, his eyes clear, his face peaceful.

A rope ladder fell from the ceiling, like something out of an Indiana Jones movie. I rolled my eyes at the escape route Amity had just sung into existence, hooked my elbow around one of the rungs, gripped Mom's wing with the same arm, and reached a hand out to Jared. We all had to be linked for this to work.

"Time to go."

He shook his head, and the chaos around us dimmed to white noise.

"Jared, you promised. We swore an oath. You have to—"

"I promised to keep you safe," he said. "Even if that means from me."

"I am safe with you. C'mon we have to—"

"I knew, Korrina."

My breaths froze in my chest.

"Before we made the oath, I knew Phorkys was your father. I knew what you were."

The rope ladder jerked under my arm. They wanted me to jerk back twice. To let them know we were ready.

But we weren't, we couldn't, because Jared...

His eyes flashed red, green fire poured from his palms, and I didn't know who I was looking at anymore. Who I'd been looking at this entire time.

"Korrina," Mom yelled. I looked past Jared. The Horde was surging toward us. Phorkys had morphed into a full-on giant sea monster. Hades and Persephone had created a smoke screen that blocked his attacks, but it couldn't hold for long.

"Go, *Elpida*," Jared growled, and his fire licked the floor at my feet.

Elpida. Not Korrina, but *Elpida*. I jerked the rope ladder twice, our feet and talons left the ground, and Phorkys's fortress rushed away.

CHAPTER 37

KORRINA

I landed on my rear with an *oomph*. Mom rolled to the ground next to me, and Luke groaned and slowly rose up on an elbow. Sunlight screamed at us, and it felt like an all-out attack after being so long without its brilliance.

Mom covered her face with her wing. The woman hadn't seen the sun in eighteen years. I wondered if she would even be able to adjust to the light.

I blinked until the sun spots danced away and I could search for clues to where we'd landed without squinting. Our surroundings were vaguely familiar. Mom was with us, so we were still on the mythical side of the Veil. A meadow strewn with multi-hued flowers and a table-shaped rock perched in the center. An ancient wood surrounded the meadow, and I knew that on the other side of the wood, the ocean beat the island's shores.

"Anthemusa," Mom purred.

The island home of the Sirens.

I'd been here before, back before I knew I was a Siren, before I knew anything.

Did I know anything now? It seemed like every time I

started to trust my footing, the world shook and I was knocked to my knees once again.

Jared was still imprisoned. Phorkys was still alive. Persephone was still trapped. The curse was still unbroken.

What exactly had I accomplished?

You freed your mother. You released trapped souls. You befriended a titaness. You—

"Not now, Ania," I muttered.

My mom gave me a you're-a-weirdo look, then cocked her head. Her gaze flew to the edge of the forest.

Four ancient Sirens emerged—Molpe, Thelma, Peisinoe, and Aggie—followed by Tanzy, Amity with her peacock-colored wings, and Cloud and Danica hand in hand. Neri fluttered in the air behind them, an iridescent beam of light. Dave was the only one missing from the band.

"This place is creepy," Danica called out.

Mom and I gave each other a confused look and took in the peaceful meadow.

"How, exactly?" I asked Dan when she neared.

She pointed at the table-shaped rock—"Sacrificial table"—circled her hand above her head—"cut off from civilization"—thumbed behind her—"forest and beach deserted and perfect for hiding bodies." She rolled her eyes in a *duh.*

"Mm-hmm." I threw my arms around her neck. "I missed you and your psychopathic theories."

She squeezed me back before she acted all tough again. "Of course you did. And if you *ever* do this to us again"—she let the threat hang, while the rest of the group formed up behind her, arms crossed, wings tight against their sides, all in all a pretty intimidating picture—"we reserve the right to sell your organs on the black market."

"Deal," I said, keeping my *Luke, I am your father* news to myself for the moment. After all, if a primordial sea god was my father and a siren was my mother, who knew what kind of organs I had.

Cloud wrapped his arms around me, holding both Danica and me at the same time. "How's Jared?" he asked, his voice low.

My throat grew small and tight, and tears threatened to spill over. I shrugged. "Not here."

Cloud's lips went thin, and he and Danica hugged me tighter. He rested his chin on top of my head. "We'll get him back. All of us. Together."

"Promise?" I squeaked. Because for once, I needed someone else to promise the impossible.

Cloud drew back, spit in his hand, and held it out. The Mischievous oath.

I cry-laughed—when did I start crying?—spit in my hand, and squished my palm to his, sealing the pact.

Danica had her hand sanitizer out before we let go. "Still gross," she said, squeezing the clear gel into our hands.

Behind the humans, the Sirens shifted. "Do you enjoy holding us in suspense, *Elpida*?" Peisinoe's tone had a glare.

I huffed and turned to the rest of the group. Molpe's and Neri's faces held expressions of concern. The rest just looked impatient.

"Phorkys plans to double-cross Hades," I announced. "He'll join his war, position his forces, and strike when the gods are the weakest. I saw the war map."

The Sirens leaned in.

"Phorkys's children are already spread across the globe—both sides of the Veil—and he has more children than anyone has recorded. I know Amity has done a good job of organizing refugee mythicals on the human side, but there are more. So many more on the human side. More than I would have ever guessed."

Everyone exchanged looks, and the less-than-celebratory mood dropped even lower.

Luke cleared his throat. "That's not the worst news," he said.

I raised my eyebrows. All focus shot to him.

He pushed himself up from the ground, brushed the dirt off his knees and elbows, and breathed in deep. "My job in the deep was to run messages." He shoved the disheveled hair out of his eyes, and it brushed against his neck. "I wasn't supposed to read them," he said, holding the pause for dramatic effect.

Amity sighed. "But you obviously did, so what do you know?" she snapped, beating me to the punch.

Tanzy just blinked her big green eyes at Luke. Seriously, what was going on between those two?

Luke ran his hands through his hair again, smoothing out the tangles in his shoulder-length waves. "Jared knew, Korrina. All of it."

The air left the world. It must have, because there was none left for me to breathe.

Luke kept a hard gaze on me, as if making sure I wouldn't look away, wouldn't deny what he had to tell me. "He knew that Phorkys was going to double-cross Hades. He knew that Phorkys could protect his family from your power"—I faintly registered a hiss of air from everyone at that revelation—"and he knew that you showing your power was the only way to get what he really wanted."

What he really wanted. That phrase hung in the air in front of me, dangling like a noose. What Jared really wanted was me. Wasn't it? But if what Luke was saying was true, I wasn't what Jared wanted, and the thought threatened to strangle me.

"And what he wants?" I gasped, unable to locate oxygen.

"For Phorkys to win," Luke shrugged, as if I should have known.

As if I should have known better.

My insides had turned to one big bruise, with my heart at the center, the source of my bleed. How had I read Jared so completely wrong?

Had anything we'd experienced been true? Did he love me even a little? Or had I just made him up in my head—the person I wanted him to be?

Had I ever really known Jared Thalassa?

Luke came close, and even though the entire group could hear, he spoke only to me. "I thought your plan would work, but it didn't. All it did was expose how powerful you are to the gods who want that power the most."

"Geez, buttmunch," Danica said. "Ease up a little."

"We don't have time for that," Luke shouted back, and everyone flinched. "Don't you guys get it? Phorkys now knows how powerful Korrina is. He knows that Jared is her weakness. He knows the only way to get Hades under his thumb is to get to Korrina before Hades does. He knows how to inoculate himself and his family against her so she can't fight him. And he knows that without Korrina, he will lose. He. Is. Coming. For. Her."

The group went silent. We seemed to shrink.

"What about Hades?" I broke the silence.

Luke's face, if possible, turned even more depressed. "We can only assume that he's coming for you as well. It's a race. Whoever owns you wins."

Anger hardened my insides. Everyone wanted to use me as their tool—the Sirens with the scepter in my body, the Council with its missions, Jared to get "what he really wanted," and both Phorkys and Hades to win a war.

"No one owns me," I hissed.

Luke's lips broke into a smile. "That's my girl."

I held a finger in his face. "I am *not* your girl," I snarled. If I'd been a werewolf, he'd have been running.

He grinned even bigger. "Exactly why you are my girl," he said, then jumped out of strangling range.

Neri fluttered in between us, her before-time-existed aura

descending on us all like a weighted blanket. "Korrina, what's the new plan?"

Amazing that they were still turning to me for plans. My heart twinged at the thought of Dad, always a man with a plan. I usually hadn't liked him taking charge, but right now, it would be nice to pass the strategizing off to someone else.

But Dad wasn't here any longer, and I was the only one of the group who'd seen the all other side had to offer.

I bit my lip, let out a deep breath. "If Phorkys and Hades are both coming for me, then I say we make it easy for them." I looked around at all my friends and glommed-together family. "Let's make it easy for them to fall into our trap."

"I like it," Danica cracked her knuckles. "Use you as bait, and then maybe you'll think twice before leaving us again."

I raised my eyebrows. Danica wasn't one to hold a grudge—well, that wasn't true. She very much was. And if needed, she delivered on her threats. But stacking punishment upon punishment was not her style.

I'd hurt her. Far worse than I'd known. I looked around the group. I'd hurt all of them.

And now, they had to do the impossible and build a trap to stop not one, but two pissed-off gods. Otherwise, it was *sayonara, Siren* for good.

CHAPTER 38

KORRINA

Everyone agreed that staying on the mythical side of the Veil was the best plan, for multiple reasons. The biggest one being that I refused to risk innocent humans on the other side when Phorkys and Hades inevitably hunted me down. Better to keep that risk to this side of the Veil, where there were fewer innocents and more immortals.

Luke and Tanzy sat beside a campfire, talking quietly and poking at the flames every now and then. Amity soared in the sunset, practicing flight with her newish wings. Molpe's sisters had just gotten back from a fishing expedition and were busy preparing a giant fish to cook over the campfire's flames.

Molpe crouched near Mom, heads bent together and, every once in a while flicked their gaze toward me. I hoped Molpe was updating Mom on all that had happened in the past year. I super-hoped that she was telling her about Dad's death. How heroic he was. How he loved her.

Because I couldn't. Not now, while it was fresh and she was conscious.

I stretched out on the cool grass, the stars above starting to pop out of a bruising sky. Cloud and Danica sat on either side of me while Neri paced from side to side, the three of them brainstorming different ways to disable a god, but I'd tuned them out. I'd been mulling this over, under, sideways, and upside-down for days, and my brain hurt.

The crux of the problem was this: we had no idea what to do. Luke's power hadn't worked. My song hadn't worked. And going by the sounds of a not-so-distant battle, we were running out of time. The gods were at war, and we were on the losing side. Hades and Demeter were having it out, finally, the long-time-coming war for Persephone's heart, and the fate of the Sirens—and Jared—was caught up in the middle.

The winged curse would not be broken until Persephone was freed. The fight for the scepter would not be over until Phorkys was defeated. Jared's heart and mind and soul would not be his again until I broke the curse and killed his god.

And to do that, we had a whole lot of monsters to fight.

Monsters I'd been made powerless to combat.

Monsters I'd come to know, understand, and even like.

I flung my hand over my face, Neri's words coming back into focus.

"—news channels are blaming it on a rapid acceleration of climate change. Record-breaking tornados in Texas, multiple hurricanes swirling in the Atlantic, earthquakes in Maine, flooding in Arizona, freak blizzards in places that rarely see snow."

I sat up. "It's that bad over there?"

Neri met my gaze. "Thousands are dying, Korrina. This war has to stop. Soon."

Danica fidgeted and interlaced her fingers around her knees. "Cloud, Neri, and I have a theory."

"About the war?" I looked between them.

Neri shook her head. "About why your and Luke's plan didn't work on Phorkys."

"Three of the smartest and most devious brains I've ever met have a theory?"

I called out to Luke, Tanzy, and Amity to join us. Amity spun down to the ground and landed with the grace of an experienced skydiver, and Tanzy and Luke walked over, bumping into each other every few steps.

Once everyone was gathered, I held my palms out in an impatient, go-ahead gesture. "Spill."

Cloud cleared his throat. "Luke's touch mutes your power, but only if he makes skin contact."

"What if"—Danica picked up the thread—"Luke's power didn't work on Phorkys because he's a shapeshifter? He could have been transforming his skin fast enough that Luke's power couldn't take hold."

Neri nodded. "His shapeshifting is one of his lesser-known powers, but a common enough power to all the gods. Gods often appear as human in order to seduce—"

"Ew. Yes, I get it. Don't need the history lesson. Move on."

Neri ruffled her feathers but closed her beak.

"So we think," Cloud continued, "that if we could find a way to halt his shapeshifting long enough for Luke's power to seep through, then you'd have a chance to—"

I held up my hand.

"We need more than a chance." I looked each of them in the eyes. "Even if you came up with some experimental potion, it's just that. An experiment. It could stop his shapeshifting, or it could make him stronger."

"Over my downy derriere," Neri piped up, and our jaws all dropped. I didn't know she knew that word. "We cannot do anything that could make Phorkys stronger."

Danica lifted her chin. "Owl has a point. Sea god's on my nerves as is."

I shook my head, trying to get all the puzzle pieces in my

brain to settle into place. "We need to work with what we know. Something that we're sure will at least diminish his power."

Silence hovered, as everyone seemed to be sorting through their own mental puzzles.

And then, just like that, my mind popped the corner piece into place. "The tattoo. That's what's giving him an edge now, and it's what's protecting the entire Horde." My heart sped up from a new idea spark. "When we were in the Deep, he scratched the tattoo to activate it. It required him touching it. Like it was an external thing on his arm. Not part of him. If we can find a way to destroy the tattoo, the Horde will be unprotected. We'll stand a chance in a fight."

No one spoke, but the fidgets stopped while they rolled my words around in their skulls.

Finally, Danica shifted. "But even if he's unprotected, what's powerful enough to hurt a god?"

I rubbed my hand over the oath scar forming on my palm. "Blood. Power comes from blood," I murmured. "It's our blood." I took a breath and spoke louder, announcement-volume. "Luke and I have to mix our blood again, like when we found a way to silence my song, only this time—"

"We shoot it at a god," Luke finished.

Tanzy nodded. "I see a path clearing where there hasn't been one before."

The group fell silent, chewing on my theory. Danica finally nodded. "We do this, and we stand a fighting chance."

Neri fluttered into the air. "I'll run it by the rest—see if they can think of anything we haven't." She soared over to Mom and Molpe, gestured for the rest of the original Sirens to join them.

"We need Dave," Amity said. "If it shoots, he's shot it before. He's the best marksman we have."

"And, as much as I hate to say it"—Luke's face twisted into a grimace—"we need my brother. Crannik is the only person I know who could figure out how to craft a weapon that could pierce immortal skin."

"Aw, I miss Crannik," I said, which earned a sharp glare from Luke, but I hadn't seen his older brother for over a week, and despite his creepiness as a priest of Demeter, I liked him. Mainly because he drove Luke nuts.

"There's something else you all need to know before we go forward with this plan." Luke looked at me pointedly.

I huffed, but he was right. They needed to know. And I wanted to tell my closest friends before Neri and the original Sirens returned.

Danica and Cloud's chins jutted out, Tanzy and Amity leaned in, and they all turned their attention to me.

I'd been dreading this moment, but bad news was like a Band-aid. The quicker you ripped it off, the quicker you'd feel better. "Phorkys shapeshifted into human form to get close to my mom and figure out where the scepter was hidden. When Mom slashed open his face, she was able to suppress his shapeshifting powers with her song, linking them together."

Eyes widened. Jaws dropped. No one moved. I didn't know if they'd followed me to my conclusion, but I wanted to make it crystal, so I'd never have to say it again. "Phorkys is my birth father. Colin was just another one of his forms."

No one moved, not for eternity. Silence thickened, glances bounced around without a single one landing on me.

Neri returned with Mom and Molpe and the other Siren sisters, and their arrival seemed to break the silent spell. Danica pressed her lips together, then threw her arms around my neck and hugged me tight, not saying a word.

Neri fluttered her wings. "What happened?"

I looked up from Danica's shoulder, squeezed her tight, let her go. "Phorkys is my birth father," I announced.

More glances, more worry, more concern.

Peisinoe stepped forward. "If that's true, then your plan will fail," she said, ever the voice of positivity. "He shares your blood. It will protect him against your attacks."

And my perfect plan lasted all of three minutes. I flopped to the ground with all the drama I could muster. "Great. That's just great."

"What if," Tanzy hummed, "we don't use your blood?"

The attention shifted.

"Continue," Peisinoe said, her gaze sharp.

"If Raelynn's power resided in Phorkys's scar and allowed her to suppress his abilities, what if all of us were to mix our blood? Combined with Luke's magical talent, it would be a powerful attack. One he may have no defenses for." Tanzy's hands raised into the air, bringing her idea to a close in her loopy way.

Backs straightened, eyes alighted, shoulders strengthened. It was like a wave passed from body to body.

"If my progeny was a part of this," Peisinoe said, "it would be a fatal shot. But yes, as such, this could work. If we could destroy the defenses surrounding his army, we win."

"Not win." Tanzy raised a finger. "Not now. For that, you are correct—we need your descendant. But this opens the path. Combining our blood gives us a future."

A future. However short. At this point, it was all we could hope for.

CHAPTER 39

KORRINA

The sky had grown dark, and the campfire burned bright. Delicious smells of roasting fish scented the air, mixed with herbs and root vegetables that Thelma picked out of her forest garden. It was a serene moment, or should have been, but a worry crept through me with a sickening aftertaste.

We hadn't thought of everything. There were unknowns. I'd wanted certainty, but our plan was based off a theory, and that plan based off another plan that had already failed.

Not to mention…Jared. He was the wrench in my every plan, my fatal flaw. I knew it, he knew it, Phorkys knew it, my friends knew it, and no one could do anything about it.

I wandered away from the light of the fire and the warmth of the group, the dark, chill night doing its magic to clear my thoughts. Truly alone for the first time in weeks, and all I wanted was to get back to the safety of my friends. But they were a crutch, allowing me to ignore all the emotions I had yet to fully process.

Dad wasn't here anymore.

I wasn't even the slightest bit human.

And I'd failed Jared.

Grief threatened to pulverize my insides. I felt it coming like a tsunami, an impending sense that if I didn't run, I'd drown. My breath shuddered, came hot, fast, and I couldn't get enough air. I braced my hands on my knees, doubled over, and allowed the first wave to hit me, to tear away at all the defenses I'd been forced to build. I'd stuffed it all into a box. Fed the scepter my emotions to take the edge off. So I could survive.

Nothing in my life made sense. Nothing was in my control. Nothing had gone according to plan. So what hope could I possibly have for the future?

Something yanked on the thread that connected me to Jared. I straightened, all my senses on high alert, and shoved all those emotions back into a shadowy corner. A strong scent of burning wood drifted across my nose. Not from the direction of the campfire, but from deeper into the forest.

"Jared?" I whispered and followed the curl of smoke away from my friends and food and safety.

The sensation that he was near faded to an echo, but the woodsy smell of burning undergrowth strengthened. Ahead, green light flickered against the underside of leaves and made eerie shadows crawl along the leaves and dirt.

I crept forward, my breath shallow for completely different reasons now. Tongues of heat licked my skin, warning me to keep my distance.

Fire stretched ahead of me, dancing in a pattern I couldn't decipher. Not normal flames, but Siren Hunter curses. Not a normal wildfire, but deliberately set, and for what purpose? He wasn't here anymore. This wasn't him sneaking me away for secret kisses.

A whoosh of wings above the trees drew my attention. Amity and Molpe circled above the flames, spotted me, and landed.

"We saw the flames from the meadow. Jared?" Amity asked, but it was more confirmation than question.

I nodded.

Molpe edged away from the fire, which was starting to spread. "We need to get back to the others. There is very little time."

"Time?" I looked between the two of them. "What makes you think we're almost out of time?"

"The fire spells out a word, Korrina," Amity said. "It says *dawn*. They're attacking at dawn."

I MADE MY WAY BACK TO THE CAMPFIRE, AMITY BY MY SIDE. Molpe chose to fly rather than waddle, and I couldn't blame her. Amity still had her legs.

Even with her wings, though, Amity was more human than me.

I shook that thought to the side and focused on more important matters.

"Why would Jared tell us when they're attacking?" I mused.

Amity shook her head. "To freak you out? To make sure there's a good fight? I don't know. The guy's sick." The ferociousness in her voice and posture almost made me smile. Amity and I hadn't had a great start to our relationship. I had the feeling she thought I was all silly and no serious—mainly 'cause she'd said so to my face. But maybe she was starting to accept me as family.

"What if"—I started, but my voice had a damper—"what if it was a message to protect us? To make sure we're ready?"

"Then why wouldn't he have stayed and delivered it himself? Why would he use fire that could curse you and Tanzy and finish the job with me?"

She has a point, Ania said.

We emerged from the woods to find everyone on their feet.

Luke passed a dinner plate he'd saved for me, and I gave him a grateful smile.

"Crannik is on his way. Neri went to get Dave," he said as I stuffed my face. "Dawn will come soon."

As if he'd conjured them by invoking their names, a crack of light popped up from the ground and Crannik appeared, robed in his priest garment, staff in hand. Dave materialized next to the stone table clutching Sully the shotgun and a large canvas bag, military-style, with Neri at his side. He looked around, eyes wide, until his gaze found Amity.

His jaw dropped, and a strangled gasp escaped his throat. He hadn't seen her with wings before.

She stepped forward, hands out. "It's me," she said, more gently than I thought she was capable of.

He took small steps toward her, until they met, and he grazed her cheek with the back of his hand. "You're an angel," he whispered, awed.

Amity blinked quickly, and a smile softened the sharp edge of her lips.

"You are aware of how little time we have," Crannik gruffed and tapped his staff against the ground for effect, but Amity and Dave seemed oblivious to his grab for attention. Oblivious to any of us for that matter. Dave wrapped his arms around Amity's waist, pulled her close, and Amity encircled them with her wings.

Crannik shook his head, as if romance was something reserved for lower creatures, set a black, metallic plate on the stone table, and tossed Luke a clear vial etched with intricate sigils and a small box tied closed with a scarlet ribbon. "You first, little brother. Show them how it's done."

Luke rolled his eyes but sat the vial and box on the flat rock and unwrapped the ribbon. Tanzy kicked at Amity's ankle, and she and Dave finally broke apart.

The box's lid fell open. Luke reached in, pinched out a small, silver blade, and without any hesitation sliced his four-fingered hand open. He set the blade on the plate with a clink. Blood pooled in his palm, and he held it there, like a cup, until he could hold no more.

When blood dripped from his fingertips, he tipped his palm over the vial and poured the glistening red liquid into the glass. When he was done, he looked up and addressed Tanzy and Amity—the only two Sirens besides Mom not of Phorkys's immediate bloodline. "Slice quickly, slice deep. Hold the blood in your hand until you feel your pulse throb through your wrist. The bleeding will slow, and it is then that you offer your blood." His voice had taken on a ritualistic timbre, and I wondered just how long he'd served Demeter under Crannik. "Place your blade on the plate before stepping away from the altar. Korrina, would you mind healing our cuts once we're done?"

The night had taken on a somber note. I nodded. "Of course."

He passed the box of blades to Tanzy, holding his still bleeding hand in the air. Tanzy grimaced but selected her blade, a white, bone-like knife, closed her eyes, and sliced. She held her hand in front of her, and it filled like a cup. Her hand shook, and Luke breathed, "Steady." She opened her eyes and focused on him, seemed to take strength from him. When it was time, Luke nodded, and Tanzy fed her blood to the glass vial and left her blade on the platter.

Amity was next, and Dave obviously didn't like it one bit. He stood behind her, hovering, protective, as she picked out a blade that looked like it had been carved from a pink shell, moved closer as she sliced her hand open, then wrapped his hands around her elbows to help her hold her offering steady.

And that's what this was. A sort of offering or ritual. From the blades to the carved glass vial to the platter that seemed to absorb starlight, this was a ritual. A ritual to create a weapon that could maim a god.

Amity added her blood to the vial, her blade to the plate, and stepped back.

A change passed over the three of them, as if they were suddenly linked. Wordlessly, they came together, cupped their bleeding hands together in a Celtic knot, and went still.

Crannik took the vial and added the blades to the blood. He began muttering something in a language I didn't recognize, and I understood Ancient Greek. Tanzy, Amity, and Luke began to sway to the rhythm of Crannik's words, then took up his chant, one step behind him. The volume increased, clashed and clanged into something I almost couldn't bear to hear. A dark light flashed from the vial, the chanters went silent, and Crannik moaned in a low, dual-tone note.

Something *other* filled the night. Whispers, a chill. The hair on the back of my neck pricked against my scalp. Molpe, Mom, and the Sirens exchanged quick glances and tightened their wings against their bodies. Fear? Or ready to fight?

I stood alone, on the other side of the fire from the rest of the group, and I suddenly felt vulnerable, in danger. I wanted, needed to get close to the others, but I couldn't move. Not because some magic froze me in place, but because every primitive survival instinct I owned was holding me still, quiet. If I moved, the something would see me, and I doubted I'd survive.

Crannik's hands shook as if something was trying to tear his hands apart. The vial burned with a black light, the whispers grew heavier, more insistent, and the something in the night wrapped itself around Crannik.

His eyes popped open, they seemed to glow silver, and from my vantage point, I was his only witness. His stare bored into me, as if I wasn't there, as if he could see all the cells and molecules that made up my very inhuman body, and he opened his mouth and sucked in the unspeakable *something*.

His hands stilled, his back straightened, and just as suddenly as it had all started, it was over.

Tanzy, Amity, and Luke let go of each other and looked around as if just waking up.

"What was that, Crannik?" I rasped. Because that silver had stayed in his eyes, and something in his expression had changed.

"That," he said, his voice torn to rags, "was how you make a weapon that can hurt an immortal." He held out his hand, and in it nested a black arrowhead.

CHAPTER 40

KORRINA

Crannik took his leave soon after placing the arrowhead in Luke's hands. He didn't offer to fight, and no one asked him to join our crew. As one of Demeter's priests, his place was by her side.

No one mentioned sleep.

Amity took one look at the arrowhead nestled in Luke's hand and sang a bow and quiver of arrows into existence. Dave slung the quiver over his shoulder, tested the weight of the bow, and headed to the far side of the meadow without a word. Soon, the dull thud of arrow hitting wood echoed back to us.

Neri fluttered into the air. "We need to reinforce the beach. Most of Phorkys's children will come from the sea."

Danica looked heavenward in a dramatic eye roll. "That should be easy since we're on an island and surrounded by ocean."

Peisinoe gazed at Danica with an admiring eye. "My sisters and I will place ramparts into the beach. Amity, sing what you can into existence by way of fortifications."

Amity nodded and flew into the air after Peisinoe, Thelma, and Aggie. Molpe stayed on the ground.

Neri's gaze followed the Sirens, then she turned her focus back to us. "What to do with you?" she muttered, eyeing Danica and Cloud.

Cloud grinned. "Oh, we have tricks up our sleeves. C'mon, Dan. We have mayhem to seed." They fist bumped and headed into the woods.

I locked eyes with Neri. "I want them across the Veil when the fighting starts."

She gave a serious dip of her beak. "Yes, agreed. They are too precious to risk." She turned her intense gaze on Luke. "You're with me during this battle."

Something dimmed in his eyes. "Haven't I proven myself?" His words were quiet, but we heard them clearly. He straightened his shoulders, strengthened his voice. "I will not betray you. Not ever again." At his side, Tanzy took his hand.

Neri flitted to his eye level. "It is not your loyalty I question, but rather how you will handle fighting your family. It is a harder thing than you can imagine." Her voice lowered, and for the first time, I wondered what Neri's life had been. Had she ever had a family? Had she ever been in love? "You and Tanzy follow me," she continued. "We need to form a battle plan. With your knowledge of the inner workings of Phorkys's army and with Tanzy's foresight, we should be able to come up with something resembling intelligent." She snapped her wings and soared across the meadow, leading Tanzy and Luke to the beach.

"And us?" I asked Mom and Molpe.

Mom's jaw tightened. "We practice."

Molpe nodded. "Let's go somewhere else." She led us to the opposite side of the meadow, and despite her and Mom's earlier chattiness, a silence had tightened between us. Mom fell into a waddling step beside me, while Molpe picked our path through the trees.

Mom kept my pace, swallowed a few times. "Molpe told me

about Michael—Dad. What he sacrificed…" Her blue eyes watered. "I'm so sorry."

My throat grew tight. I still hadn't had the space I needed to really mourn Dad, and now was not the time. So I nodded, blinked back the burning in my eyes, and pressed forward.

We reached a somewhat secluded glade, open to the pinpricked sky with scraps of grass underfoot. Waves brushed against the sand somewhere close, but hidden. The beach was near, secreted away by the copse of trees.

Molpe settled at the edge of the clearing to watch. "Show us what you have learned about the scepter."

Mom stayed close.

I took a deep breath in through my nose, held it in the center of my chest, and fed the scepter my worry. Worry about what would come for us at dawn, worry if I'd be able to fight Jared, worry that once all this was over I might not overcome any of my tucked-away grief.

The scepter brightened in my mind's eye, and the weighted worry-stone in my chest lightened. I let out my breath, and with it, my nails began to glow scepter blue with a tint of Korrina purple. Since my time in the Deep, the scepter had changed. No longer an orb that separated from me, it was a part of me. It had infused itself into my body, my brain, and I no longer believed that someday it could be removed.

Like Ania, the scepter was a part of who I was. It made me into something more, and the moment I'd accepted it fully and completely, it had stopped tearing me apart.

"Korrina…" Mom whispered.

I opened my eyes—hadn't realized I'd closed them—and looked about the glade.

Spring had bloomed in the last few seconds. Where before there were old-barked trees and dull grass, the glade burst with color. Golds and blues, pinks and oranges. Fireflies flitted between flower petals, and a night bird sang. Even the sound of the waves brushing the beach seemed calmer.

Molpe straightened. "What were you thinking about just now?"

I shrugged. "I fed the scepter my worry, as Mnemosyne taught, but then I started thinking about how the scepter was a bit like Ania, in that I've had to accept it as part of me and stop spending energy fighting it."

"And you felt…" she prodded.

I looked around the glade. "Weightless. Like everything in me was harmonized."

Mom nodded. "In that moment, you weren't thinking of your worries. You were existing only in the present."

"Like meditating," I responded, already at the conclusion they were leading me to. "Mnemosyne mentioned that what I fed the scepter impacted its power, and I've seen it happen. But how do I know what to feed it to get exactly what I want? All I know is that if I feed it a positive emotion, I get a healing response. If I feed it a negative emotion, it becomes a weapon." I threw my hands up in the air.

Mom's eyebrows raised. "Well that's useful, isn't it?"

"Not if she wants to use it in combat," Molpe said.

Her understanding of my underlying fear made the breath whoosh out of me. "I can't go out on the battlefield like this. I'm like a toddler with a grenade. Just as likely to hurt us as I am to hurt them. And what if I run into someone that I actually like on the other side, like Ben or Isa or Lydia? Or—"

"Jared?" Mom finished for me.

I nodded, my throat tight. "What if I see him and do nothing but grow a field of flowers?" My chin dropped. "What if I get one of you killed?"

My mom and ancient grandmother closed in, circled me in their wings, their warmth, and pressed their heads to mine. Not offering false comfort but giving me the rock-solid love I so desperately needed.

Molpe was the first to break away from our huddle. "Walk me through those last moments in Phorkys's throne room."

I raised my brows but did as she asked, detailing my scepter-song scream attack that had brought the Horde to its knees, before Phorkys had reinforced their protections with the emblem tattooed on his arm.

"You used the powers of the scepter and your song, together. Not one to prompt the other or to feed the other but wove them together and used them in equal measure?" It wasn't so much a question as it was a musing.

I nodded. "I thought it'd be more powerful, and since they'd silenced my Siren power, it was eager to be used."

Molpe pursed her lips, shot a questioning glance at Mom, and Mom gave her a go-ahead nod. "Okay. Do that again. But this time, use your song to direct the scepter's power. Feed the scepter your intent, and then sing your song."

Mom squeezed my shoulder. "We'll be right here to help."

I jerked my head, exhaled through my nose.

You can do this, Ania whispered. *You've already done this.*

I took another breath, more confident this time.

Across the glade was a tree that had escaped my earlier magic trick. Rotted and hollowed out, bark singed from a long-ago lightning strike or fire, it needed to return to the earth. It needed to become soil once again, nourishing and life-affirming. I focused my intentions—to reduce the tree's corpse to loam—and fed them to the scepter. It hummed deep within my bones, hummed to the point I could no longer contain it.

I let it free.

The scepter's light poured from me, hummed into the ground at my toes. I sang a melody, strong and directive, one that spoke to the north winds and to the ocean that lay just beyond the rotting wood. The bluish-purple power that poured from me turned into a path of light from me to the decaying tree, as if I was casting a light-filled shadow.

The light grew more intense, and though only a few seconds had passed, it felt as if I was watching the tree decay in real time, turning soft, crumbling in on itself, branches dropping to the ground with dull explosions, the trunk eaten down by insects and birds, until finally, the only hint that a tree had ever existed in that space was a pile of warm, fertile soil and a placeholder of emptiness.

It was Mom who broke the silence. "I don't think she needs our help."

Molpe laughed and Mom whooped, and then they were both hugging me again, only this time to celebrate, not to comfort.

"A few more hours of practice," Molpe said, "and you'll be able to hold your own on any battlefield."

I wanted to smile with them. I wanted to join in and celebrate. I wanted to enjoy this small win. But something niggled at the top of my spine. A sixth sense, a feeling of something-not-right.

I pulled in a tight breath and focused on my surroundings, and even then, it took me a moment to realize what had changed.

The waves.

They no longer swished against the beach.

The ocean made no sound at all.

CHAPTER 41

KORRINA

My heart rammed into my throat. It wasn't dawn. We had hours to go until dawn. Jared had said dawn.

I pushed past Mom then Molpe, stomped through the decomposed tree, exploded onto the moonlit beach. The stench of rotten eggs filled the air, and I covered my nose and mouth with my sleeve.

The water had pulled away from the island. Fish flopped in the sand, and crabs scuttled around, confused. I scanned the beach for enemies. Empty. I searched farther out, my heart thudding in my ears, because we weren't alone. The enemy was here.

Molpe and Mom landed next to me. "Gaia save us," Molpe whispered, her voice low, and I traced her focus through the unnaturally wide beach, past the dying fish and scavenging crabs, out to the horizon, where the stars should have shone.

My mouth went dry. Every one of my bones buzzed. I grabbed onto Mom's wing to steady myself. In the distance, the ocean had risen, higher and higher, and the moon glinted off the top of an impossibly tall wave.

"Tsunami," I gasped.

Molpe and Mom launched into the air. As they rose, Mom wrapped her talons around my shoulders and lifted me with them. We reached the meadow at the same time as everyone else.

"They're coming," I shouted. "Now. Neri, get Cloud and Danica out of here!"

Cloud's and Dan's eyes widened. Before they could protest, Neri opened a portal, grabbed hold of them, and yanked them through.

Overhead, flocks of birds screeched and flew away from the island, sensing what was coming. Sensing that we were on a death trap.

But I doubted they could get away any more than we could. Both birds and the elder Sirens could fly, but we'd never reach the mainland with a tsunami chasing us and Phorkys's monsters hiding like ocean-deep land mines between us and safety.

I looked at the rest of my team. All of our preparations were for naught. No amount of ramparts or fortifications or Mischief and Mayhem traps were going to work against a tsunami.

Still, they deserved a choice. "Run or fight?" I asked.

"There's nowhere to run, and we can't fight a wave," Amity said, her eyes wide, Dave at her side.

At least I wasn't the only one to understand our impossible dilemma.

"We can create a barrier though," Aggie offered. "It'll protect the island from this first attack. Take up your positions, Sisters."

Molpe, Aggie, Peisinoe, and Thelma leaped into the air, separated in four different directions. Precious seconds later, their songs washed over the island, and an iridescent dome curved over our heads.

"Will it hold?" I asked Tanzy.

"They know what they're doing," Mom answered, but I kept my focus on Tanzy.

She hadn't taken her eyes off the rising tsunami, hadn't stopped analyzing the dome, hadn't unclenched her fists.

The water towered over the island, blocked the moon, sank us into its shadow. If we survived the next few minutes, I'd never forget its sound. The tsunami roared as if it had swallowed a dragon, the noise low but piercing, thick and heavy. I lost my balance, fell to the ground. The island shook, knocking the rest of my team to their knees. Our ancestors might create an impressive barrier, but we needed something more.

"Tanzy, Amity, Mom, we're forming a back-up barrier," I shouted above the roar. "Luke, Dave, get in the middle." I pushed Luke to the center. Dave joined him, still clutching that military canvas bag and Sully. I grabbed Tanzy's and Mom's hands. They grabbed Amity's, and she began to chant. Tanzy took up the harmony, and Mom and I filled in the gaps, lacing it with steel strength from the scepter and my intentions to save us from this sure death.

The barrier cracked. The ocean pressed against it. The roaring thundered. In one, heart-splitting moment, the wave paused above us, held impossibly still.

And then came crashing down.

The ancient Sirens' barrier held, barely, water leaking through the top in rivulets. Tanzy met my gaze, hers frantic, telling me what I already knew.

If we didn't get our own barrier up, we weren't making it out of here.

The rivulets turned to waterfalls. A screeching hiss popped around us as the barrier gave way, as our smaller barrier snapped into place, as the ocean fell on top of us.

I squeezed my eyes tight and fed the scepter all that I had. Every fear, every hope, every belief that this was not our time to die. Water swirled around us, buried us, but our bubble remained. I raised my voice, set the tone, inspired the song.

Amity changed the words, began speaking in Ancient Greek, and Tanzy led us through the melody, hurried yet strong.

The roaring lost its earsplitting volume and settled to a grumble. We—my Siren sisters and I—were defiant. The ocean quieted further, so much so I heard Luke whisper, "That's my girl." For the first time, I didn't think he was talking about me.

"And mine," Dave said, unmistakable notes of pride lifting his voice.

For a microsecond, I felt alone. Unbearably alone. My guy wasn't here to be proud of me. Instead, he'd tried to kill us.

Tanzy squeezed my hand.

I peeked open my eyes.

Our bubble had grown.

It had not only grown—it'd pushed the entire ocean back into its rightful place.

Amity brought the lyrics to a close, Tanzy tied off the melody, and I let go of the scepter. Our bubble melted away with the sound of our voices, and we surveyed the damage.

We were still here.

But little else was.

The stone table had toppled over. Trees had been ripped out of the ground from their roots. The beach had fallen back into the ocean. In the few minutes that the island had been underwater, the soil had eroded away, and the island's rocky undergarments were left vulnerable.

Peisinoe returned first, drenched and bedraggled. "We couldn't hold it. Too much ground to cover." She sounded winded.

Aggie and Thelma landed next to her. "You survived," Thelma gasped and threw a wing around Tanzy.

"Yes, I foresaw the collapse, so we created our own barrier," Tanzy said, as if we'd simply thought ahead to bringing an umbrella, instead of creating a tsunami-proof bubble.

Mom searched the dark skies. "Where's Molpe?"

"She hasn't returned?" Peisinoe's voice went sharp, and she lifted into the air without a moment's hesitation. Her black feathers were the perfect camouflage for night, and she quickly disappeared.

Aggie and Thelma exchanged looks. "She took the north side."

I looked back at where we'd come from, where the tsunami had originated, where the once gentle beach had been replaced by a sand-encrusted cliff that dropped sharply into the ocean.

Neri appeared. "The humans are safe." She looked around the group, saw the panic in our eyes, became our reflection. "Where's Molpe?"

The soft hush of wings beat the air, and Peisinoe dropped into our midst. "I cannot find her."

In the past year, I'd only seen Peisinoe a handful of times, but she had cemented herself into my mind as a hard, unbreakable creature, one comfortable with setting a foot inside dark decisions, one who may have orchestrated Persephone's kidnapping and triggered a future with cursed Sirens and a stolen scepter.

But now, in this moment, I saw her cracks.

She loved her sister. And she feared the worst.

Currents of concern electrified my head to my toes. I looked from Neri to Molpe's sisters. "But she has to be okay. Molpe's immortal, right?"

Aggie shook her head. "We may be ageless and difficult to kill, but no creature is immortal, god or otherwise. We all have our weaknesses, death being one of them."

Neri stilled, cocked her head to the side, then shot into the air. She hovered above us like a suspended star, then snuffed out her light and landed. "The Horde has arrived."

We were exhausted, our defenses were shattered, and we were down one of our strongest fighters. I pressed my lips together, ran to the edge of the island, and forced out the scepter. Its energy spread wide and far, lighting up the night.

The sea and sand squirmed with bodies, and what seemed like a thousand eyes looked back at me. Amity and Tanzy joined me on either side, and we took each other's hands without a word.

No words were needed. Like Aggie had said, no one was immune to death.

And ours was crawling toward us with a steady, incessant creep.

CHAPTER 42

KORRINA

At first glance, it would have been easy to mistake the teeming Horde for waves under the stars. The moon had set, dawn was creeping closer, and I wasn't sure we'd see the sun rise.

Amity's hand squeezed mine. "Tell me again how we fight this, Korrina."

"If the Horde is protected against my song, we have to assume they're protected against all Siren songs. I doubt the ancients created a symbol that only makes my song useless."

Tanzy nodded, her hand limp in mine, but there nonetheless. "But we may still use our songs."

"Right. We can't shut them down, but we can use our voices to make things much more difficult. And we have Luke, who can still cancel out their powers."

"And Dave," Amity reminded us.

"And us," a voice said from above. Mom landed behind us, followed by Peisinoe, Aggie, Thelma, and Neri. Dave and Luke weren't too far behind.

"Ten of us, about a thousand of them," I breathed. "Amity, what can you do to slow them down?"

She grabbed a stick, cleared the debris at her feet, and started writing. "Plenty," she murmured, and a thick, stone wall began to rise around the edge of the island.

Amity sucked in a breath, shuddered, and fell to her knees. The wall stopped growing. Dave was on the ground with her so fast I hadn't seen him move. I knelt beside her.

"Sorry," she wheezed. "Between the tidal wave and spending all night creating defenses…"

"You're exhausted," I finished for her. Our powers used a part of our energy, and we required rest after using them.

"That's why Jared told you they were coming at dawn," she said, her eyelids fluttering with fatigue. "So we'd drain ourselves before they got here."

Acid settled into my stomach—she wasn't wrong. There was a reason he was Phorkys's *strategos*. Jared knew our secrets from observing me, knew our power wasn't endless. He knew we would have spent all night preparing, without ever imagining it would all be useless.

Tanzy swayed at my side. "They will come to us. We need to make our stand in the meadow."

"That's the least defensible position," Peisinoe snarled, but Thelma placed a quieting hand on her arm. Her lip still raised, she showed her teeth. "Fine, but if you're wrong, it'll be a complete genocide. The entire race of Sirens is on this island."

Tanzy dipped her chin, rocked side to side on her toes, her hair swaying around her neck. "Not the entire race. There is still one more, Peisinoe, whom you well know." Her voice was monotone, the way it went when she was reading a possible future.

Peisinoe's eyes went went wide. "Molpe? Or—"

A whisper hissed through the air. "Sticks and stones, *Elpida*. We're coming to break your bones."

I knew that hiss, that snark. Echidna was somewhere swimming in the ocean—her serpentine body made to glide through waters deep.

My first encounter with one of Phorkys's children had made a lasting impression.

Mom bent her head close. "Is he out there?" she whispered.

I wasn't sure if she meant Jared or Phorkys, but I closed my eyes, felt for the thread that tied me to Jared, and followed it beyond the half-formed wall, past the first wave of creatures, into the heart of the army. My chest tightened. "Jared's there, and I doubt Phorkys would miss this."

"Incoming," Tanzy gasped, leaped for Luke, and pushed him to the ground. I threw the scepter's energy into the air, attempted to deflect whatever Tanzy saw.

The air whistled, something cracked against my power, and a large, spiked boulder skidded into the trees in an explosion of dirt and debris.

"Rocks?" Peisinoe *pftted*.

The boulder moved, stretched, unfolded. I shook my head, gripped Mom's arm, but she stared at the shifting stone. "Thanos," she gasped.

My stomach sank. I hadn't gotten to know him well, but I'd seen him up close, I knew how he liked his tea, and he was good to those who served under him.

Thanos stretched high and flexed his arms. His thorny flesh jutted out like he'd had a fresh injection of steroids. The air whistled again, louder, more piercing.

I didn't bother to look at who landed next to him. I grabbed Mom, threw Neri into the air, and led the run for better cover, Echidna laughing behind us. The island shook with the impact of more spiked, rocky creatures. Indestructible creatures whose very skin was a weapon.

"Get to the meadow," I shouted over my shoulder, sensing rather than seeing the rest of my team following close behind.

Those with wings quickly overtook us, made it to higher

ground seconds before the rest of us did. The rumble of another approaching tsunami sounded.

"You have got to me kidding me." We reached the meadow. I spun around. The sky had lightened, the stars had dimmed, and a dark shadow rose from the ocean. Not another tsunami. It was too dark in the growing light, too uneven to be a wave. But that didn't make me feel better.

A thousand of Phorkys's children was equal to ten thousand of any other army, and as dangerous and inevitable as a tsunami.

They teemed in, frothed against the harsh edges of the island, spilled over the wall Amity had attempted. Thanos and his buddies balled back up and rolled uphill toward us.

Peisinoe, Aggie, and Thelma grabbed what they could and rained down boulders and trees and shots of power at the onslaught, but Thanos and his troop were unstoppable. They dodged the physical attacks, and our Siren songs bounced off their skin as if they were made of rubber and not divine energy.

I turned to Amity. "Take what you need. We can't do this without you." I grabbed her shoulder, hummed my power into her. Tanzy did the same.

Amity grabbed a rock and scratched words into the hard earth, words of defense, leeching our power from us. Power we needed, but right now, we needed hers more.

Rocks rose in front of us, sharpened into points, and the ground began to rise under our feet. The decimated stone table at our backs splintered, but didn't spray. Amity was controlling it, refashioning it into something we could use.

Mom's song wove through the air, dove into the fray, built up a barrier of debris…

Thanos swatted it away as if it were cobwebs.

The rocks grew, fortifying our front, and the ground rose, giving us the high ground. Thanos rolled to a stop. He and his comrades unfolded themselves, Crox and Silent Bob taking positions at Thanos's back, and the entire force crackled their bones at the base of Amity's cliff.

She stopped, took a breath, collapsed to the dirt.

Thanos raised one arm and slammed it into Amity's sharpened defenses. His troop mirrored his movements, and our one defense shuddered.

Tanzy grabbed my arm. "Korrina, look." She pointed to the distant ocean…not so distant anymore.

"They're bringing the ocean to us," I said, my voice grim. "We've got to get Dave to Phorkys and destroy that tattoo. Luke, get Amity somewhere safe, then find me. We're going to need you when they get close."

Judging from the way Thanos and his troops were slamming away at the rocks, it wouldn't be long. Already the ocean was halfway up the hill to the meadow, lapping against the base of the forest.

I burst out a bladed note, two, three, shot them like knives at Phorkys's forces. They bounced off, ineffectual, the tattoos on each breast or arm or leg or back glowing with each hit. "Let's see what this scepter can do," I muttered.

Ania readied herself in the back of my mind, ready to lend her strength. I pulled on the scepter's energy, bathed us in its crystalline blue light, wrapped the light in the purple power of my song, and shot it into Crox, who'd advanced ahead of the rest.

I just wanted to stop him, make it so he couldn't move, and I fed those intentions to the scepter. I couldn't stomach killing him. Any of them. Not after I'd served them breakfast and lunch for the past week. Not after I'd rocked their babies in the nursery.

Crox froze, and a small bubble of triumph welled up in my chest. Mission accomplished.

The edges of Crox's stony form crinkled, then he began to crumble from his head to his toes. Before I could process what was happening, his body disintegrated, turned to dust and rubble.

The entire Horde stopped.

Bile surged up my throat. I wanted them defeated, not dead.

I dropped to my knees, changed my song. I could create. I'd made flowers bloom. *I can bring Crox back. I didn't mean to, didn't mean to.* The remains of his body soaked into the ocean and drifted away.

I stuffed my fist into my teeth and screamed.

The Horde's disbelief, the force of their rage, transferred to me in a lasered stare. Their endgame muddled, and I felt the shift as if it were a changing wind.

If they weren't out for blood before, they were now.

CHAPTER 43

KORRINA

The Horde moved as if they were one mind. No longer was it just Thanos and his boys assaulting Amity's cliffside, but also Phorkys's cyclops children and Luke's ogre cousins. Any of Phorkys's kids who had more muscle than bone were at the base of our cliff, chiseling away at Amity's defenses.

A screech filled the air.

I got to my feet, my fist bloody from my own bite, my stomach queasy, and surveyed at our battlefield.

Peisinoe, Aggie, and Thelma had kept Phorkys's winged children occupied, but there were too many, and a few slipped through. They angled their pointed wings at our position, their slimy bodies as aerodynamic as one of Amity's crazy skydivers. I'd glimpsed a couple of the creatures swimming outside Phorkys's fortress, their wings as proficient in the air as they were at gliding through the ocean currents. Their nails were as deadly as knives, laced with poison that would kill you if the stabbing didn't, with screams loud enough to be heard through leagues of ocean and shrill enough to break eardrums.

Tanzy planted her feet at my side, rolled her eyes up and into her head, and began to sing-chant. "Two coming at you from above and behind. Don't worry about the one in front. Thelma's got it."

I turned, forced the scepter's energy into an arrow, and shot it up and out, using my song as its guide.

The two creatures came into view. Easily dodged my attack.

"Take two deep breaths and do it again. Same spot," Tanzy hummed.

I did as she said and flung the scepter's energy into a blank point in the sky. It was weaker than before, as if I were scraping the bottom of my power's barrel. The creatures crisscrossed in a dive, too steep to pull out, and ran straight into my fire. They plummeted to the ground, and when they hit, they didn't move.

Luke appeared at my side with a crossbow and a grim smile on his face.

"Where did you get that?" I asked.

"Dave. That bag he's been babysitting is full of gear." He took aim and shot at the edge of the cliff. "They've got ladders up. Let's take 'em down," he shouted, waved his arm in the air, reloaded, and took aim again.

Dave gave me a split-second tutorial on how to load the arrows, grabbed his own crossbow, loaded up, and began shooting at the heads of creatures who had made it up a ladder.

Seemed too little too late. I dropped my crossbow, ran to the edge where the prongs of a ladder intruded our not-so-safe spot, braced my heels against the uneven stone, and pushed it backward with all my strength.

It wavered in the air for a moment, as if it were a tick-tock clock with a broken gear, then tilted backward, spilling the creatures who had been climbing the rungs. They splashed into water, deep enough that they thrashed back to the surface, unharmed.

The day broke, and the ocean continued its steady crawl, bringing Phorkys's sea-dwelling children to the foot of our cliff.

I shaded my eyes from the rising sun, low and orange on the horizon, and did a recount.

There weren't thousands of Phorkys's children as I thought. But there may as well have been.

All the celebrity kids were here.

Echidna, the giant, sassy sea serpent, danced at the submerged tree-line of the forest, as if she were at a party rather than a battle. Her sister, Skylla, scurried at the base of the cliff, a giant crab who had definitely received more of her father's features than her mother's, poor thing. Further out, Ladon, a hundred-headed sea serpent, twisted and churned up the water. He alone accounted for probably half the eyes I'd seen glinting in the starlight.

Someone yanked me away from the edge, just as a pointed barb shot where my head had been. My powers muffled, and I jerked out of Luke's grasp. I needed whatever power I had left.

He held up his hands. "Just didn't want you to lose your head."

A drop of water dripped on my head. More dripped on Luke's.

"How about if you lost *your* head, pretty Luke?" a voice hissed directly above us. Echidna. Our defenses had been breached. Why hadn't Tanzy...

I caught a glimpse of Tanzy, curled on her side, knocked out.

Hopefully just knocked out.

"Though a quick death is too good for one such as you," Echidna continued. "If I had my way, barnacles would feed on your flesh for centuries while our father's power kept you alive for every excruciating second."

Echidna reared back, her snake fangs gleaming in the sunrise. I tugged on the scepter, but it wouldn't respond. Instead, my song flew out of me and made a shield around us, even though I knew it would do no good.

The giant serpent darted in, and a rainbow of light exploded between her and us. Echidna flailed back, and Neri appeared out of the light.

"You and your ilk are done causing harm to this young man," Neri said, her voice calm and steady, rather than the posturing she usually flung at Echidna.

Echidna scoffed. "You would fight for this one? And here I thought you deserved my respect."

Neri flashed again, whorled around, and cut at Echidna's trunk. "Your respect has rarely crossed my mind."

The snake's fangs flashed, glinted with poison, and she lunged to the right. Neri mirrored her movements while Luke readied another arrow in his bow.

Time slowed. They didn't see her tail, rising from the edge of the cliff. They didn't see the snapping fangs at the end of her serpentine figure. They didn't catch the triumphant glint in her eyes.

I dove for Luke. "Neri, watch out!"

Luke released his arrow. It went far, wide, harmless into the brightening sky. Echidna's tail hissed past Luke's shoulder, slammed into Neri, and the iridescent owl, my first mythological friend, went spinning into the ground.

Echidna's bare chest heaved as her tail pinned Neri to the earth and she spun to face us. "Finally, Betrayer, we will be rid of you. And you, *Elpida*, will be my plaything."

Neri struggled against the weight of Echidna's tail.

"Neri, through the Veil!" I screeched.

She shook her head.

Echidna smiled. I hated it when she smiled. "Did the rodent not tell you? Immortal flesh is her Achilles's heel."

My gaze dated from Neri to Echidna. "My touch makes it so she can only exist in this realm, this time, this place. She can't vaporize out of here, love. She's just as vulnerable as you."

An arrow soared out of the corner of my vision, plunged

into Echidna's tail. Dave. After making sure his aim had been true, he spun on his heel and found another target.

Echidna jerked, and Neri pushed free. Echidna roared, and before I could move, she snapped forward, clipped Luke's shoulder. He flew through the air, hit rock, slumped still. Blood trickled then poured from an open wound, staining his shirt, pooling onto the ground.

Echidna reared back for a finishing blow.

Neri flashed into existence before her, wings spread wide, colors brighter than I'd ever seen.

"He is no longer the betrayer," she said, her voice strong and steady, weaving the air with its vibrations. "His brave heart is worth more than yours, and certainly worth more than mine. Korrina, see to him. Keep them safe." Neri let out a loud screech, an otherworldly tone that shivered through me at a cellular level, and dove into Echidna.

Not at. Into.

She disappeared into Echidna's chest, and at first, I thought she'd set the snake on fire. But the fire was white, frozen on the edges, a gel-like substance I didn't recognize, had never seen. Flames grew from the substance and burned a hole into Echidna's scaly flesh. Though we could no longer see her, Neri's voice strengthened, rose, and with it, the hole in Echidna's body widened. Echidna lifted her face to the sky and screamed, but whatever Neri had done, there was no stopping it. It was like a small nuclear bomb, and Echidna was its containment field.

Echidna's flesh turned black, withering and turning to ash from the center of her chest and spreading outward. There was a flash of light, blinding, brilliant, and something final in its magnitude.

The light faded. Neri and Echidna were nowhere to be seen. And, though dawn was now fully in effect, the sunrise seemed dim compared to the light Neri had wrought.

I darted to Luke and whispered a song laced with scepter

power over the wound in his shoulder. The spill of his blood ceased. His tendons and muscles and flesh knitted back together. He sat up, dazed, and we surveyed the damage.

Echidna was gone. Never to return.

But so, too, was Neri.

CHAPTER 44

KORRINA

There is a connectivity that exists in battle. A link forged between all soldiers, no matter the side, when the first attack is struck. That link surged now, a blinding awareness that a devastating blow had been dealt, a quiet pause while both sides reeled from the impact.

The Horde breathed in. My heart clenched behind my ribs. I'd seen this before.

I spun around, no time for grief. "Take cover," I screamed as the Horde super-sized.

Luke's eyes went wide, and he scooped Tanzy into his arms, ran for what was left of the trees. Dave retreated to a pile of displaced boulders just in front of where Luke took cover. He knelt to one knee, took aim, and fired a barrage of arrows at Phorkys's forces, who were spilling over the edge of the cliff.

Mom, Aggie, Thelma, and Peisinoe dove for the ground behind Dave, and I ran for them all.

We needed to retreat, regroup. Neri's sacrifice had saved Luke's life, but it had made the Horde even more ready for our blood.

The Horde's tattoos flared—as if we needed the reminder

that our Siren powers were as effective in this fight as feather pillows—and an agonizing, deep roar rumbled through the ocean waves and shook the bruised island. Phorkys. Perhaps realizing the loss of his serpentine daughter.

I skidded into Mom as another attack began. Black tar flew through the air, sizzled where it landed, burned holes into the earth. One splatted against a boulder near Dave. He retreated closer to us, still keeping his crossbows busy, firing one after another after another. The tar began to eat through solid stone.

"We have to get to Phorkys," I panted. "We don't stand a chance with those tattoos blocking our songs."

"Phorkys sits at the back, well protected," Peisinoe said, her teeth clenched. "We'll be dead before we even get him in our sights."

"Or captured," I said, my voice quiet.

Mom shifted next to me. "What is going through your head?"

I took a breath. "I'm the reason he's here. He'll kill the rest of you to get to me."

Mom shook her head.

Luke crossed his arms.

Peisinoe narrowed her eyes. "You want to surrender yourself."

I nodded. "Phorkys will buy it—he knows I'd do anything for my family."

"But we're not escaping," Thelma prompted.

"No. But if I surrender, Phorkys will want to make a ceremony of it. He'll come to me."

Peisinoe bared her teeth. "And we'll come to him." If she had hands, she would have rubbed them together.

"Yep," I agreed, glad to have at least one original Siren on board. "Then Dave can get close enough to take his shot with Crannik's arrowhead."

Luke ducked as another tar ball came soaring overhead. This

one closer. They were getting more accurate. "You want the rest of us to hide where?"

"I can help with that," a weak voice said from the ground. Amity rose up on her elbows, eyes narrowed against the brightening day. She drew in the dirt, and distant clouds formed in the sky, low and thick. A brisk wind picked up, and the clouds moved toward the island. Steady enough that the clouds would be here soon. Not so sudden that Phorkys would notice.

I hoped.

I locked eyes with Amity, then the rest of the group. "Reserve whatever power you have left. No one uses their energy until that tattoo is destroyed, got it?"

Nods all around.

"Once I destroy the tattoo, then what?" Dave asked, crossbow still trained on the skies.

I shrugged. "We sing. Send them back to the depths. Make them understand that if they come after us again, it won't be without consequences."

"I don't like it," Mom said, her wings brushing my shoulder as if ready to use herself as a shield.

"No one likes it," Tanzy groaned from the ground. "But choice do we have?"

"We're in agreement?" I checked the group. No one looked away, no one dissented, but the thin line of their lips showed they understood the stakes.

"This is a risk. A big one," I went on, "but worth it."

They looked from one to the other, exchanging glances as if they were condolences.

The tar balls became a flurry of destruction. Our shelter was quickly disappearing.

"Wait until I've got their attention, then leave." I turned around because this next part had to be said but I couldn't face Mom while I said it. "If this fails, keep flying. Deal?"

There was a sharp hiss of breath at my back, but I walked

away from the group, away from shelter, before anyone could protest.

The scepter's energy went out before me, and I hummed a song that shaped its power into a glowing blue circle around my frame. The attack slowed, then stopped. They knew who approached.

The Horde who had scaled the cliff made room in their ranks for me to pass, and it was not unlike my first day in Phorkys's fortress. Only this time, I knew what I was getting into.

I reached the cliff's edge, and Thanos was waiting for me, arms crossed, carapace spiked. He wouldn't forgive me for Crox. I wasn't sure I would either.

The ocean lapped at the lip of the cliff only a few feet down, and I sensed the Horde close rank above and behind me. Water-bound members of the Horde churned angrily a short distance away, frothing the ocean, but staying in formation.

Thanos cast his gaze into the sky, eyes narrowed at the other Sirens. "The rest try to escape. Flyers, fetch." He slung his arm in the direction they'd flown, and returned to his stony stance. I could only hope that Mom and the others had a large enough head start to stay safe and hide in Amity's cloud cover.

The rest of the Horde waited in silence.

Near the cliff's edge, the water began to bubble, then boil. A crown of red spikes rose from the water, followed by the grotesqueness that was Phorkys. He'd gone back to his clawed self, though he'd ditched the tail in favor of legs, and he'd grown.

I tightened the scepter's energy around me, as if his claws could somehow pop my protection.

The water lifted him high and formed a throne, while Jared stood at his side, dry, breathing normally, and scarlet-eyed. But for once, it wasn't the color of his eyes that made it feel as if I'd been shot in the heart. It was the deadness in them. The lack of anything human.

Any trace of my Jared was gone.

"Are you offering your surrender?" Phorkys boomed, yanking my attention back to him and my plan, and the Horde tittered.

I raised my chin, stood tall. "In exchange for you letting my friends go, unharmed, I offer my surrender."

"And why would we do that, when we have you here and could easily kill them now instead of later?"

"This way you get what everything you want." I called back to his words in our last moments together in the fortress. "Respect for your children. Protection for them. I can offer both. I will help you win that respect, and I will extend the unmatched protection of my power."

"We win the whole war by simply sparing your family and friends? Seems too good to pass up."

I nodded, drew my power in close, and held out my hand.

Phorkys eyed my outstretched palm but didn't lift his own. "*Strategos*, what make you of this bargain?"

Jared closed his eyelids, and behind his lashes, his eyes moved erratically, as if he were a robot processing data. I didn't know how he'd answer, but the more time he took, the more time my friends and family received. "She has not proven herself worthy of your trust, my *dimiourgós*."

My heart sped up, but I fought the urge to defend myself—it would only make me look desperate—and kept my hand extended. The almost-smile on Phorkys's face disappeared.

"But she is without options," Jared continued. "Her power has dwindled in fighting off our attacks, as have her Siren companions' powers. She needs to rest, as do they, and if she does not make this bargain with you now, none of them will see tomorrow. So in this, I believe you can trust her intentions."

I fought another urge, the urge to murmur a thank-you to

Jared—not that he deserved one. He'd said exactly what I needed him to say. The *strategos* had advised Phorkys to accept my surrender.

The cloud cover that Amity had written into being reached us.

Phorkys fixed his cold hard gaze on me. "You will swear it to me with your blood, and we will have no more of your treachery."

I looked from Jared to Phorkys. Resisted looking at the clouds. Phorkys extended his arm, morphed his claw into a human hand, and grasped my still-outstretched palm. Not a handshake but a claiming.

A high-pitched whistle whisked through the air. Phoryks screamed, let go, and clutched his arm.

An arrow wobbled in the center of the tattoo on Phorkys's bicep. Dave's aim had found its mark. I held my breath as the glowing boundaries of the raised mark faded.

Fresh hope surged in my chest.

I searched out Thanos, his tattoo no longer large and in charge, but fading, fading, gone. A guttural screech filled the air above, and two of Phorkys's flyers plummeted from the sky, crashed into the ocean, and sunk into its depths.

Siren songs filled the air.

CHAPTER 45

KORRINA

In an instant, the battle turned, but I was still lost in a sea of enemies, and I'd just made enemy number one very, very mad.

Phorkys Klingon-death-screamed, mouth open wide to the sky, and if hatred had a sound, it was this. Guttural and raw. Primordial.

He transformed into a creature redder than blood and more sea-demon than crab. "Again. You have done this to me again," he roared, and he focused all that ancient, pure hatred at me. "I begin to question whether the scepter is worth keeping you alive," he seethed.

I shrugged. "Let's dance, old man."

"I think I'll cut in." Jared flexed at Phorkys's side. This was not one-on-one but two-on-doesn't-stand-a-chance.

Jared's foot moved back into a defensive stance I knew well. He'd used it on me in the training room. Back when he'd promised he'd never allow me to be hurt again.

His eyes flashed scarlet, and green fire leaped into his palms. His dagger stayed in its sheath on his hip, easily accessible, ready to deliver my curse.

I didn't think he uphold his promise now.

I scraped together what Siren power I had left and coated my body in its energy. The scepter battered at my chest, begging to be used, but Siren song was zapped and without its strength, I couldn't contain the scepter's power. Couldn't promise I wouldn't annihilate the tortured guy that held my heart's tether.

My mind acknowledged pieces of the battle scene around us—each Siren battling several of Phorkys's soldiers. Dave, Luke, Amity, and Tanzy fighting with their backs to each other, the Horde crumpling at their feet. But those sounds fell away as the world narrowed to just me, just Jared.

I didn't wait for him to make the first move—I had to end this. Quickly. Before my power deserted me.

I went for his ribs. He deflected like it ain't-no-thang and blocked me with his shoulder. I threw my leg around the back of his knee, tried to force him to buckle, but it only brought us face-to-face, limbs locked together.

His fire didn't touch me. Maybe he knew it would be pointless until my shield failed. I met his gaze, the scarlet in them mocking any belief I'd had in us. But something was different. In the past, he'd had a manic, almost zealous slant to his eyes, and a cruel smile had etched his face. Now, the fight had left his gaze, and his motions seemed more automatic than fueled by hate.

He wrapped an arm around my waist, threw me to the ground, braced our impact with his arms. The he lowered his mouth to my ear. "Stop holding back," he growled. He sprang off me, fell back into a fighting stance, and his Hunter fire played with his fingertips.

"I'm not," I growled back, and the light coating my body dimmed, as if it needed to prove to him that I was tapped out. I spared a second to search the skies for any of the Sirens. I needed a rescue op, but everyone's talons were busy.

When all else fails, survive, Dad had taught me. Go down fighting, never give up.

I leaped to my feet. Phorkys had retreated to a safe distance, a vulture watching its dinner die.

Jared lunged, forced me back. I blocked his punches, using what little power I had left to protect me from the touch of his fire. It wouldn't be enough.

Not true, Ania whispered at the back of my mind.

You've been quiet.

I've been busy, she responded, sounding tired. *You've made friends in the spirit Void. They'd like to lend you their energy.*

Seriously?!

Super serious. After taking so much from you and Raelynn, and after you freed so many of them, it's the least they can do.

The air cooled, chilled, turned frostbitten almost instantaneously. Everyone, monster and Siren alike, paused and looked around. Pricks of cold pierced my skin, sank into my bones, and with each hit of ice, my Siren power grew stronger.

I breathed in, breathed out, and lit the battlefield with my purple glow, boosted by lost-and-found spirit energy. "Now we're talking," I said, twirled into a spin-kick fueled by Siren power, and connected with Jared's ribs.

He went down.

He didn't get back up.

I landed in a crouch, covered his prone body with my shield, sang my song.

The scepter's energy poured from my skin, and I fed it with my need to protect my family, my friends, innocents, and Jared. My song shaped the scepter into a disk of light, and with the spirits' help, I boomeranged it into the monsters attacking my friends and my family, freeing them from their skirmishes, before directing the energy at Phorkys.

For half a heartbeat, he transformed his face into Colin's,

and his expression wasn't one of shock or defeat, but disapproval. As if I had somehow disappointed him.

My energy collided into him, sliced into his side. White ichor dripped from an open wound, and Phorkys roared. The ocean lifted him high, a king sitting on a skyscraper of teeming water.

Tanzy screamed my name.

I pulled the scepter back into my body, sucked in the remaining energy the spirits had gifted me, and threw up a barrier that coated the entire battlefield just as Phorkys released his attack.

No time to define it to just my people. To save them, I had to protect all.

Water crushed the island, rammed into my energy, but it held. I held.

The Horde stopped fighting and looked around as the ocean attempted to swallow us, but we remained dry. All under the shield of my protection.

I scanned the battlefield. Amity and Tanzy stood, brushed themselves off. Luke had a cut just above his brow, and Dave leaned against him for support. Peisinoe held a creature against the ground with a talon, her teeth bared. Mom, Aggie, and Thelma were nowhere to be found, and I could only hope they had flown high enough to stay safe.

Thanos walked forward and held my gaze. "The Horde repays its debts," he shouted, loud enough that his voice echoed through the dome, and he dropped his weapon at my feet.

The Horde followed suit. Silent, heads bowed, one by one they sank outside my barrier and into the ocean. Thanos knelt by Jared's body, picked him up, and after the last of the Horde had disappeared into the swirling ocean, walked through my barrier, Jared in his arms.

I wanted to scream, to stop him from taking Jared, but I couldn't stop my song, couldn't allow the barrier to collapse.

Green energy coated Thanos and Jared, and they were spirited away, supposedly safe.

"What just happened?" Amity said, hands by her sides, wingtips trembling.

"The Horde has honor," Luke said, walking toward me. "Korrina saved them along with us, so they've spared us today."

Tanzy knelt by me. "You are weary."

"Come close," I gasped. Even with the spirits' adrenaline shot of energy, the scepter and my song had begun to weaken. I tugged the edges of our dome closer, collapsing my energy, and when everyone was huddled around me, I inhaled, and pushed it all out.

Water exploded from the island in a glittered geyser. I fell to my knees as saltwater rained down on us, as the ocean regained its boundaries.

"Why didn't Phorkys keep his children safe?" Tanzy asked, her brow crinkled.

Luke shrugged. "More than likely the tsunami wouldn't have harmed them, but honor requires them to reciprocate. A life for a life."

But this wasn't over. Not by a long shot.

The Horde was gone. Phorkys was gone.

Jared was gone.

For the moment, we were safe. But Phorkys had tried to annihilate us. And one way or another, he'd want the job finished.

CHAPTER 46

KORRINA

The island sparkled as if it had been through a storm. Seaweed hung from broken tree branches. Mud and sand were left in random piles against the trunks of trees, many of which were half-uprooted. What leaves were left on the forest trees dripped water and held onto their branches, bedraggled and limp.

Thelma and Mom landed near our group, and Mom waddle-ran to me. A tear tracked down her dirt-dusted cheek—I'm sure mine looked no better—and I met her halfway, let her gather me into her wings.

"Where's Aggie?" I asked against her cheek.

She leaned back, eyes shining. "With Molpe."

I couldn't breathe.

"We found her on a nearby island. Hurt but alive. She needs her sisters."

Relief dragged a ragged breath out of my lungs.

Peisinoe heard her words and launched into the air, Thelma close behind. The rest of us took stock.

Bruised and battered, beyond filthy, but alive. Tanzy helped Luke clean his cut the best she could—my healing power was down for the count. We all needed about a week to rest and recover, but I doubted we'd be granted much time at all. This was nothing more than a reprieve. Phorkys and the Horde would want to strike while we were still weak.

Dave limped to Amity's side. His ankle was swollen to the size of a softball. Amity tried to write a bag of ice into existence, but the effort made her drop to her knees. Dave balanced himself on one foot, helped her to stand. "I'll just heal the human way, babe," he said and kissed her temple.

I left the couples to kiss each other's boo-boos and walked to the place Neri had given up her life, strategically avoiding the spot Jared had fallen. Our tether was intact—I'd know if he was fatally wounded, but it didn't stop me from worrying about him.

Mom's eyeballs followed me, but she left me be, perhaps her mother's instinct advising her I needed to be alone.

Impossibly, the area Neri and Echidna had fought and died was clear of debris. Standing by itself, a plant stood tall and proud, and at the end of its stem, two flowers bobbed in the breeze. The petals were as iridescent as Neri's feathers, the stem of the plant as serpentine as Echidna's frame.

I knelt beside the plant, packed the dirt in around its stem. There was no way it could have survived a tsunami, a battlefield, and the ocean falling on us, but there it was. I picked one of the flowers, leaving the other to hopefully flourish, and walked to the water's edge.

The ocean was calm—and not for the first time I wondered what Poseidon thought of Phorkys using his ocean like he did. Phorkys was God of the Deep and Father of Monsters. But Poseidon was God of the Ocean. Perhaps they had some agreement where they both looked the other way.

Or perhaps they are on the same side, Ania whispered.

You're a glass-half-full kind of gal, aren't you?

I felt her roll her eyes. If Ania was right and Poseidon and

Phorkys had teamed up—and if Phorkys teamed up with Hades—we were in deep doo-doo.

The ocean rolled peacefully onto the beach, no indication that it could turn into its own kind of monster. But perhaps that's what it was there to teach us—everything and everyone had different aspects to themselves. Sometimes, we were as peaceful as water kissing the beach. Sometimes we raged as violently as a storm. But always, we're contained within the vessel of who we are...no matter what that vessel looked or sounded like.

A monstrous form did not a monster make. What it did do was make the lines of good and evil, right and wrong, all blurry and indecipherable.

Phorkys and the Horde believed they were fighting for the good of their family.

The Sirens also believed we were fighting for the good of those we loved.

Demeter believed she was fighting for the good of her daughter.

Hades believed he was fighting for the good of his wife.

Persephone...Persephone just seemed to be fighting.

When looked at from that perspective, the enemy could have honor. And maybe Jared was capable of walking both sides of the line.

But where did that leave me? Where did that leave us?

The water brushed against my shoes. I didn't fear it. The ocean itself had no agency—it was driven by the influence of others. Others who, for the moment, had decided to give us a break.

A song welled up in my throat. Not one backed by power, but just music, just notes. I sang my grief, my confusion, my torn conscience, and let my tears fall freely. For Dad. For Neri. For Jared. For all the times I'd been forced to say goodbye.

A voice joined mine, the notes sad and quiet, filled with their own tones of mourning, and Mom's feathers brushed my side. Tanzy took my hand and blended her song into ours. Amity harmonized. No power backed our voices. We were spent—every one of us—but power wasn't needed for this.

Saying goodbye carried its own kind of power.

Our grief and worries about tomorrow blended together, but still, we could sing. We were alive and we could sing.

I let the wind catch the flower in my palm and carry it out to sea.

On the horizon, three Sirens appeared in the sky, carrying a fourth between them, limp and wounded, but alive.

CHAPTER 47

KORRINA

We gathered around the fire. Even though it was midday, the air still retained a crisp chill, as if the spirits that had given me their energy lingered. Molpe was propped up on the other side of the flames, her wing in a makeshift splint, an angry bruise swelling up the left side of her face, her features drawn in grief at the news of Neri. The tsunami had focused its energy on Molpe, had overcome her, had swept her out to sea. It had been at that point that the ancient Sirens' barrier had failed.

They really didn't like it when I called them ancient.

"We need to talk," Tanzy said, when everyone had settled.

I perked up. Tanzy never took the lead, preferring instead to act as a compass and let someone else take the first steps down the path.

Luke let his knee touch her thigh, his eyes seeing nothing but her profile. Whatever had been building between them had reached some sort of crescendo, and despite my own inability to have a relationship, they warmed a cold corner of my heart.

"Peace is impossible for us until Demeter's curse is broken. Demeter's curse cannot be broken until Persephone is saved from

Hades. And Phorkys stands in the way with his Siren Hunter as the wielder of the curse, with the power to take us down." Tanzy stared at me as she talked, and I knew her words were for my ears. We all knew all this, of course, but apparently, I needed the reminder.

Jared was dangerous. And there could no longer be any rogue attempts to save him. I'd tried. I'd failed. I had to learn my lesson.

I met her unyielding gaze with my own and nodded. "No shortcuts. To break the curse and save everyone"—especially Jared, I added mentally—"we have to free Persephone."

She turned her intense gaze on the rest of the group, seemingly satisfied by my response. "We are incomplete. Until we have restored all our families, Persephone cannot be saved, the curse cannot be broken, and we cannot defeat Phorkys."

Peisinoe straightened. "My line did not continue." But there was a waver to her confident tone, a betrayal in her stony facade.

Tanzy shook her head, smiled. "It did. And we must find him."

Amity and I exchanged looks.

"Him?" she said.

"Yeah. This is a girls-only club," I protested.

Tanzy shrugged. "We have to go back. He's alone, his powers have been activated, and if Phorkys or Hades gets to him before we do, we cannot win."

Molpe struggled to her feet. Her sisters rushed to support her. Something had changed in them, in all of us. Our dynamic had shifted from being a bunch of individuals shoved together to something cohesive.

"Tanzy's sight is strong," Molpe said, "and perhaps this is the reason we thought your line had failed, Sister." She raised her good wing and brushed Peisinoe's cheek. The intense Siren I'd always been so intimidated by sniffled and ducked her head, and before she reassumed her gangsta-like vibe, her eyes glistened, her lips softened.

Peisinoe shook her head, and though her tough shell returned, a bit of the softness remained around her mouth. "Sisters, help me open a portal. It's time to send these hatchlings home."

Mom gathered me in her wings, squeezed tight, then pulled away and held my gaze. "We will see each other again, very soon." She placed a kiss on my forehead. "Be well, my star."

I let her let me go and stepped back into the circle of my friends and Siren sisters. We took hands, Tanzy and Amity holding on tight to Luke and Dave, and the four ancients and my mother surrounded us. A soft note hummed in their throats, gaining in intensity, until the Veil peeled back and we were pulled into the cold vacancy of the Void.

The black space remained seemingly unchanged, but we rushed through, not stopping to see the sights. Still, the memory of those floating rocks, inhabited by untethered spirits…it made the Void less, well, Void-y.

The cold slipped from my body, and we fell into a familiar room. In the year that we'd been gone, a delicate layer of dust had covered the furniture and floated fairy-like in the slatted sunlight.

I stood and brushed off my knees, noting a bucket in the corner of mine and Dad's living room with a mop propped up next to it, and the scent of something baking.

Danica walked in from the back room, a red and white checkered handkerchief around her hair, rubber gloves on her hands. She stopped, raised an eyebrow, and wiggled her lip ring. "Hey Cloud," she shouted up the stairs, "the cleaning crew finally got here."

Footsteps thundered from upstairs—clearly more people than Cloud and Danica were in my house—and unrhythmic *clickity-clacks* of our surprise welcome-home party made their way down the three flights of stairs of my old brownstone.

I tried to catch Tanzy's and Amity's eyes, but they acted like they knew exactly what was going on. Dave too. I nudged Luke. "Why are they cleaning my house?"

Tanzy walked over to the mop and bucket, just as Cloud leaped off the second-to-bottom step. "Nice of you to join us," he said, not surprised at all.

Behind him, a woman descended the steps. A naked woman, though that wasn't quite fair, as her entire body was covered in fur. Amity stepped forward and enveloped her in a hug.

"Danica, why is there a yeti in my living room?"

Danica gave me her wide, shut-up-Korrina eyes.

Dave shook the woman's hand, then turned and said, "This is the new headquarters of the Alliance of Humans and Mythicals. A-HAM for short."

"A ham," I repeated.

Amity stepped forward. "And this is Callie."

"First recruit," the naked fur-woman said with a grin and held out her hand. "Not a yeti, by the way."

I took it, shook it limply. "And how many recruits are there, exactly?"

Amity shrugged. "Last count, over two thousand spread over the country. Right now, everyone is gathering at our various locations, to prepare."

"For the war," I filled in.

Callie nodded. "Humans have no idea what is coming, and there's no way for them to protect themselves."

"And you care because…?" It was rude, and I didn't like the question, but this not-a-yeti was here, in my house, with my most precious people, and I needed to understand why.

"Because I know what it's like to be the gods' plaything, and I want a safe place to live. Not on the mythical side of the Veil, but here."

"Here," I repeated. I was doing that a lot.

Callie nodded, and Amity looked ready to launch into a defense argument on why we were suddenly allowing mythicals to stay in the human world, which was expressly against the Council's rules, but Tanzy gasped and fell to her knees, seconds before the world trembled.

Luke dropped next to her, supported her against his chest. The rest of us fought for balance.

The quakes stopped. A distant scream from the streets broke the sudden silence, followed by another, followed by a symphony of ambulance sirens and terror.

Tanzy's chin snapped up, her eyes glazed over, and she wobbled against Luke. "Hades has closed the gates of the Underworld. The dead are trapped among the living."

Her air left her in a wheeze, and she fell forward, barely catching herself with her hands.

My heart finally restarted. Tanzy's words and their consequences tumbled around my head. While my friends demanded more details from Tanzy's gift, I rushed to the stairs, ran up to the third floor, and threw open the window.

Shouts and screams and sirens grew infinitely louder, and smoke curled into the air a few streets over.

I grabbed my pair of dusty binoculars, slid over my old, Siren-embellished toy chest, and scanned the streets for my first zombie sighting. "Nice welcome home, Brooklyn."

CHAPTER 48

JARED

I hadn't planned on surviving. Surviving changed everything. Pain etched Thanos's features, and it made me question my debts.

He'd saved my hide, and now I must punish his.

I'd pinned Thanos down per Phorkys's orders, driven hooks into his carapace, and fused those with more hooks that were sunk deep into an ancient stone wall in the Grotto. I arced back my arm, cracked the whip through the air once again. The tail met his shelled chest, and though his skin was his armor, it wasn't impenetrable. He flinched, his face twisted in fresh pain, but he made not a sound.

Thanos had acted with honor, upholding the most basic contract of existence. Owe nothing to none. This was the one thing I couldn't have anticipated—the extent of Korrina's compassion and how it would affect others. Korrina had saved the Horde, and so Thanos had repaid the life debt by allowing her and hers to live. He owed none.

I could not say the same for myself.

Thanos held firm, taking his fifty lashings with strength. And if my arm did not throw as much power as was expected, if my aim occasionally hit the wall instead of him, who was to know?

Perhaps some of my debt could be repaid.

The Horde had been quiet since our return—not abashed, but waiting. We had tasted the demise of the Sirens, had sampled the sweetness of victory, and wanted more.

The Sirens were not infallible. They could be destroyed and our father's place would be restored in the hierarchy of the gods. He had come before Zeus, Poseidon, and the Ancient Greek race. Son of the Titans Pontus and Gaia, his power far exceeded the young pantheon.

And it was time for them all to recognize the God of the Deep.

My veins burned, I felt a tug on my mind, and the order to report to Phorkys in the war room came through clear. His thoughts reflected into mine, stronger and more willful after the injection of Siren Hunter power I'd chosen to take. But this time, something was different.

This time, somehow, I had choice.

Phorkys's summons burned through my veins. But no longer did my muscles clench and respond before my brain told them to. My body waited on me. On my decision.

My. Decision.

I laid the whip down. Helped Thanos slump to the floor and called for a medic. I waited for the medic to arrive and let Thanos sip water from a cup I held while the minutes passed.

The summons came again, stronger with a touch of fury. My *dimiourgós* was not used to waiting.

And still, I squatted next to my head of guards and infantry commander. He said not a word, and not a word would be said of this small sign of weakness. This was the aftermath of battle. This was how our bonds were forged.

Eventually, I made my way to the war room. Phorkys paced

the interior, his claws clicking against the floor in an irritated rhythm.

"What has held you from my summons?" he asked.

"I was carrying out your first orders, to punish Thanos for his rebellion."

His black eyes narrowed and his nostrils flared, as if he could smell the not-quite-truth.

"Hades has shut the gates to the Underworld," Phorkys said, choosing to not question my statement. I would need to be more careful.

"He has made his first move, as predicted." I spread my feet, clasped my arms behind my back, at attention. Colin was gone, and there could be no more brotherliness between us.

"And so we must make ours. Summon my children. Summon *all* of them."

My stomach went hard. " I urge you to reconsider. That is not what we planned. It will show our strength before we are ready."

Phorkys shot me a sideways glance. I didn't often disagree with him.

"Echidna must be avenged," Phorkys whispered, his black eyes wetted in pain.

"And she would want you to reserve your display of power for the right moment," I argued.

The color of his skin angered, going at once to a deep, dark red. "Do not dare to assume to know Echidna's mind. My daughter is dead, and the world will know. Summon her brothers and sisters. Summon them now." He slammed his hand on the polished stone table, and the mirrored black surface sparked to life.

Phorkys's children were dim lights on both sides of the Veil, in place but unrevealed.

I walked across the room and took an ancient horn off the wall. Made of bone, the cracks filled in with the ichor of fallen demigods, it was heavy, ancient, and not an instrument for mortals.

Good thing I was no longer mortal.

I placed the cold bone to my lips and let out a single breath. A single breath that roared through the bone-carved sides and amplified, a tone that made the fortress shudder, a sound that echoed deep in the ocean, a vibration strong enough to rattle continents.

One by one, the lights of Phorkys's children brightened, covering the mythical world, surrounding the human world, enumerating more than the stars.

The full extent of the Horde had been summoned. Our victory was in reach.

And yet, my thoughts were full, not of the impending battle and the strategies that would lead us to victory, but of a girl. A girl with crystalline eyes, a sacrificial heart, and power beyond measure.

Power that could win wars.

Power that could save souls.

A NOTE FROM KRIS FARYN

Dear Reader,

    Thank you for taking a chance on this series. I hope you have enjoyed Korrina's story!

    If you did, I would be eternally grateful if you would write a review on Goodreads (even if it's only a sentence or two). Every review matters to authors and helps other readers discover the book.

    I look forward to continuing Korrina's journey with you.

    To Good Books and Living From Joy,

    Kris

KORRINA WANTS TO KNOW - BOOK DISCUSSION

1. The person you're in love with is giving you some serious mixed signals. How do you respond? *settles in with colored pens and a bullet journal*
2. So...my mom's alive. And awake. And a Siren that can't cross to the human side of the Veil. How would you go about getting to know your mother if you were in my shoes? I mean, pedicures, coffee dates, and shopping trips are out.
3. While in the Deep, I had to confront a lot of misbeliefs about my so-called enemy. Maybe the most important thing I learned was that just because someone has different ideals or motives than me, that does not automatically mean they are my enemy. (Looking at you Isa, Ben, and Lydia.) The Horde and I have a drastically different belief system, and yet, I made friends while there. Have you ever become friends with someone you thought was your enemy? Or if not, is there someone you don't get along with, but maybe could if you better understood their ideals, motives, or situation?

4. Do you think Luke is trustworthy? Or is he still acting in his own best interest?
5. What have I done since arriving in the Deep that you would have done differently?
6. Do you think Persephone wants to be rescued? Do you think it's possible to rescue her? And if so, what effects would her rescue have on the weather? Or for that matter, the balance of the living and the dead? ('Cause Hades will be *enraged*.)
7. Neri sacrificed herself to save Luke, and in doing so, took out Echidna. Do you think Neri is actually gone? And if so, do you think I'm ready to be without a spirit guide?
8. Peisinoe is my least favorite Siren aunt. But do you think I've misunderstood her just as much as I misunderstood the Horde?
9. What should we rename the Void, now that we know it's not actually a Void? And what are we going to do about all the souls who are stuck there?
10. Toward the end of this book, I made a huge mistake. I thought I had my power under control, and I really thought that I'd learned enough and trained enough to direct the scepter, but I hadn't. And Crox paid the price. What do you do when you've tried so hard, and it still isn't enough?
11. The war between the gods has begun in earnest, and it's having real world consequences on the human side of the Veil—storms are more destructive, food is becoming more scarce, and finally, the dead can no longer enter the Underworld. How would you prepare to survive this apocalyptic world?
12. If given the chance, would you save your enemy?
13. *Takes a deep breath.* *I will not cry, I will not cry.* Do you think Jared can be saved?

KORRINA'S MYTHOLOGICAL CHEAT SHEET

SIRENS

Aglaope (ag-l-OW-pee)
In her own words, she is "the daughter of the Muse Melpomene, granddaughter of the Titaness Mnemosyne, blood of Gaia, and handmaiden to Goddess Persephone." No, I don't think she's stuck up. Nope, not at all. And I'm sure she loves her new nickname, Aggie. She's the OG of Tanzy's line, and they are considered the maestros of the song, mainly because they can see what happens next.

Molpe (mole-PEE)
Molpe is my gajillion-great Siren grandmother. We've gotten to know each other a little better, and I now believe she's not evil. Not sure about her sisters yet, but Molpe's cool. A bit too formal, but I'm good at loosening up ancient mythical creatures. Our Siren line carries the power to heal, and we are the passion behind the creation of music. Of course we are.

Peisinoe (pee-see-NO-ee)
Another one of Molpe's sisters and another one of my ancient great aunts. Her raven-like fathers reflect her shining personality. But Peisinoe came through when we fought against Phorkys. I still think she's not on the up-and-up, but she loves her sisters, in her own way. I think.

Thelxiepeia (thel-ksee-EH-pee-ah)
Thelxiepeia is Molpe's sister, so that makes her my ancient great-aunt. She's also Amity's gajillion-great grandmother. Amity nicknamed her Thelma—as one does with ancient beings. Amity's line was "blessed with the ability to cast words as power," though I doubt Amity agrees with the word 'blessed.' Essentially, Amity and her line are songwriters.

GODS, GODDESSES, AND A TITAN(ESS)

Aphrodite (a-fruh-DAI-tee)
Goddess of Lurve (I'm saying this in my Barry Manilow voice), Daughter of Zeus, and Wife of Hephaestus, though she's actually crushing on her half-brother Ares, God of War. She's declared for Hades in the war.

Apollo (uh-PAA-low)
God of Sun and Light and acts as the Jiminy Cricket of the gods. He's the son of Zeus and Leto, the twin brother of Artemis, and has declared for Demeter in the war, which I think gives our side the moral upperhand.

Ares (AIR-ees)
God of Courage and War, Son of Zeus and Hera, and dating his half-sister Aphrodite. As one does. He is definitely on Hades' side in the god conflict, given that he loves all things war.

Artemis (AR-tuh-muhs)
Goddess of the Hunt, twin sister of Apollo, and daughter of Zeus and Leto. She's declared for Demeter, and a good thing too, because she's got great aim.

Athena (uh-THEE-nuh)
Goddess of Wisdom and War, daughter of Zeus and Metis, and on Demeter's side. Thank the gods we have at least one of the gods of war on our side.

The Council of the Gods
A tribunal of the Greek gods, led by the three Fates, who determine how the mythical world should interact with the real world. When I met with the Council—in a Chinese restaurant no less—Zeus, Poseidon, Hades, and Hestia held Council seats, with one empty seat saved for Demeter.

Demeter (dee-mEE-teer)
Goddess of Agriculture and Mother of Persephone. Now that Demeter has been restored—thanks to mwah—there is a tentative peace between the Sirens and the goddess. We're on the same side of the fight against Phorkys and Hades, though at the moment, she's MIA.

Dionysus (dai-uh-NAI-suhs)
God of Wine and Parties, and Son of Zeus. You'd think he'd be fun to be around, but he's sided with Hades in the war, so I doubt I'll have a chance to get to know him.

The Fates
So, I met Fate, or rather the Fates. At the Council of the Gods meeting in the Chinese restaurant. (Please tell me you find that as ridiculous as I do. I mean, we didn't even get a fortune cookie.) They are three sisters whose figures change at any given

moment. At times, they appeared beautiful, with long, cascading hair as white as the moon, and at other times they appeared as three hags, with missing teeth and curled, yellowed nails. Probably the most disturbing body image they chose to take on was that of a Frankenstein version of a Siren, with goose bodies and old hag heads in place of beaks. Shudder.

The Fates are goddesses who weave the threads of destiny together. Apparently they also hook them to your insides like tapeworms and attach them to other people who have influence on you or you on them. Ask me how I know.

Hades (HAI-deez)
God of the Underworld, kidnapper of Persephone, and starter of wars. Our fight against him is purely out of self-preservation, but he's teamed up with Phorkys and that spells disaster for both sides of the Veil.

Hera (HAIR-ah)
Goddess of women, marriage, and childbirth, and wife-y of Zeus. Also, sister of Zeus...

Excuse me. I just barfed a little.

Hera's declared for Hades against Zeus's wishes, 'cause she's a drama momma.

Hephaestus (huh-FAY-stuhs)
God of Blacksmiths and Artisans, Son of Zeus and Hera, and said he's staying neutral in the war. Given that he's basically the armorer for the gods, it would be a huge win if we could get him on our side. Technically, he and I should have a lot in common, given my artistic talents. Unfortunately I've had zero

time to dedicate to my art. So he'd probably give me a lecture about not making time for my creativity. Whatevs. I have a world to save.

Hermes (HUR-meez)
Though I haven't actually met Hermes, I heard him mentioned in a vision of Demeter and Phorkys, so I'm including him in this cheat sheet. He's known as the messenger of the gods and witnessed Persephone's kidnapping. He's sided with Hades in the war.

Hestia (eh-s-t-EE-aa)
Goddess of the Hearth, Hestia is basically the perfect home economics professor. She even sent Luke and me home with cookies. She seems friendly enough, but I've learned that you can't trust a goddess. She sits on the Council of the Gods with her three brothers, Zeus, Hades, and Poseidon, and her sister, Demeter, and has sided with Demeter against Hades.

Melpomene (mel-poh-mEN-ee)
Melpomene makes me sad. She used to be known as the Muse of Singing and Dancing, but she transformed into the Muse of Tragedy. And well, that's sad. She's also the mother of the Sirens, so we're related.

Mnemosyne (mm-nee-mow-sEEn-ee)
A Titaness. Specifically the Titaness of Memory, Time, and Tales. She's also the mother of the Muses, which makes her the grandmother of the Sirens, and the original owner of the scepter.

She showed up in Phorkys's fortress to meet me—I mean, who wouldn't?—and taught me the ways of the scepter. Not that I'd ever given much thought to titanesses before, but Mnemosyne is nothing like what I expected. Irreverent and cool, I'm proud to claim her as part of my bloodline.

Persephone (pur-SEF-uh-nee)
Got kidnapped. Ate a pomegranate. Lives in the Underworld. Her husband, Hades—God of the Dead—is hot. Hot, but deadly. For half the year, Persephone lives above ground, which makes Demeter, her mom, happy, and so we have spring and summer. For the second half of the year, Persephone lives in the Underworld with Hades, and Demeter pulls a fit and causes crops to wither and die—fall and winter.

Persephone believes that Molpe's sisters helped Hades kidnap her. She only trusts Molpe, which saved my life. But Persephone also doesn't seem to hate her position with Hades in the Underworld. Is this Stockholm syndrome, or is she actually in love with the God of the Dead? Which begs the question—does Persephone need to be saved? Must explore this more...

Phorkys (fOR-keez)
Phorkys, primordial God of the Deep and Monsters. Among his many powers, he's also a shapeshifter. Can't tell you much more than that as I don't want to share spoilers, but let's just say I like Phorkys even less now. Thanks to me, he's back at full power and strength, and he's figured out how to protect his army, the Horde, from Siren songs.

Super fun.

Poseidon (poh-SEE-duhn)
God of the ocean, father of Triton, grandfather of Ariel—who is a mermaid, not a Siren. There is a difference. He also sits on the Council of the Gods and has a resemblance to The Dude. He

hasn't officially taken a side in Hades's war, but we believe he'll eventually side with Phorkys as a fellow god of the ocean.

Zeus (zee-oos)
Zeus is the George Clooney of the skies. An obvious choice for the Council of the Gods, though he is a bit theatrical. As the king of the gods, I guess he's entitled to be dramatic whenever he pleases. For the moment, he remains a neutral party in the war between the gods.

CREATURES

Ben*
We don't know what Ben is, other than an overgrown grub with a *lot* of teeth. He's super sweet though, if you can get past his looks.

Callie*
She's not a yeti. But she looks *exactly* like a yeti. She's apparently the first recruit of A-HAM, the Alliance of Humans and Mythicals. I haven't gotten to know her well enough to ask her the name of her species.

Chimera (KAI-mir-ah)
An indecisive mashup of a goat, a lion, and a serpent. I kicked one's butt back to the mythical side of the Veil in typical Korrina-fashion.

Cyclops (KEE-klohps)
One-eyed grandsons of Phorkys. We had a short meet-and-greet right before I sent them back to their side of the Veil in *Song of Destiny*.

Daimones Proseooous (day-MON-eez pro-see-OH-us)
I met these six sons of Poseidon six months ago, back in *Song of Destiny*. They are essentially demonic, sea-ghost guns for hire. Poseidon banished them from his realm—they were cursed and, in their madness, attacked their own mother—and Phorkys must have taken them under his wing—er—claw after their banishment.

Echidna (eh-KEED-nah)
Snake from the waist down, woman from the waist up, and not a fan of wearing clothes. She does have a pretty awesome belly ring. Echidna is one of Phorkys's favorite daughters, and she's known as the mother of monsters.

Griffins
I haven't seen an adult griffin but oh-em-gee the babies are soooo cute! Can you hear me squealing? 'Cause I'm squealing. Part lion, part eagle, and totally cuddly. Also, they skyrocket the hot boy temperature into the danger zone. Do you have a fan? I need a fan.

Harpies (HAIR-peez)
These are also bird-women, but much smaller than Sirens, and not nearly as beautiful. They look like they were spliced with turkey vultures, but of course, I only got a quick glimpse. Their name means *snatcher* in Greek, and sometimes they're accused of snatching souls. Creepy.

Isamarine*
Besides kissing Jared and seeing my mom alive, Isa may be my favorite part of the Deep. She's a Double Trouble firecracker compressed into a tiny frame, a total girl boss in her role as deputy head chef. Smelling of freshly cut onions, Isa wears an

apron to cover her food-stained clothes. Her hair is dark and wiry and falls in a long braid to her waist. Her skin is the color of seaweed, and her eyes an orange sunset. Her scraggly, bat-like wings and slightly hunched back don't look like much of a threat, but I've learned not to guess someone's threat-level based on looks.

Isa's most dangerous feature is her chain. It's a bit like an earthworm, in that it can be split in half and regenerate. Phorkys used her chain to fasten a Siren silencing charm to my neck. A charm made from Luke's crushed finger. No. Don't make me say it again. I don't want to even think about it. And by the way, no amount of exfoliating can remove *that* memory.

We couldn't find records of her species in our research, but not every mythical creature has been recorded. In Isa's own words, she's "the one who drags sailors to their deaths."

Minotaur (meen-oh-TAR)
Disturbing monster. Man body. Bull head. His mom—Pasiphae, wife of Minos—had an affair with a white bull, got preggers, and birthed this thing. I wonder if mythological creatures have access to a good therapist.

Neri* (nair-EE)
An interdimensional owl who claims she existed before time itself. She's my spirit guide, my *pneuma*, and yes, she does guide me, and yes, she can yank my spirit out of my body, so yes, she's my spirit guide.

Thanos, Crox, and Silent Bob*
Yet more mythical creatures I met who don't appear in our research. Thanos is the head of guard in Phorkys's fortress and

leads the infantry during war. Crox and Silent Bob are his top two guards. Their skin is actually a hard shell, and they can throw spikes out of their pores for protection and as a weapon.

PLACES

Anthemusa (an-the-MUSE-ah)
Island home of the Sirens, and a really difficult place to defend. FYI.

Cathedral Rock Vortex
A female vortex located in Sedona, Arizona. People are supposed to feel calm and comforted while there. We. Did. Not.

Headquarters for the Alliance of Humans and Mythicals*
Also known as home. Located back in my old townhouse in Brooklyn, Amity set it up as the world headquarters for the army she's forming. An army made of humans and friendly mythicals, who just want to stay safe on the human side of the Veil. They plan to fight Phorkys's forces with us.

The Grotto*
Phorkys's special dungeon. I used to think it was a place he kept those he hated most, but now I know it's the place he keeps those he wants to forget. Mom spent almost two decades there. I spent almost two days there, and it was more than enough. At least the floors are cushy.

Tartarus/Underworld (TAR-tar-us)
Persephone's home away from home. Also, where mythicals go after death. Some humans who live behind the Veil go there as well. Like Guardians. My dad. He's hopefully in the Elysian Fields, if Demeter got there in time.

KORRINA'S MYTHOLOGICAL CHEAT SHEET | 289

The Veil*
A magical barrier that protects the human world from the mythical world.

The Void*
An interdimensional space that sucks in lost souls and keeps them there for all eternity. Or so I thought.

Vortices
Swirling centers of energy that are conducive to healing, meditation, and self-exploration. Or, you know, link to a goddess gone crazy across the Veil.

CEREMONIES

The Lesser Mysteries
Part of the Eleusinian Mysteries and the cult of Demeter and Persephone, each spring those who wanted to join the cult were invited to sacrifice a piglet to Demeter and Persephone. They then ritually purified themselves in the river Ilissos. I have no idea what that entailed.

The Greater Mysteries
Held in early fall in Athens, initiates who had been through the Lesser Mysteries ritual in the spring would walk the Sacred Way from Athens to Eleusis and reenact Demeter's search for Persephone. Many parts of the ritual are lost in history but, lucky me, I got to experience it firsthand. The point of the ritual is to learn how to hold peace while surrounded by the darkness of death—supposedly like Persephone does in the Underworld.

*You may have noticed that my author revealed some creatures and places that aren't included in Greek mythology canon. I've asterisked *those so you don't, you know, write an essay on the wonders of Isamarine or something like that.*

ALSO BY KRIS FARYN

The Siren's Call Series

Song of Destiny

Song of Wings

Song of Curses

Free Novelette | The Nefertiti Curse

The Muse Island Series

Mark of the Gods (Book 1)

Power of the Song (Book 2)

Rise of the Storm (Book 3)

Curse of the Night (Book 4)

Book 5 ~ coming soon!

Muse Island Short Stories

Finn's Call

Gryla's Gift

ABOUT THE AUTHOR

Kris Faryn is known for her love of bean burritos, of traveling, and of her patooties at home, including the grown-up one and furry ones. She also loves baking, cooking, a good book, and a crackling fire.

Kris Faryn is a multi-award-winning author of Young Adult Fantasy books and Adult Suspense. Most importantly, Kris believes in turning dreams into realistic goals and that everyone has something special and unique to offer the world.

Get to know Kris Faryn at:

- facebook.com/KrisFaryn
- instagram.com/booksandfuzzysocks
- bookbub.com/profile/kris-faryn
- goodreads.com/krisfaryn
- amazon.com/author/krisfaryn
- patreon.com/KrisFaryn

Ingram Content Group UK Ltd.
Milton Keynes UK
UKHW012050040723
424555UK00007B/525